Praise for UNDERGROUND FUGUE

Winner of the Edward Lewis Wallant Award
one of *ELLE*'s "Most Anticipated Books by Women"

"The characters . . . are constructed with depth and richness . . . Singer's London emerges as a place of missed connections, miscommunications and misinterpretations."
—*The New York Times Book Review*

"In this extraordinarily accomplished debut novel, Margot Singer confronts life's essential losses—aging, illness, accidental death—but also the scalding, self-inflicted wounds of alienation, estrangement, and prejudice. The book's tender, questing spirit imbues even these dark recesses with a kind of luminosity, making *Underground Fugue* a pleasure to read from beginning to end."
—Geraldine Brooks,
Pulitzer Prize–winning author of *March*

"Singer's novel travels up and down the scale of sorrow, reflecting the musical and psychological connotations of her title . . . This haunting story . . . feels suspended in a murky state between memory and presence, happiness and despair."
—Ron Charles, *The Washington Post*

"A beautiful novel about affinities, assumptions, and family mysteries. We know less than we think we do, and we need each other more than we thought."
—Allegra Goodman, bestselling author of *Intuition*

"*Underground Fugue* swept me away. I could not put it down. Here is a writer aptly named—Singer. Read and savor the music, even as your blood jumps."
—Richard Bausch, author of *Peace*

"I haven't been able to get *Underground Fugue* out of my mind. Haunting and breathtaking, this debut sticks, the way good literature always does, because it awakens us to the majesty—all the pain, all the joy—our lives contain."
—Lee Martin, author of *The Bright Forever*

"Singer gracefully weaves the fugue motif throughout her debut novel . . . The result is a nuanced, realistic exploration of themes of loss and identity, which seem particularly relevant in these uncertain times."

—*Library Journal*

"Singer's introspective tale of displaced characters casts a subtle light on current events." —*Booklist*/American Library Association

"An unusually layered debut. In short, taut chapters, [*Underground Fugue*] alternates between two families who have suddenly become neighbors . . . When terror strikes, the plot accelerates and the novel's strands converge brilliantly."

—*Publishers Weekly*

"Subtle, affecting . . . The novel shimmers between meanings, never settling on the single one. It . . . continues to reverberate in the mind after its final words." —*The Columbus Dispatch*

"*Underground Fugue*—an absorbing, deeply poignant intersection of lives and histories—establishes Margot Singer as a world-class writer. May the literary gods rejoice." —Bob Shacochis, author of
The Woman Who Lost Her Soul

"A riveting, deeply affecting novel I will be thinking about for years."

—Eileen Pollack, author of *A Perfect Life*

"Intense, unblinking, elegant and smart, Margot Singer's *Underground Fugue* had me—sometimes by the heart, sometimes by the throat—from its first striking sentence to its last." —Laird Hunt, author of *Neverhome*

"Thrilling, tender, and dangerously seductive, *Underground Fugue* is an exhilarating journey into the perilous depths of London's tunnels and the bewildering labyrinth of the human heart."

—Melanie Rae Thon, author of *The Voice of the River*

"Margot Singer writes like the dark angel cast down to live among us in these troubled times." —Brad Watson, author of *Miss Jane*

"Deftly handled, this novel's characters reflect a time and place and the attitudes gripping much of the Western world still."   —*Read It Forward*

"*Underground Fugue* is a literary novel of moral heft and stylistic grace."
—Laurie Loewenstein, author of *Unmentionables* and
president of the James Jones Literary Society

"Elegantly written and extraordinarily timely, *Underground Fugue*, a recipient of the James Jones First Novel Fellowship, is clearly one of the most accomplished and powerful winners to date."
—Kaylie Jones, author of *The Anger Meridian* and
co-founder of the James Jones Literary Society

UNDERGROUND FUGUE

MARGOT SINGER

A NOVEL

MELVILLE HOUSE
BROOKLYN · LONDON

UNDERGROUND FUGUE

First Melville House Hardcover Printing: April 2017
First Melville House Paperback Printing: May 2018

Melville House Publishing
46 John Street
Brooklyn, NY 11201
and
8 Blackstock Mews
Islington
London N4 2BT

mhpbooks.com   facebook.com/mhpbooks   @melvillehouse

Die Sonette an Orpheus by Rainer Maria Rilke,
first published 1923 by Insel-Verlag. Germany.

The Library of Congress has catalogued the hardcover as follows:
Names: Singer, Margot, author.
Title: Underground fugue : a novel / Margot Singer.
Description: Brooklyn ; London : Melville House, [2017]
Identifiers: LCCN 2016044061| ISBN 9781612196282 (hardback) |
    ISBN 9781612196299 (ebook)
Subjects: LCSH: Domestic fiction. | BISAC: FICTION / Political.
    | FICTION / Jewish. | FICTION / Sagas. | GSAFD: Suspense
    fiction.
Classification: LCC PS3619.I572447 U53 2017 | DDC 813/.6—dc23
LC record available at https://lccn.loc.gov/2016044061

ISBN: 978-1-61219-730-2
ISBN: 978-1-61219-628-2 (hardcover)
ISBN: 978-1-61219-629-9 (eBook)

Printed in the United States of America
1   3   5   7   9   10   8   6   4   2

M'amour, m'amour
　　　what do I love and
　　　　　where are you?
That I lost my center
　　　fighting the world.
The dreams clash
　　　and are shattered—
and that I tried to make a paradiso
　　　　　　　terrestre.

—EZRA POUND, Notes for Canto 117 et seq.

UNDERGROUND FUGUE

No one sees him fall or jump. No one sees him swim, shoes awkward in his hands, arms stretched above the swell. No one sees him splash onto the shore, the loose stones giving way beneath his feet. He simply appears as if from nowhere, a lone figure stumbling along the beachfront road near Sheerness: dripping wet, barefoot, dressed in a white shirt and formal suit.

In the midnight stillness, the sea and sky hang gray along the shadowline of the coast. From here at the mouth of the estuary, the North Sea stretches eastward to the rim of the horizon and beyond it to the continent: Ostend, Zeebrugge, Dunkirk. Only on this night there's no horizon, just one flat, unbroken surface, water indistinguishable from air. There's just the throaty hiss of waves on pebbles, drawing near and then receding, like a lapping beast. Points of light flicker on the headland. The grayness hovers: an erasure, a wiped slate.

The police car slows, the driver's window opens, an arm extends. A head cranes out.

—Oi! You! What's your name?

The man half turns and shies away, continues walking. He walks with his head tilted, carrying his shoes. He's a piece of flotsam, washed up, mute. He looks blurred around the edges, drained of color, a charcoal rubbing in tones of gray.

At the hospital he shivers beneath a blanket, unyielding as a wave-

washed stone. His pockets contain nothing. The labels have been cut out of all his clothes. On the inside collar of his jacket there are just two stubs of fabric, looped with thread. At the neck of his shirt, a jagged hole. On the waistband of his trousers, the perforated outline of a square. All identifying marks have been rubbed off his shoes. His gaze slips sideways. He has no notable scars or birthmarks, fillings or tattoos. He does not speak. He has no language, no history, no memory, no name.

In the photograph that will run in all the papers, the camera has caught him standing in a grove of trees outside the hospital, wearing that black suit, that white shirt buttoned to the neck, clutching a plastic folder of sheet music to his chest. Tall and thin, he stands slightly hunched. He has cropped blond hair, a pale prickling of beard. The sun is at his back, whiting out his head and shoulders in a blaze of light. He takes on the colors of his surroundings, like a container made of glass.

The expression in his eyes is what you will remember. It is both vulnerable and wary, pleading and accusing, as if he's begging you to look away, to leave him be. But in the instant of the shutter's click, everything has changed. He has been transformed into a body of pure speculation: a plot to be unraveled, a projection of your desire, a myth.

Given a pad and pencil, he sketches a grand piano, all eighty-eight keys in fine detail, the lid raised like a wing. On the old upright in the mental hospital chapel, he plays the Moonlight Sonata, *some Lennon and McCartney tunes, the theme from Tchaikovsky's* Swan Lake. *He plays for hours, his body swaying, his fingers tracing patterns along the keys: chord progressions, arpeggios, halftones, quavers, counterpoint.*

Listen: everything you want to know is in the music.

The voices rise and fall, call and answer, take flight.

ONE

ESTHER

The plane descends toward Heathrow on a cold, gray April morning. It is just past 6:00 a.m. in London and Esther has traveled through the night, shed five hours of it over the Atlantic, and now her eyes feel loosened in their sockets and her feet are swollen and everything is vibrating with fatigue. She rests her forehead against the window. Square green fields bisected by hedgerows, snaking subdivisions of redbrick houses, rain-wet motorways, tiny cars. The landing gear whirrs. The flaps adjust.

She folds her arms across her chest, crosses her fingers, tucks her thumbs into her palms for luck. A useless superstition. The man seated beside her doesn't seem to notice. He is an American, a petroleum engineer, he told her back in the friendly moments at the beginning of the flight before he fell asleep. He's on his way to a rig in the North Sea. Something to do with pressure control valve design. Hated traveling, he told her. Didn't like to be away from his wife and kids. He barely fits into the coach class seat, overlapping its borders like an adult wedged into a child's chair on parents' night at school. He fell asleep quickly, the dinner trays not yet cleared away, the cabin still abuzz. At one point in the night his head lolled onto her shoulder, heavy as a melon, trusting as a sleeping child in the strange intimacy of strangers on transatlantic flights.

Esther used to love to fly. She loved the promise of the city

names clicking over on the departure boards, the way the sylla-
bles turned over on her tongue: Dar es Salaam, Helsinki, Riyadh,
La Paz, Berlin. She loved the weightless lift of takeoff, the earth
dropping away and spreading out below, the bunting of clouds,
the sun appearing like a gift. She misses it, that lightness she once
felt at thirty-six thousand feet, the substance of her life below as
unreal as the vanished earth beneath the strange cloud sea. But
now she knows she'd mistaken the illusion of lightness for possibility. She'd thought that if you kept moving forward, you could
leave the past behind.

Rain spatters against the windows. They are low now, nearly
there, the squat terminal buildings and hangars stretching larger,
into scale. The blue blink of runway lights. Then the thump of
the wheels on tarmac, the chest-slam of the reverse-engine thrust.
She uncrosses her fingers and arms. On the ground now, the jet
lumbers, awkward on its little wheels.

The engineer bends and lifts his duffle bag onto his lap. He
has to catch a connection to Aberdeen, he has told her, then hop
a helicopter to the rig. She's seen pictures of those wave-battered
platforms, those men in orange coveralls, the men who kept the
oil pumping, the oil that wars were fought for, that viscous blood-
line deep beneath the sea.

The engineer turns to her and nods. "Good luck," he says.

Esther has come to London because her mother is dying, her
death a matter of time—of weeks or months—not luck. Her
mother is eighty-three and has lived her life, Esther knows, but still
the word *dying* drops inside her like a stone. Since she was last in
London, Esther has lost her son, quit her job, left her husband. The
world has changed. One by one, the moorings have been cut free.

The jet jolts to a stop at the gate. The cabin lights blink on, and
then everyone is standing, pushing into the aisles, reaching overhead for coats and bags, pressing toward the doors.

———

Esther takes a taxi to her mother's house, a semidetached Georgian on a quiet street just off Finchley Road. The two halves of the house are mirror images of one another. Parallel front steps lead to side-by-side blue doors. Matching windows align beneath the eaves. In back, twin gardens share a wisteria-covered wall. The right side is her mother's. The Last Resort, Esther dubbed it years ago, a little joke that stuck. She presses the bell and waits.

A woman Esther has never seen before comes to the door. For a moment, the familiar shifts. The woman has a wide moon-face, blond hair pulled back tight.

Esther takes a half step back. "Oh, I thought—my mother—is she—?"

"I fetch her. A moment, please," the woman says. She has an accent—Eastern European, perhaps. She is wearing a blue smock with white trim around the sleeves and collar; an ID badge hangs on a lanyard around her neck. The district nurse—of course.

Esther lugs her bags over the threshold. The house smells of mildew and furniture polish, same as always. She steps into the sitting room. There is the sofa with the crocheted afghan folded over the back, the green-tiled hearth, the mantel clock, the vitrine crammed with china teacups and figurines, the piano, the Persian carpet worn in spots to threads. Through the doors at the far end of the room, she can see the branches of the weeping mulberry swaying in the breeze. A gray cat is crouching on the garden wall. Weathered brick, slate-tiled rooftops knobby with chimney pots. A green scrim of trees.

"Esther."

She turns and her mother is there. She is wearing a cable-knit cardigan and slacks, pearls glinting at her neck. Her thinning white hair has been brushed and set. She approaches slowly, her shoulders bent. She smiles, holds out her arms.

She looks the same, Esther thinks as they embrace. She looks the same, although she feels smaller and more fragile than Esther expected, or remembered. Loose skin over jutting bones. She is shrinking, in old age, in illness, consolidating into herself. But she smells the same—a powdery scent. You wouldn't suspect those unstoppable cells—*malignant, metastatic*—dividing, multiplying, spreading through her blood and lymph.

In the kitchen, the radio is on, the familiar descant of the BBC news. Her mother fills the kettle, shakes a few biscuits onto a plate. Esther leans against the counter. She could be twenty-two again, she thinks, back for a quick obligatory visit, the rest of her life not yet even the nucleus of an idea. Somehow, inside, she is that person still.

"Mum, sit. Let me do that."

"Nonsense." Her mother sets out a cup and saucer, sugar, cream. The newsreader drones on. "They're burying Pope John Paul today," her mother says. She spoons coffee from a canister into a French press. Her hand shakes, a little spills. "Do you know, the Poles wanted the Vatican to send his heart to Kraków, to be buried there?"

Krack-uff, her mother pronounces it. She was born just fifty miles from Kraków, across the former Czechoslovak border in Moravská Ostrava—Mährisch Ostrau when it was part of Austria-Hungary, Ostrava in the Czech Republic now. Another world. Her mother would be about the same age as Karol Wojtyła, the departed Pope.

"Just his heart?"

Her mother's lips twist into her old ironic smile. She waves her hand. "Cut it out and send it here, they said."

"That's horrible!"

"Quite. In any case, the Church refused. He is to be buried in one piece, in the crypt beneath St. Peter's, in Rome."

"I'm glad to hear that."

Her father was buried in the Jewish cemetery up in Willesden. Noah was buried out in Queens. Esther tries to picture the Pope lying in state in his polished casket: the red robe, the peaked hat, his dead face gray, his stilled heart thick with congealed blood inside his chest. She does not want to, cannot, imagine her mother dead. She wonders if her mother envies the Catholics their faith in heaven and the eternal life of the repentant soul. She wonders if she's afraid. *She's failing*, the doctors said, as if life were an exam.

Her mother sets the French press onto the table and pushes down the plunger. "He was a good man, the Pope. Now come and sit."

By *good man*, Esther knows, she means, *good for the Jews*. She can't recall what this Polish pope did to earn that praise.

In the other room, the mantel clock sounds its noonday chime. The newsreader murmurs on the radio. Her mother pours the coffee. There is comfort in the surfaces of things, here at the still point of the morning—in the stained wood of the tabletop, the growl of the refrigerator, the old pots and pans hanging from their hooks, the flat gray English April light.

It's 2:47 a.m. Esther fell asleep early, but now she's wide awake. She can hear her mother moving—the mattress creaking, the toilet whooshing, the water gurgling through the pipes—and wonders if she's in pain. Surely they've given her some meds to help her sleep? Esther should have asked. She's supposed to be here to help. Everything is always worse at night, her mother used to say when Esther was little, stroking her hair with cool fingers, pulling up the covers, tucking them back in. But now her mother is dying and Esther is alone in this familiar, unfamiliar place where the pillow is too soft and the duvet is too hot and the old mattress dips into a rut and the alarm clock on the bedside table has a too-loud tick.

She gets up, pulls on her dressing gown and slippers, and tiptoes downstairs. The house is webbed in shadow, blue and cold and still. She pulls on her raincoat over her robe and fishes a pack of cigarettes out of her purse. She eases open the front door and sits down on the top step, wrapping her coat around her legs.

The parked cars and dark houses across the street float in shadow. The streetlamp emits a faint, high-pitched buzz. A siren sounds in the distance, not the old *nee-nah* but an American-style wail. It is cold. She pulls a cigarette out of the pack, flips the lighter. She guesses it is a very un-English thing to smoke out on the street in the middle of the night with a coat over your night-gown like a bum. But there is no one around to see. The tip of the cigarette flares orange in the dark.

Sometimes, in New York, she used to go up onto the roof of their building on nights she couldn't sleep. The tarpaper roof was flat and bare. There were just a couple of sooty planters of bamboo and a few weathered folding chairs. From there, twelve stories above the Upper West Side, she could make out the dark slash of the Hudson, the red and white streams of taillights flow-ing south along Columbus, the blank gap of the park. Beyond floated the sodium vapor galaxies of the East Side, Brooklyn, and Queens, a vast, sparkling net of lights.

In Noah's room, the ceiling glowed with constellations they'd stuck up there when he was little, a yellow-green array of plas-tic stars. His shelves were still lined with his model airplanes, propped on angled stands: B-52 bombers and F-16 fighter jets, a Sopwith Camel and a Gulfstream and a spindle-nosed Concorde. She and Gil had bought the model kits for him, helped him with the early snap-together versions, then just stood by and watched as he hunched over the tiny plastic parts of the more complicated models, surrounded by little bottles of glue and jars of colored paint. It didn't seem possible that this boy who spilled the cereal and tracked mud onto the living room carpet and didn't seem to care or even notice whether his shirt was on backward or inside out could manage such painstaking work. He'd painted the F-16 in jungle camouflage. The Sopwith Camel had targets like a moth's eyes stenciled on its wings.

On the wall above his bed, Noah had taped a photograph

of a jet plane flying above two swirling vortices of cloud. The plane was a thin black boomerang above twin spiral curls, undulating striations of gray and white. It looked almost as if the plane were flying into a tunnel. It was wake turbulence, Noah had explained, waves of air created by the wingtip during lift. The clouds looked to Esther like a strange sea, each vortex the scroll of an Ionic column, or an enormous waterspout. The image was beautiful and terrifying. It seemed as if the plane had lost its way, had crossed into another dimension of time and space.

She doesn't hear the footsteps, doesn't see the figure approaching until he is nearly in front of her, climbing the steps next door. A man. A young man. She draws back into the recess of the doorframe, rubs out her cigarette. Her heart stutters. It is very dark. She hopes he hasn't seen her. She pulls in her legs and holds her breath.

In the dim illumination of the streetlamp, like a freeze-frame caught in a camera's flash, she registers disjoined details: a black knit cap pulled low, dark hair curling underneath, a black hoodie, wet and muddy boots. An older couple lived next door, or used to. They had no kids. Who was this, then? Panic flushes through her limbs. Jesus. He was breaking in.

He pauses before the door and swings his backpack off one shoulder, turning toward the light. And as he turns, he looks up for just a second, and their eyes connect. His eyes are what she will always remember. She knows them intimately, even though she has never seen this boy before. They are the eyes of a Byzantine icon: large and heavy lidded, nearly black, intense.

She cannot move. There is a pounding in her head. She is aware of him taking in her bare shins and slippers, the light blue satin of her dressing gown sticking out beneath her coat. She is aware that he is aware that she is looking back at him.

Then he is reaching into the backpack, stepping closer to the door, keys jingling in his hand.

She lets out her breath.

Just sneaking in.

And then he is pulling the door open and stepping inside and the door thumps shut behind him and the London night settles once again around her, strange and cold and dark.

JAVAD

He is dozing on the sofa, his book splayed spine-up on his chest, when the thump of the front door startles him awake. He meant to rest his eyes for just a moment, not sleep. He groans, sits up, and runs his fingers through his hair. He picks up his mobile off the coffee table, squints at the screen.

2:58 a.m. Bloody hell.

The house is dark and hollow beyond the light circle of the gooseneck lamp. He listens to the soft creak of his son climbing the stairs. The cat leaps onto the coffee table, arching her back. He pulls her onto his lap and ruffles her fur. It's cool and damp. "So where's the lad been off to, then, cat?" he says. The cat's chest vibrates with a purr.

Javad puts on his glasses, stretches his arms overhead. It's Friday night. Probably he's been to a party. Possibly there's a girl, although Javad rather doubts it. "Just hanging out with the blokes, Baba," Amir always says, his eyes shifting away. He's nineteen now, but still there's something in him that's not yet fully formed—a stress fracture, a hairline crack.

Slanted rectangles of light from passing cars drift across the wall. "Magic movies," Javad and his sister Darya had called them when they were children, back in the old house on Hesabi Street in Tehran. That life, long vanished, seems no more substantial than these projections of moving light. He wonders if everyone experiences childhood that way, or if it's just the nostalgia of an exile he's condemned to bear.

He heaves himself up off the sofa and climbs the stairs. His lower back aches. Water is running in the bath. The old pipes groan. A bath, at three in the morning? He pauses outside the bathroom door but doesn't knock.

He is glad to have Amir living here with him now, although proximity has only made him even more acutely aware of how little he knows his son. What did he expect? It was a good deal for the boy, certainly—far nicer than any grotty student digs and free to boot. At the end of all those alternating weekends—as he watched the boy climb the dodgy steps to Caroline's flat, his dark head bowed, his kit bag slung over a skinny shoulder—Javad always felt as if he were casting him out to sea in a leaky skiff. After all these years of shuttling and negotiation, of passing him back and forth like a relay baton, it's good to have him here.

He had always thought that by now he'd be remarried, living a normal life, if there was such a thing, or at least a life less complicated than this. Well, he did what he had to do. He did what he could. He did his best.

It is nearly noon when his son comes downstairs the next morning. Javad is at the kitchen table, surrounded by a pile of papers, working.

"Baba," Amir says, yawning, "you work too hard."

Javad looks up, the half-formed sentence that was revolving in his head scattering like molecules of light. His son's dark hair is sticking up, his cheeks stubbled. He has Javad's coloring but Caroline's nose and her gap-toothed, soft-lipped smile. He's wearing workman's trousers and lug-soled boots, which make him look, as usual, as if he were a builder or a lumberjack rather than a university student. He's a bit taller than Javad and broader across the shoulders, his boyish slenderness solidified into strength.

"Good morning," Javad says, glancing at his watch. "Only just."

Amir rolls his eyes. "It's Saturday, Baba. In case you hadn't noticed." He picks up the cafetière and shakes the coffee dregs into the bin, turns on the tap.

"You were out late last night," Javad says.

Over the noise of the water, Amir says, "Not that late."

"Three's pretty late."

A shrug.

"What did you lot get up to?"

"Just hanging around. You know."

Javad does not know. At his son's age, he was already on his own, here in England, in medical school. There had been a revolution in Iran.

Amir glances over his shoulder. "Will you have another cup?"

"Please."

Children, he thinks, are like the vestiges of light from distant stars. By the time the rays have crossed the light-years of the galaxy to reach your retinas, the stars have long since disappeared.

The sound of the piano comes through the wall as if through water: a muffled melody in a minor key. Javad is lying on the sitting-room floor in *shava-asana*, corpse pose, his knees bent and arms outstretched, palms up at his sides, with two paperbacks beneath his head, trying to relax the muscles of his back. He's never heard the piano being played next door before. Surely it's not the old woman, his neighbor—he's spied her once or twice, shuffling in and out of taxis like a hunch-necked bird, although they've hardly exchanged a word since he moved in. There's a ripple of arpeggios, a nimble run of notes along a chromatic scale. Whoever it is plays very well.

He inhales and exhales as the physio instructed, directing the air in and out through his nose, trying to visualize his breath. He is supposed to imagine it flowing like a stream, in through his nostrils and down along his spine, easing the knotted bands of muscle, allowing the damaged vertebrae to float gently apart, those thirty-three bony butterflies curving from the brainstem to the buttocks—cervical, thoracic, lumbar, sacral, coccygeal—that form the spine. He's got a compressed disc just above the iliac crest, the consequence of too much sitting, too lanky a frame, too little exercise. Or maybe it's just the price one must pay for carrying a body through the world for forty-some-odd years. Mostly there is just a dull ache and stiffness, but when the muscles spasm he is overwhelmed by a clenching agony, zoned out on muscle relaxants, flat on his back in bed for days. He lives in wariness of his back and its betrayals. He treats it like a fickle lover, with tender vigilance and distrust.

Through the wall, the music continues. Voices chase each other up and down the octaves, the melody moving from treble to bass and back again. It's Bach, he thinks. He rolls over to his side, carefully sits up. The cat steps over his legs and rubs against his hip. His stomach gurgles. It is late and Amir is out and once again he has neglected to pick up anything to eat. Amir had said he was going over to Caroline's, he recalls. Javad pictures his ex-wife, her bleached-blond hair cropped short, a drink in hand. Always, of late, a drink. Amir standing by. The role Javad refused to play.

Amir brought home one of her new works the other day, a collage of photographic negatives, vintage postcards, Ordnance Survey maps, and pages ripped from encyclopedias and telephone directories, the layers glued on thick, then scraped away and rubbed with what might be chalk or charcoal and shellac. "Memory maps," she called them, according to Amir. A pretentious title, Javad thinks. But of course, the hippocampus—the seat of memory—does function as a sort of spatial map. Clever, then, perhaps.

On the other side of the wall, the piano plays on. Louder now, the notes cascade, then consolidate into chords. If this goes on, he thinks, he'll never be able to work or sleep. Neighbors, bloody hell. He pulls on his leather jacket, shoves his mobile and keys into his pockets, and heads out into the night.

On Monday morning, Javad stands at the demonstration table at the front of the UCL lecture theater; the brain before him rests on an aluminum tray. It is a human brain, tinged yellow by formaldehyde, lumpy as a cauliflower and roughly the same shape and size. Three pounds of jellylike gray matter, soft enough to ooze like toothpaste out of a hole drilled in the skull. A remarkable organ, capable of contemplating its own mechanism of contemplation, like a mirror reflected in a mirror—an infinite regression. Within each nerve fiber pulse a hundred billion neurons, a hundred trillion synapses, most of it as unmapped as outer space.

Grasping the brain beneath the frontal lobe, he holds it up before the audience, pointing out the fissures that faintly demarcate the lobes, rotating it like a fruit. He sets it down and pries apart the outer layers of the cerebral cortex to reveal the gray matter underneath. Taking a scalpel, he slices down to expose the cingulate gyrus and the corpus callosum, working his way through the lateral ventricle to the hippocampus and the almond-shaped amygdala buried deep inside. The amygdala: hard nut of anger, anxiety, fear.

This is a healthy brain from a healthy body. Whomever it belonged to was relatively young and died of something that does not do much damage to the brain—a heart defect or drowning; a suicide, perhaps. He sets the brain back on the tray, peels off the latex gloves. He has long since stopped considering cadaver organs as connected to living, human bodies, thinking of it no more than he thinks of a cow when he eats a steak; although there was a time, early on, when he'd been unable to stop himself from picturing the corpse—headless and eviscerated, its bits and bobs "donated to science," the family members grieving around a closed casket or diminished urn of ash.

He moves back to the computer mounted in the podium. Behind him, the screen lights up. Things have changed since his student days—it's all prosection and PowerPoint now. A PET scan image appears, a radiant inkblot of blue and yellow and red, a normal brain. The next scan, an image of a brain atrophied by Alzheimer's, reveals a much larger dead area of cobalt blue and black, limned with gold, the temporal and parietal lobes choked with the weedy plaques and tangles of the proteins beta-amyloid and tau.

"It wasn't until relatively recently, you know, that we have come to understand the function of the brain," he says. "Aristotle thought it was a sort of radiator designed to cool the heart. Descartes conceived of it as a machine filled with 'animal spirits,' rather like hydraulic fluid."

The course participants—students, consultants, trainees—regard him in silence. Javad always thinks that people will find his bits of historical trivia amusing, but they nearly never laugh. They want the facts, not the messy reality of science—the confusion and the ambiguity and the mistakes.

"The German phrenologist Franz Joseph Gall, of course, believed that a person's character and personality could be discerned by reading the cerebral convolutions of the brain," he continues. He clicks to the next slide, an illustration from a mid-Victorian phrenological journal, a detailed diagram of a human skull, each part of the brain mapped and labeled with a little line drawing: a history book, a numerical equation, a cupid holding a bow and torch.

"We now know that phrenology was mostly a load of racist bunk," he says, "but Gall's assumption that thoughts and emotions were located in specific regions of the brain is actually not so far off from what neuroimaging is now starting to reveal."

This is his research terrain. The fuzzy borderline between the psychological and the physiological, the question of how emotion may or may not manifest in the functioning of the brain. He is interested in breakdowns of memory, awareness, perception, identity: dissociative amnesia, psychogenic fugue. The neurological puzzle of the "self."

"With damage to the frontal lobe, for example," he says, aiming his laser pointer's red dot at the screen, "we see increasingly irrational behavior, the loss of ability to plan, sometimes loss of inhibition, even an increased tendency for violence, as well. Damage here, to the parietal lobe, causes disorientation, an inability to locate the body in space. Damage to the occipital lobe makes it difficult to recognize people's faces. And damage to the temporal lobe, of course, causes problems with memory, language, speech."

He thinks of the first case diagnosed by Alois Alzheimer back in 1906, Auguste D. Her famous words: *I have lost myself.*

The piano starts up again that evening as he is lying on the sofa, *The Guardian* spread out across his chest. Javad takes off his glasses, closes his eyes. The melodic voices rise and fall in rippling symmetry. The music washes over him as color: indigo, lapis, cerulean, ultramarine. Deep water blue. Moon-shadow blue. The azure halo of the earth as seen from outer space. The blue of arterial blood beneath the skin.

His grandmother, he recalls, had that sort of translucent skin. Veins like rivers on a raised relief map snaked along the backs of her arthritic hands. At the end, they told him, she hallucinated ghostly figures. Lewy body dementia, it must have been. By then, of course, he'd long since left Tehran.

Amir is clomping about overhead. He has been restless since the third term began, staying out late, lying in, spending the rest of his time in front of the computer, earphones in. Javad can't keep track of what his son is studying, all that Middle Eastern history and politics, none of which interests him one whit. God only knew what one did with a degree like that. Everybody said that the School of Oriental and African Studies, SOAS, was a prime recruiting ground for MI6, but it was difficult to imagine the lad—dreamy, scruffy, clever, but not especially hard working—as a spy. Honestly, it was hard to imagine Amir doing much of anything. Even now that he was here, living with Javad at last, he remained stubbornly opaque.

The other day Javad had found him stretched out backward on his bed, his feet propped on the headboard, reading the Qur'an. Javad thought of the mullahs in the mosques back in Tehran— barefoot, robed, and turbaned, mumbling into their beards. He had come to England to leave all that behind.

"You're not going all religious on us, are you?" Javad had said.

Amir glanced up. "I am, actually."

"What?"

An eye roll. "Baba, I'm cramming for my exams."

Now Javad opens his eyes at a thumping on the stairs; he fumbles for his glasses. Amir steps into the doorway, rucksack slung over one shoulder, earphones looped around his neck. He has on jeans with white-stringed gashes at the knees. He could use a haircut, Javad thinks.

"Off to the salt mines?" he says.

"Yep."

"Don't you want anything to eat? What time is it?"

A shrug. "I'll pick up something over there, I guess."

"Right. Let me know if you'll be out late."

"Okay." A smirk. "I'll be out late."

"Don't be a cheeky bastard."

"Baba, leave it."

And then his son is gone. Javad hears the front door bang shut. Next door, the piano abruptly stops. For a moment, the last notes linger on the air and disappear.

ESTHER

T here will be good days and bad days," the nurse, Zofia, says on Monday morning. They are sitting at the kitchen table, drinking coffee, weak daylight filtering through the curtains above the sink. Esther's mother is still upstairs, asleep. Today is not such a good day. Zofia's moon-face is smooth, her body solid, the bones and muscles invisible beneath her doughy skin. In her calm, Polish-accented voice, she explains to Esther how to monitor her mother's caloric intake, her blood pressure, her mental state; how to help her to the loo; how to administer her meds—Fentanyl, Ativan, morphine—when she's in pain. You might think she was describing how to tend a garden rather than the stages of impending death. Pull weeds. Spread mulch. Hope for rain.

"It is not necessary, of course, to worry about addiction," Zofia says, with a small smile. Esther gets it. A little hospice-worker joke.

An array of booklets lies between them on the table. *How to Be a Supportive Caregiver. What Does Someone Dying Need? A Guide to Grief.* The hospice logo is a stylized bird flying across a blue ground toward a yellow sun. Esther feels overwhelmed. She is afraid she will screw up, break down, fail. She would like to grab Zofia's arm, like a child, and beg her to stay.

Esther is not good with illness. Gil was always the one who
held Noah over the toilet when he was throwing up, picked out
splinters with a blackened needle, dabbed peroxide on his bleeding cuts. Often when Noah got sick he'd sleep in the big bed with
Gil, and she would banish herself to the study's pullout couch. She
is ashamed to admit it even now, her inability to summon a calm-
ing presence. Her selfish fear. The worst moment was the time
Noah tripped on the playground and broke his new front teeth—
she will never forget the sight of him standing in the doorway, his
lip swollen and bleeding, his forehead scraped, his beautiful new
teeth now jagged stumps. She'd burst into tears and turned away.
She will not forgive herself for that.

"You will manage very well," Zofia says.

Above all, her mother wants to stay at home. No more hospi-
tals, no more treatments. Even over the telephone, long distance,
Esther could hear the determination in her voice. It was the least
she could do, Esther thought, to give her that. Although now, as
she hears her mother's plaintive calling from upstairs, she wonders if she's gotten in over her head.

Upstairs, her mother is sitting up in bed. Cords of wrinkled skin
drape along her neck. She says some words in Polish. Zofia smiles
and reaches for a bottle of lotion and squirts a stream into her palm.
Her mother shifts her legs out from beneath the duvet and Zofia
lifts them onto her lap and begins to massage the lotion into her
mother's feet, which are swollen and knobby and purple veined.
Between Zofia's capable, soft hands, they look less like feet than
organs pickled in an autopsy-room jar. Esther turns away.

Outside, the sunlight brightens and then dims. Time hangs
loose around them. It's hard to believe Esther hasn't even been
here a week. She has hardly left the house except to walk over
to Waitrose for groceries. So far, she hasn't been of much use.
At least she can cook. Today, perhaps, she'll bake a cake. Maybe

later she'll play the piano. The other day, she raised the keyboard
lid and played for the first time in years. Amazingly, a piece she'd
memorized so long ago came back—one of the fugues from *The
Well-Tempered Clavier*. From where?

The top of her mother's chest of drawers is lined with photographs in silver frames: Esther and Gil on their wedding day,
her hair blow-dried straight and feathered in awful 1980s-style
wings. Snapshots of Noah as a baby and little boy. Noah at his bar
mitzvah, draped in a tallit, rocked back on his heels by the Torah
in his arms, with Gil and Esther, proud parents, on either side. An
old portrait of Esther's parents, a studio shot in black and white.

In that photograph her father is seated on a chair, her mother
perched on his lap with her arm around his shoulders. Her hair
is set in a dark bob, her blouse unbuttoned at the neck, revealing
the strand of graduated pearls she has worn for as long as Esther
can recall. Her father's jaw has not yet slackened into the jowls
Esther remembers; his hair has not yet thinned to baldness on
the top, although his forehead and chin have already hardened
into the angles of a much older man's face. His lips curl beneath
a protruding nose and heavy-lidded eyes. His face is as impene-
trable as a carapace, and as self-contained.

They orbited him, Esther and her mother, like two moons
around a planet. Without him, they flew apart.

She waits until early afternoon to ring Gil at his office, punching
the string of numbers into her mother's clunky British Telecom—
issue corded phone. Even now, in 2005, her mother has no computer, no Internet access. Esther and Gil have always talked on
the telephone, in any case, and she feels obligated to call him now,
even though everything has changed. A *trial separation*, they were
calling it. Don't rush into things, everybody said. But she has
flown across the ocean. She has crossed the line.

"Feinman," Gil says. It is his work voice, rough. It is early morning in New York. She can almost smell his smooth-shaven cheeks, the starch of his laundered shirt. How well she knows him after all these years.

"I just wanted to let you know I'm here."

He clears his throat. "How's she doing?"

"Okay. You know. More or less."

"Please give her my best."

She hears him exhale. The distance vibrates between them, the seconds ticking like a meter in a cab. Time dropping into the void. Were telephone calls still carried beneath the ocean on fiber-optic lines? Or was it all done by satellite these days? And how exactly were sound waves transformed into pulses of light? She presses the phone against her ear. There's street noise in the background, New York morning sounds: a honking horn, the screech of brakes.

Gil clears his throat again. "So how long are you planning to stay?"

"I don't know." She feels a flush of irritation. "How should I know?"

More silence.

She takes a breath and says, "It's better this way."

"Is it?"

"I think so. Yes."

Nothing will be the same again, Gil had said. It was the autumn before Noah's death. They were standing in front of the TV, staring at the silent plume billowing into that oblivious blue sky, as if they were watching from a much greater distance than a hundred or so blocks uptown, as if the sirens already sounding on the streets below couldn't possibly be real. Then they walked over to Seventy-Eighth Street and picked Noah up at school. *Nothing will be the same again*. She hadn't believed Gil when he said it. They were the lucky ones, she remembers thinking then.

———

By late afternoon, her mother has dressed and made her way downstairs. Between them on the kitchen table is the apricot cake Esther has baked. *Aprikosenkuchen*, her mother's recipe. It is too early for apricots, yet there they were in Waitrose, blush ripe, imported from Iran. Persian apricots! "Esther, Esther, Queen of Persia," her father always sang to her at Purim, making her feel as beautiful and brave and clever as her namesake, the secret savior of the Jews. She has done a nice job with the cake. Overlapping slices of apricot spiral around the top like the petals of a flower, the fruit sunk like islands in a golden sea.

Papers and folders are piled on the table in a stack. Her mother slides them across to Esther, one at a time. There is a plot in the Jewish cemetery in Willesden, beside her father's. Everything is arranged. Esther will only need to take the death certificate to the Registrar for Births and Deaths and ring the Burial Office to make arrangements for the funeral. No flowers, no speeches, nothing maudlin, please.

"Have a piece of cake, Mum," Esther says.

Her mother continues handing over papers. Direct debit forms. Telephone numbers for the solicitor, the accountant, the bank. Her NHS card, insurance papers, library card, passport. A fat folder of medical paperwork. The hospice pamphlets, bird-and-sun logo facing up. The property deed. Her will. Esther gathers the papers into a heap and sets them on a chair. It is too soon, too much.

"This house is the only thing left of any value, I'm afraid," her mother says.

"Come on," Esther says, nudging the cake plate toward her mother. "Have a little piece. I made it just for you."

"I'm told the place next door sold for over a million quid!"

Esther looks up. "Who bought it?"

"An Arab. A doctor, I think they said he is." Her mother shakes her head. "It's all Arabs, these days, isn't it?"

"For god's sake, Mum."

"Everything has changed."

"How old is he, this doctor? Does he have a son?"

"What did you say?

"A son," she repeats, louder. "Does the doctor have a son?"

Her mother frowns. "I've got no idea."

Esther is thinking of the boy. He reminds her of the icon at Santa Katarina in the Sinai—the two-faced Christ. One eye direct and knowing, the other lazy-muscled, inward looking, swiveling away.

The disordered sleep of jet lag is slow to fade. Esther falls asleep easily enough but wakes up nearly every night at two or three in the morning with a headache grinding behind her temples, unable to get back to sleep. She tries drinking warm milk, performing relaxation exercises, cutting back on chocolate and caffeine, but nothing seems to work. The few hours of sleep she does get are disrupted by frenetic dreams filled with crowds pressing around her, people who all seem to want something from her that she cannot name, tugging like beggars at her sleeves. She is always traveling, always in a desperate hurry, always irrevocably late— for an appointment, an exam, a plane. The action surges and slows, as in a fever dream, although she is not sick. She wakes up sweaty and out of breath, her nightgown sticking to her skin.

In the darkness, Esther listens for her mother the way she'd listened for Noah when he was small. The floorboards click. Sometimes, at odd hours, she thinks she hears the sound of water running, faint as the vibration of traffic through a tunnel or a gentle rain. She tiptoes down the hallway to her mother's room and leans over the bed and listens to her breathe. The breathing changes just before you die, Zofia has said, but her mother's shoulders rise and fall regularly beneath the duvet's heft. In the dim glow of the hall light Esther watches the movement of her mother's eyes as they flick back and forth beneath her lids, chasing the trajectory of a dream. How obliviously the heart pumps on; how stubbornly the lungs inflate.

Downstairs she pauses by the piano, ghosts her fingers across the keys. She presses gently; the hammers creak as they swing up, stopping just before they sound the strings. The sheet music is piled inside the bench, where she abandoned it years ago: faded blue Henle Verlag and dull green Peters editions, the glue crumbling along the spines. Bach inventions, Chopin etudes, Beethoven sonatas, Scarlatti, Mozart, Liszt. The pages are annotated with slashes of colored pencil highlighting the arcs of phrases and the angles of crescendos, marking trouble spots with vehement lines and loops. Here and there her teacher's notes are scribbled in the margins: *passion, prayer, incantation, ghost.*

She hasn't played in years. She'd worked hard at it in high school. She'd played dutifully, perhaps even with occasional moments of real passion, but then she went off to university and her mother was no longer there to make her practice and she never seemed to have the time or space for a piano in the city after that. Her mother took the Blüthner with her when she moved back to London from Boston, and here it has remained, mute, unplayed.

Now, surprisingly, the pieces she once knew come back. She plays the same bits well; she makes the same mistakes. The melodies wake and sing. "You must practice until the notes are in your fingers," her teacher always said. Now it is as if they have been there all this time, folded into the synapses of muscle memory, tucked inside her cells like the music books inside the piano bench, waiting to be released.

In the morning, her mother is already in the kitchen, eating breakfast, when Esther comes downstairs. It's a good day—a relief. The news is droning on the BBC. A new pope, a German, has been elected. Two Israelis have been wounded in a Palestin-

ian sniper attack. The inflation rate is up. Her mother's lips cinch
like a drawstring purse. Triangles of toast are cooling in the rack.
Esther reaches for a piece.

They are two old women, wrapped in their dressing gowns,
eating toast. They are mother and child. Who knew that growing
up would take so long? Where was the wisdom, the sureness that
was supposed to come with age? Her younger self has not been
left behind, the way you'd think. It's still there loose inside her,
like unlashed cargo shifting in the hold of a ship.

As a toddler, Noah would wrap himself around her legs each
morning when she dropped him off at preschool. The more desperate and guilty she felt, the more fiercely he would cling. He'll
be just fine, the young teachers assured her, prying him away.
The moment you're out of sight, they said, he'll be all smiles.
Esther had to run off like an escaping convict as he kicked and
flailed and screamed. Separation anxiety is normal at this age,
the teachers said. But she was the one who'd suffered from it, far
more than the boy.

Her mother sips her tea. Her hair is as fine as milkweed, her
eyes watery and faded, like liquid at the bottom of a glass. She is
wearing her strand of graduated pearls, as always, tucked beneath
the neckline of her nightdress. Only the tiniest ones show, white
as baby teeth, against her crinkled skin.

Pearls are living things, her mother always said. You must
wear them right against the skin.

A pearl, of course, was the mollusk's way of protecting itself
from irritants or parasites: a kind of gorgeous cyst. Their lustrous
nacre a response to pain.

All these years, her mother has lived alone. Perhaps she too is
like the mollusk, her losses calcified inside her, iridescent, out of
sight. There are so many things she never speaks of: her childhood, the war, her husband's death. If she's been lonely, she's kept
it tucked away. Her mother chews her toast, swallows, her face

a crinkled shell. The silence hangs between them like a weight. Esther sighs and takes another piece of toast. If only you could tell which moment would be the last.

The last time Esther saw her father was a wet late-summer day. She was just thirteen. She and her mother were flying to the States—going on holiday, she'd been told; he would join them in a couple of weeks. He opened the door to the taxi and hoisted up their luggage. *Safe journey*, he said. Esther pushed down the window and leaned her head out into the rain and waved as the taxi lurched away.

She reaches across the table now and takes her mother's hand. It is the sort of unthinking gesture she might once have made toward Noah or Gil. Her mother's hand is bark on knotted knuckle, twigs of bone. Her mother gives a start, looks up, surprised, and her expression surprises Esther, too. Has she been so distant all this time?

She runs into the doctor from next door a few days later. She's just climbing the steps to her mother's door, returning from a trip to Waitrose, as he steps out of his. She has a clutch of carrier bags in each hand. He's wearing a leather jacket and sunglasses. Their eyes connect.

He pushes his sunglasses up onto his head. Kind eyes, dark hair. A few threads of gray about the ears. She has the immediate, irrational sensation that she knows him—a prickling of recognition, as in a dream.

"Hello," he says. "Have you just moved in?"

"No, I'm just here staying with my mother for a while." She sets down the bags of groceries, reaches across to shake his hand. "She's not well."

"I'm sorry to hear that."

He speaks with a British-tinged foreign accent that she can't place. The sun is shining on the puddled street. It is one of those windy April days that shifts without warning from sun and sweeping nimbus clouds to rain, the air pungent with the scent of hawthorn and flowering pear, those stinky harbingers of spring.

She shifts her weight. "So, I hear that you're a doctor?"

"I trained as one. Now I primarily do research."

"What kind of research?"

"Neurology. Cognitive neuroscience."

She raises her eyebrows. "Wow."

His lips turn up slightly at the corners, as if he's on the verge of smiling, but not quite. "You know what they say about neurologists, of course."

"What's that?"

"That we're a clever lot, but completely useless. Can't actually cure anyone of anything."

She smiles. "I'm sure that's not the case."

"It's quite true, I assure you." Wrinkles like tiny parentheses mark the crease between his jawbone and his ear. Forty-something, if she had to guess. Like her.

"So you must be the pianist?"

"You could hear?" Heat rises to her cheeks. "I'm so embarrassed. I'm sorry about that."

"On the contrary, you play very well."

"I haven't practiced in a hundred years."

He smiles. "All the more impressive, then."

The sunlight brightens, dims. They trade brief details of their displacement: she tells him she was born here but has lived in the States since she was a kid; he tells her he is from Iran but has lived in London for nearly thirty years. So Aryan, not Arab, though presumably a Muslim still. She feels a reflexive clench. She is as bad as her mother. Of course, everyone is paranoid these days. The wind gusts, damp with the smell of rain. She pushes her hair out of her face, reaches for her bags.

"All we eat is takeaway, it seems," he says, eyeing the groceries. "I should make time to cook."

"We—?"

"Amir and I. My son."

The boy. His son. Her stomach quirks. "I think I saw him, maybe, the other day?" she says. "How old is he?"

"Nineteen. He's finishing up his first year at university."

Again she sees the boy glancing over at her, wet and muddy at three in the morning, sneaking in. Did he know his son had been out that late? What was it about the way the boy had caught and held her gaze, as if she'd been entrusted with a secret and promised not tell?

He takes his sunglasses off his head. "And you? Married? Kids?"

Clouds scud across the sky, billowy as spinnakers, racing past. She shakes her head. "No." She flings it away from her, the half truth, like a snake.

LONIA

Lonia drifts upward into brightness. Squinting, she makes her inventory: lamp, chair, dresser, pictures, vase. Her daughter. Esther is standing at her bedside, arms crossed, the corners of her mouth drawn down, her brow creased. It was difficult to get used to one's daughter being middle aged. Her hair is still thick and dark. But you can see where the folds are starting to harden, how the skin is growing pinched. The lines of pain. A pity. She has had no luck.

Lonia's own face surprises her in the mirror. The skin reptilian, crumpled and webbed, barnacled with spots. She only recognizes the irises of her eyes, as if the young woman she once was were still hiding there behind that mask of age.

"Mum, can I bring you something to eat?"

Loss of appetite is one of the items on the list provided by that Polish girl, the nurse. What to expect when dying. Lonia feels quite hungry, she decides. A good sign.

Esther disappears. She has always had a sort of serious dutifulness to her nature that Lonia could never quite understand. She remembers her as a child of three or four, dressed in a pea coat and sagging tights, clutching her little handbag, humorless as the Queen. *Such a good girl*, people always said. One always had the impression she was trying hard—rather too hard, perhaps—to do the right thing.

Lonia sees Esther at the age of five or six, home from primary school, sitting at the table having her tea. Esther, kicking her heels against the legs of the chair. She was not going back to school, she declared.

It is the sixties. Lonia's dark hair is bobbed, her dress a sleeveless sheath.

"Why not?"

"Because I'm not."

Kicking the chair. Averting her gaze. Breaking her biscuit into pieces, pressing the pieces into crumbs. How did one reason with a child?

"Of course you are."

"I'm not!"

"What happened at school? Did something upset you?"

"I'm just not going."

Naturally, something had happened. It wasn't difficult to get her to confess. Esther began to cry, and it emerged that she had picked the eye off a classmate's glued construction of a snake that was hanging in the hall. They'd been queued up, waiting to go outside to play, and she had reached out and picked the glittery eye right off. It is still there, in her pocket. She stuffs her hand in, pulls it out. It lies on the table, the eye, a crumpled wad of foil and a shiny button, blind.

"Well, what did you do that for?"

"I didn't mean to do it."

"Tomorrow you will apologize properly."

"I can't!"

"Yes, you can."

"I can't! If I say I did it, whoever made the snake will be cross, and if she's cross then she'll go and ruin the picture *I* made, and then I'll ruin hers back again, and then it will go on and on like that forever. It will never end!"

She had it all worked out, Esther did, at the age of six. The endless chain of hate.

Time is dissolving. The shapes of the furniture and the outlines of the window and the doorframe shift. A wardrobe hunches in the corner. A tram rumbles along Nádražni Street below. In the dimness, the wallpaper's stripes thicken into bars. Somewhere a dog barks. Lonia's father comes at night to tell her a story. He has small round spectacles, thinning hair, blue ink stains along his middle finger from his fountain pen. He sits on the edge of the bed, the mattress tilting inward with his weight.

Es war einmal, he begins. Once upon a time.

Lonia's favorite story is of the twelve princesses who escape the locked doors of their bedroom to dance throughout the night. No one could work out how the soles of their dancing shoes were worn right through every single morning. "Finally," her father says, raising his eyebrows, "an old soldier, hired by the King, wrapped himself in an invisible cloak and followed the youngest princess through the trapdoor in the floorboards, down steep stone stairs, and to a long, dark passageway that led to a subterranean grove of trees with silver, gold, and diamond leaves. The grove stood at the edge of a vast underground lake. There, twelve princes waited by twelve rowboats at the shore. Across the lake stood the castle where they would dance all night."

The black lake water slapped the oars; phosphorescence glittered in the rowboats' wakes. Faint strains of music drifted through the darkness. Lonia has learned in school about the dolomite caves in Bozkovské: dark and dripping, hung with stalactites, clear green water underneath. Here in Moravská Ostrava, coal mines were everywhere underground. From time to time the grownups spoke of mine disasters: explosions, cave-ins, floods. Was there a secret underground lake here as well?

She interrupts. "Is the castle like the Slezskoostravský hrad?"

"I should think so," her father says, "only even bigger and much more grand."

"And then?"

"Well, after following the princesses for three nights," her father continues, "the old soldier went to see the king. He told the king all about the trapdoor, the underground passage, the lake. As proof, he gave the king a gold-leafed bough he had plucked and a golden goblet from the prince's banquet spread. The king was grateful. The underground passage was filled up with dirt and the trap door in the princesses' bedroom nailed firmly shut. There would be no more nighttime dancing, no more escapes."

Lonia pities the poor princesses, especially the eldest, married off to the nasty old soldier as his reward. Weren't they furious that they'd been betrayed?

"But what happened to them after that?" she said.

"That's the end of the story, Lonia, *schatzi*. Now it's time to sleep."

Another story floats upward toward the light: Lonia and Hugo, ages six and ten. Hugo: pale, angular, all jutting knees and elbows, sagging socks and too-short sleeves. Clever, infuriating Hugo. Lonia always trailing behind, tearing her skirt scrambling after him over chain-link fences or slip-sliding on the forbidden Ostravice river ice.

An autumn afternoon in the park. A bright, cold sun. Hugo setting dead leaves on fire with a magnifying glass. He crouches, angling the glass. A tail of smoke curls upward from a spot of light.

"Hugo, stop! Someone's going to see!"

He blows on the leaves and the bright spot flares like magic into flame. He looks up, triumphant.

"I told you it would work!"

"You'd better put it out."

"You'd better shut up."

The leaf blackens, curls. Hugo piles on a handful of twigs and leaves. The flames spread and rise. Of course, the air is already smoky. It's always smoky in this Silesian city with its blast furnaces and coking plants and steel mills. Soot and ash on everything. Always the sulfurous smell of burning coal.

Hugo crouches lower. A trail of black ants skirts the burning leaves, furring a crack along the pavement.

"Ants build entire cities underground," he says, "layers of tunnels connecting rooms where they store their food and lay their eggs. I saw a picture in a book."

He stands and blocks the ants' path with his big scuffed leather shoe. The black line bends toward the flames. Lonia frowns. Why don't the ants just run away?

"Hugo, stop, I'll tell!"

Her voice blows away like leaves. In her memory, as in children's stories, there are no adults to tell. The world she inhabits with Hugo exists next door to that other world, the one of proper meals and music lessons and school, of timetables and rules. They slip into it through a trapdoor in the floor, Hugo in the lead, Lonia following behind. Sometimes he takes her hand and instructs her how, should he be in danger, she should go for help. The secrecy worms a worry-hole inside her chest. It makes her feel as important as a thief.

They are just two children playing in a park, three-quarters of a century ago. The burning leaves will blacken and thin to ash. The flames will soon snuff out. The ants will continue on their way.

Again the light blurs and shifts. Lonia blinks. How long has she been asleep?

Her daughter is looking down at her, annoyed. "You said you wanted an omelet, but you haven't taken a single bite!"

Lonia cannot remember asking for an omelet. But there it is before her on a tray beside the bed, shiny and yellow, cheese oozing out, congealed.

She should let them put her in a care home, she thinks. She did not want to be a burden to her daughter, should not have agreed when Esther said she was coming over to stay with her. But she couldn't bear the prospect of spending her last days warehoused among all those quasi-corpses parked incontinent and drooling in wheelchairs before the telly, catatonic from the drugs. And there is her daughter, looking so very earnest and uptight.

She sits up straighter, forces herself to swallow a few bites of egg. She has lost all sense of taste. One always forgot. She gives her daughter her best approximation of a smile.

Seated by the side of the bed, Esther crosses and re-crosses her legs. "When you're feeling a bit better, Mum, maybe I'll take you for a nice walk in the park. Would you like that?"

Lonia almost snorts. Stick her in a pram, take her on an outing to the park! It was just as everyone said—they treat you like an infant when you're old. Before long Esther would be changing her nappies, wiping her bum, spoon-feeding her stewed prunes.

Her husband, Isaac, had been lucky—a swift blow to the heart and that was it. Well, at least she has survived. She has raised their daughter, lived out her life. She has done her best. Now it was time.

"I am ready," Lonia says to Isaac, wherever he is. Lately she has felt that he is closer. She often senses the shadowy presence of other people here in the room with her, fleeting as bats at night. She knows it is some sort of hallucination—a sign that her mind is going, in all likelihood—but to her surprise it doesn't frighten her. Rather it gives her a kind of comfort to think that Isaac is here with her now. Sometimes her brother Hugo and her father are there as well. The lost, returned at last.

Everything ended in loss, of course. That was the way of life. It no longer angers her. She is old enough to accept it. She feels lucky to have found Isaac, to have had that kind of love, even if for too short a time. She hopes her daughter finds someone to love again sometime soon. Or if not love, she hopes at least that Esther finds the person that she needs.

TWO

ESTHER

She is sitting on the front steps, smoking. She tucks her skirt between her thighs, presses her knees together. Today the neighborhood is peaceful. Parked cars shine in the morning light. It is May Day. Elsewhere girls are twirling ribbons around maypoles; men are high-stepping Morris dances in the streets. She flips the word over like a coin inside her head.

May Day. Mayday. *M'aider.*

The sun is warm on her face, the sky a slip of wedgwood blue beyond the leaves. Across the street, a dumpster blocks the pavement, heaped with broken boards and chunks of drywall and empty sacks of dry concrete. Usually the racket is horrendous, but happily, there's no work going on today. It's a basement conversion, by the looks of it. Probably some rich investment banker turning the Victorian-era coal cellar into a fancy media room or a suite for the nanny or a private gym. Esther has even heard of people putting in full-size swimming pools underground.

The windows on the other side of the semidetached house, the doctor's side, are reflective, dark. She cranes her head, half watching for the boy, his son. It was odd that you could live so close to other people and hardly ever see them. The two sides of the house adjoin along the upstairs hallway; downstairs the two sitting rooms share a common wall. But mostly she forgets the neighboring side is there at all.

Amir. It's a common name in both Arabic and Hebrew, and with those dark features he could pass as either Muslim or Jew. But it is the icon that she pictures when she thinks of him. Those heavy-lidded eyes, that flat and knowing gaze.

At this hour on a Sunday she would imagine that he's still asleep, bare shouldered, wrapped in rumpled sheets, the sun pressing at the edges of the blinds. She wonders how he feels about living at home with his father instead of at university. She wonders what he is studying, whether he has a girlfriend or a job, what sorts of things he likes to do. She wonders again about that cat burglar's dark cap, that dark hoodie, those muddy boots. She almost laughs out loud at the thought of herself sitting out there like a fool, imagining that he was breaking in. But what *had* he been up to that night, so late? What was the meaning of that look?

The gray cat slinks along the sloping whitewashed balustrade that divides her steps from the doctor's. It must belong to him. It regards her as if it wants to tell her something, its head cocked to the side, its tail flicking like a metronome. Esther reaches out and wiggles her fingers, and it comes and rubs its head against her hand, then shies away.

She stubs out her cigarette, tosses the butt into the bushes, brushes off her skirt, and goes back in. Her mother is still upstairs asleep as well. It is exhausting, it seems, this work of dying, although it is not happening as quickly as the doctors seemed to expect. In the meantime, Esther shops and does the laundry and prepares the meals. She makes roasts and stews, boils stock from root vegetables and marrowbones, decorates butter cookies with dabs of jam and powdered sugar, bakes baguettes and *boules* of sourdough bread. Today she'll make croissants, she thinks. She goes back down to the kitchen and pulls out a canister of flour, a large bowl, a packet of dry yeast.

She likes these hours in her mother's kitchen, the radio droning in the background, as she chops and measures, stirs and sifts. It is not unlike her work in the conservation lab at the museum, days spent dabbing at a varnish-encrusted canvas with a swab or scraping gently with a scalpel at six-hundred-year-old paint. She loved the physicality of it, the chemical transformations that brought the images back from beneath the accumulated centuries of grime and neglect. She almost misses it. She could go back—she has only taken an extended leave. But she doubts she will. She feels the same way about her abandoned career as she does about her failing marriage: a toxic amalgam of regret mixed with relief. From here, her life back in New York—the life she has lived for over twenty years—feels almost like a story that belongs to someone else. It is good she got away. Her mother needs her here, at least.

She bends down and pulls a tray of croissants out of the oven. Just for a moment, considering the golden pastry flaking like gold leaf, she feels she has created a perfect, lasting thing. But she eats little and her mother eats even less, and much of what she makes she ends up throwing away.

In warmth of the afternoon, Esther helps her mother outside to the garden. The park is out of the question; she doesn't know what she was thinking, imagining she could push a wheelchair all the way to Regent's Park or Hampstead Heath. This will have to do instead.

"The garden is a sight," her mother grumbles. She perches on the wooden bench, wrapped in a cardigan and a scarf and gloves.

Birds are twittering in the mulberry, hidden in the branches that trail to the ground like a Victorian lady's skirt. There is the damp green smell of grass, the forsythia's bright flare. New shoots, furled as tightly as tiny umbrellas, are pushing their green tips through last fall's rotten leaves. There will not be many more days like this.

Her mother gestures to the flower beds along the base of the garden wall, beneath the thicket of wisteria vines. "If you could just tidy them up a bit. Clear away those sticks and leaves."

Esther is not much of a gardener. Her potted plants turned brown and withered; her Christmas cactus flowered in August, not December, and soon died. She can manage cut flowers, just about. "I'll do my best," she says.

"In Opava—Troppau—my grandparents had a lovely garden," her mother says.

Esther leans her head back and shuts her eyes. A red planet pulses behind her lids. Her mother tells the same stories over and over. All her life she's heard these stories, bedtime stories, fabulous as fairy tales. Her mother's body warm beside her in the shifting darkness. The mattress tilting beneath her mother's weight. She'd like to know what lies behind the well-worn contours. The details hidden in the seams.

"I loved to visit there when I was a little girl," her mother continues. "In Moravská Ostrava we had only a flat and there was no place to play outside except on the street. But my grandparents had a villa with a garden. My grandmother grew runner beans on poles, tomatoes, cucumbers, peas. My grandfather was famous for his roses. They were big and round, almost like peonies—quite unlike anything you've ever seen.

"It was forbidden to play near the roses, of course. But one day, my brother Hugo managed to toss his ball directly into the rose-bushes. He came in for dinner with scratches right up and down his arms. We were certain he would catch it! But my Oma stepped out of the kitchen, hands on her hips, and fixed my grandfather with a look. 'He's just a boy!' she said. And then my grandfather did not dare to say another word."

In Esther's mother's stories, there is no war. There is only the *before*: the vegetables and the roses, thorn-scratched Hugo, her grandmother's defense. Of what happened to her brother, lost during the war, her mother never speaks.

Esther says, "What happened to the villa?"

"What's that?"

"Your grandparents' villa," she says, louder. "After the war. Did they get it back?"

"My grandfather died in 1938. My grandmother came to live with us. She did not live much longer after that. Perhaps not even one year."

"So the villa was sold?"

"I don't know." She purses her lips. "I was just a girl."

"Didn't you ever want to go back? To visit?"

"Go back? No. It was impossible."

"Now, I mean. Since the Wall came down. Didn't you want to see it again? The place where you grew up?"

Her mother blinks like a lizard in the sun. "No."

A commotion of flapping and squawking erupts in the mulberry. The gray cat is crouching on the garden wall, its gaze fixed on the tree.

"It's always prowling about, you know, that cat," her mother says. "It belongs to the Arab next door."

"Will you stop calling him that? He's from Iran." Esther stands and waves at the cat. "We could have gone back together, you know," she says, turning back. "It's a shame we never did it. I would have liked to go. It would have been fun."

"There's nothing there to see."

"I don't know about that."

"The place I knew is gone."

Esther sits down again. "I hear that all things Jewish are trendy, these days, in Poland. Can you believe it? I read about it the other day. Apparently there's a big Jewish culture festival in Kraków, with klezmer bands, 'Jewish' food, Hasidic dancing, lectures, movies—the works. Ten thousand people attend! Who knew?"

"Nostalgia comes easily when there are no more Jews," her mother says dismissively.

"At least they're doing something to preserve the past."

Her mother frowns. "Ostrava was no shtetl. We spoke German and Czech, not Yiddish. The Rothschilds and the Guttmans owned the coal mines and the iron works and the steel mills. The Jews were kings."

"Maybe that was the problem."

Her mother ignores this comment. "My father trained as a lawyer in Prague. He was very intelligent, a cultured man. He loved Wagner and Beethoven and Goethe. He loved his country. He fought in the Kaiser's army. He had great faith in the triumph of rationality over primitive superstition." She shakes her head. "*Nebbich*. My poor father."

Not happily ever after. This is how her mother's stories always end. Her mother has no faith. Because of that, or in spite of it, she had Esther baptized in the Church of England, as if a sprinkling of water and a mumbled prayer would protect her from future persecutions of the Jews.

The cat uncoils and springs toward the tree. The starlings flap upward from the branches in a puff of black, like smoke.

Later, she sits on a chair pulled up beside her mother's bed, watching the evening news on television. A report of Oxford students injured jumping into the Cherwell off the Magdalen Bridge. Esther freezes, remote in hand, her arm outstretched. It's a May Morning tradition, this jumping from the bridge—only this year, the water, always shallow, is not even knee deep. More than fifty students have required treatment from paramedics and a dozen have been taken to hospital with spinal injuries and broken limbs. The soprano voices of the Magdalen College boys' choir warble from the college tower as rescuers pull an injured boy into a rubber raft. A mob of students crowds the low bridge span. A girl climbs onto the parapet. The camera zooms in. Esther holds her breath. The girl's white dress billows as she leaps.

On other afternoons, after the nurse arrives, Esther walks. She wanders along the leafy streets of Swiss Cottage and South Hampstead, long blocks lined with regency mansions and Georgian terraces with their graceful, arched bay windows and white-railed steps. Some days she ventures farther out along Belsize Lane to the green expanse of Hampstead Heath where, from Parliament Hill, she can see, delicate as a watercolor landscape, the dome of St. Paul's, the crosshatched Gherkin, the BBC tower, the Knightsbridge Barracks, the slim bangle of the London Eye. One day she walks as far as Camden, crossing Regent's Park to the canal. She used to bring Noah here sometimes when he was little to watch the narrowboats go through the locks. They would walk along the towpath, reading the names of the crazy sisterhood stenciled on the low-slung hulls: *Medusa*, *Ophelia*, *Topsy Annie*, *Lorna-Anne*, *Lady Jane*. The water was a milky brown in the sunlight, dark green and dappled in the shade, thick with smells of weeds and diesel fumes, cigarettes and toast. On the boats' flat rooftops, they'd spy a gargoyle, a satellite dish, a string of prayer flags, a jolly garden gnome, a foil pinwheel scattering trapezoids of light.

Years ago, in New York, from her first apartment near Gramercy Park, she'd also walked, taking long excursions south along the paved path by the East River—passing the immigrant families gathered for their Sunday picnics, the children chasing each other across the dusty grass; turning at the Williamsburg Bridge toward the old tenement blocks of the Lower East Side; crossing onto Orchard Street and Hester and Canal, with their Jewish schmatte shops and synagogues and delis turned bodegas and Chinese laundromats.

Everyone came from elsewhere in New York. They came from the Dominican Republic, from Jamaica, Russia, Taiwan, Sri Lanka, New Jersey, the Midwest. Layer by layer, they made the city theirs. But London was different, or at least it was back when she was a child here. You couldn't *become* English; it was something you inherited, part of your genetic code. London was full of foreigners, now more than ever, but somehow the boundaries seemed fixed. You could assimilate—perfect your accent, make a fortune, change your name—but the real England remained as inaccessible as the city's private clubs and gardens, locked away behind wrought iron gates.

She remembers once, as a child, going over to a classmate's house to play. She must have been seven or eight. A grandmother or great-aunt was visiting, and the adults had gathered in the dim, upholstered sitting room, the children called in to be introduced. Little bowls of sweets had been set out on all the tables: foil-wrapped toffees and Bendicks mints. Esther took a toffee and hid it in her fist.

"Fagin," the old woman said, peering at Esther over her spectacles' rim. "An Irish name, is it?"

Esther shrugged. Not Irish, she didn't think.

"Are you Catholic?"

She shook her head.

"Protestant, then?"

Another shake.

"No?"

The classmate's mother spoke up with an embarrassed smile, her lips tight.

"Your family's Jewish, isn't that right, darling?"

Esther looked down at her feet, her brown Oxfords, scuffed at the toes. She clenched the toffee in her hand. When she tried to unwrap it later, the foil would not come off.

She wakes in the middle of the night to the muffled sound of running water. It rises, faintly, above the other night noises: the creaking floor joists, the whine of a distant motorcycle, the ticking of the bedside clock. It's 1:57 a.m. The noise must be coming from somewhere in the walls. It's just the faintest trickle, like the runoff from light rain. Is it raining? Or is there some kind of leak? She can hear it, then she can't. The minutes click by. She shuts her eyes. Through the darkness the sound of the water rises, mingling with the whooshing of the blood inside her veins. It pulls at her like a strange sea, the calm surface a deception, the current tugging underneath. She jerks awake, squints at the clock. It's 3:16 a.m. The house is silent. She turns over, pulls the pillow over her head.

In the morning, she checks the bathrooms, but the toilets are not running and none of the taps appear to have a leak. She crouches down and feels inside the kitchen cabinet beneath the sink, but it is dry as well. She goes down the creaky stairs to the cellar, dank and dim and crammed with boxes and oddly shaped objects draped in sheets, and shines a flashlight around the pipes, furred with a century of dust and grime. There's no sign of moisture anywhere. She pictures the pipes stretching through the walls like organic matter, twining around the joists, winding tendrils into cracks: lead intestines, copper arteries, polyvinyl chloride veins. She knows nothing of plumbing beyond the strangely anthropomorphic language: couplings, elbows, waste arms, slip joints, traps.

She eases open the door to her mother's room. Her mother is propped up in bed, leafing through a magazine. Esther wonders how long she's been awake. The windowpanes are rattling from the thudding roar of the excavation machinery across the street.

"You haven't noticed any leaky taps, have you?" Esther says. "I could have sworn I heard something—the faintest drip."

"A what?"

She clears her throat. "I thought maybe I heard something dripping?"

Her mother's mouth turns down. "I don't know how you can hear anything whatsoever with that infernal racket across the street. You should ring the police. This shouldn't be permitted in a neighborhood like this."

Esther sighs. "You're probably right."

"I know I'm right. What was it you said you heard?"

"Forget it, Mum. Just something dripping. I'm sure it was nothing. I checked all of the toilets and sinks."

"It was probably coming from the Arab's house next door."

"You really need to stop calling him that."

"Go over there, Esther, and tell him to ring the plumber." Her mother shakes her head. "With neighbors, there's always trouble, believe me."

Esther steps out the front door. The sky is raw and white, the pavement damp. Probably the rain was all she heard last night. She shakes a cigarette out of the pack and lights it. Across the street, workers are maneuvering a fat hose that appears to be sucking dirt from beneath the foundation and spewing it into an idling dump truck. She wonders what they'll find down there, beneath the ground. London's marshy soil was always giving up its relics: potsherds, Roman coins, marble statuary, medieval paving stones, bones from Anglo-Saxon mass graves.

She thinks of Noah as a toddler, running to her along the beach on Fire Island, palms extended and filled with shiny pebbles, bits of driftwood, broken shells. She remembers showing him how to tunnel through a sandcastle, scraping away at the cool, wet sand from both sides of the mound until her fingers poked through and met. There was something uncanny about the feeling of her sandy fingertips touching one another deep inside the tunnel, as if the other hand belonged to someone else.

She can see him so clearly, lying on his back on the beach at Fire Island, tracing sand angels. Overhead, clouds fled across the taut blue sky, chased by the salt wind off the dunes. She sees the three of them as if from an enormous distance, her and Gil and their little boy, three tiny figures on that tiny spit of sand.

The dump truck is bleeping now, backing up, a new dump truck behind it waiting to pull in. Traffic is backed up down the street. The giant machine is roaring. Everything is vibrating with the noise. She can feel it in her teeth. It wouldn't be surprising if all that excavation had caused a pipe to break.

She steps down to the pavement and turns around to look back at the house. The twin blue front doors, the two rows of mirror-image windows, the symmetrical white trim. On the doctor's side, the blinds are halfway up in one of the upstairs windows. She moves a little closer and squints, but she cannot see in.

She turns their names over on her tongue: Amir, Javad, Javad, Amir. The other day she'd walked over to the public library in Swiss Cottage and clicked through websites on the computer until she finally found him: *Dr. Javad Asghari, University College London Institute of Neurology, Alexandra House, 17 Queen Square.* The thumbnail photo was rather blurry, and the biographical details revealed little, but the official confirmation pleased her, as if without it he didn't really exist. On a whim, she typed *Amir Asghari* into the search bar too, but turned up only references to some mathematician in Birmingham and an Iranian civil engineer.

Across the street, a workman yells; the dump truck belches smoke. It is too early in the morning to knock on anyone's door. She can hardly ask Javad to call a plumber, anyway; she should just call one herself. Again she sees his not-quite smile, feels that odd sense of déjà vu. Again the lie she told gives off a little twinge.

JAVAD

The clamor of construction noise wakes him before the alarm, the roaring and banging jolting him out of some annoyingly overcomplicated dream. Bloody hell. He swings his feet out of bed and groans. His lower back is stiff. He shuffles to the bathroom and splashes water on his face.

Today he's due in Kent by ten. He's been called in to consult on a patient down at Little Brook—some fellow who turned up lost in April, out on the Isle of Sheppey—amnesic, aphasic, a possible case of dissociative fugue.

Trousers on, shirtless, towel around his neck, he steps into his study and jiggles the mouse on his computer. He checks his email, sends one off to his secretary saying he should be back at the Institute by two, clicks on the news. Polls are open today for the general election; Labour are expected to win a majority again. Another roadside bombing in Iraq. Weather chilly and unsettled, showers lingering with sunny patches later in the afternoon.

He could really do with a holiday someplace warm. Malta, maybe, or Greece. Perhaps he'll take Amir when he's finished his exams. They haven't gone away together in god knows how many years.

Behind the closed door of his bedroom, Amir is still asleep. Some days they hardly see each other, as if they lived in different time zones. Downstairs, he grabs an overripe banana from the kitchen counter, snaps shut his briefcase, switches off the lights, turns back to refill the cat's bowls with food and water, and then he's out and down the steps. He's on his way.

The sky is white, the pavement damp. His glasses blur with mist. That blasted digging machine is spewing dirt all over the street. He skirts the workmen in their orange vests and heads toward Finchley Road. He'll catch the Underground and then the overground south to Kent.

It would not be so difficult, he thinks as he walks, simply to keep on going, to give up all intention, all conscious will, and hop onto the first train, any train, and let it take you wherever it might go. That's what happened to people in a fugue state. They forgot themselves. Took off. Jumped tracks.

There was an outbreak of so-called "fuguers" in late nineteenth-century Europe—young men, mostly, who wandered away on strange, compulsive journeys that took them hundreds or even thousands of miles away from home, from bourgeois villages in France and Germany to Constantinople, Moscow, Sevastopol, Algiers. *Les aliénés voyageurs*, the French called them. Mad travelers. They'd scrape for money, get arrested for vagrancy, dragged off to hospital, shipped back home. When they finally "awoke" they could not say why or how they'd gotten where they'd been. "Yet another escapade," one fuguer noted in his diary. "What a calamity."

Dissociative fugues were rare but not unheard of these days as well. Fuguers turned up from time to time in railway stations or wandering, disorientated, on nearby streets, unable to give a coherent account of who they were or where they were going or where they'd been. Some were autistic, others suffered from dementia or epilepsy or posttraumatic stress.

Javad was intrigued by the phenomenon of neurological symptoms that seemed to lack any organic pathology in the brain. *Hysteria* was the word used by Charcot and Freud. Their patients were mostly women, of course, in whom hysteria tended to present as paralysis rather than as flight.

It's all in your head, people always said about conversion disorders, and of course that was exactly right. It was all in the anterior cingulate cortex, in the dorsolateral prefrontal cortex, in the hippocampus, in the medial temporal lobe. It was uncharted territory. They were just beginning to explore it now with functional imaging studies. Slowly, a new map was starting to emerge.

He crosses Finchley Road and joins the commuters funneling into the entrance to the Tube, a bustle of damp umbrellas and swinging briefcases. He swipes his Oyster card over the pad, pushes through the ticket barrier, and he is on his way.

The patient is tall and thin, with short, light hair and pasty skin. A twitchy, agitated affect. He cowers on the examination table, bare legs very white beneath the gown, arms crossed tightly over his chest, as if he were trying to fold himself away. He might be Northern European—a Pole or Finn. Early to mid-twenties? Difficult to tell. Javad checks the chart. Normal body weight, normal blood pressure, normal temperature, slightly elevated pulse. He notes the odd, fixed stare. Mild catatonia, perhaps.

Javad manipulates the patient's head toward his chest, from side to side. The patient flinches at the touch but gives no sign of pain. Javad shines a penlight in his eyes. The pupils dilate and contract. He moves the light from side to side and the eyes follow. Normal. By miming the action that he requires, he gets the patient to open his mouth and stick out his tongue—soft palate, uvula, pharynx—nothing unusual there. Gag reflex is fine. Taps the tendons of the elbows and knees. All normal. He sets down the reflex hammer and again tries asking a few questions, but the patient does not seem to understand. He demonstrates the Luria sequence with his fist, also to no avail. There is not much else he can do. There is no way to administer a diagnostic questionnaire to a patient who will not speak. He'd be keen to get an MRI. He wonders if he can make a case for that.

"There we are," he says out loud. "That wasn't so bad, was it?" The man's eyes flick toward him and away, quicksilver as fish. He thinks he catches the tiniest inclination of the head, the faintest intimation of a sign.

Fuguer or feigner? The difference was a matter of whether or not his symptoms were under his conscious control—and it was nearly impossible to tell. What might the man stand to gain by malingering? Either way, it seemed clear that he was trying to run away from something. Some kind of trauma, presumably. But what? What had caused this break?

The Little Brook hospital staff have gathered round the conference room table. Motivational posters hang on the walls: a sculler on a lake lit orange by the sun ("Achievement!"), a ring of sky-divers holding hands ("Teamwork!"). The room smells of cleaning fluid and cheap cologne. He takes a sip of coffee, vending machine fare in a flimsy plastic cup, which, as always, manages to be simultaneously bitter and weak. Through the sealed windows, he can hear the faint hum of traffic along the motorway. The taxi from the railway station drove him along streets of tidy redbrick cottages, lanes flanked with hedgerows and rosebushes in bloom. Far in the distance, he could see the tops of the high white stanchions of the Queen Elizabeth II Bridge. The white sky was as open as a dome. As always when he left the city, he felt the lightness of escape.

"I'm afraid that at this stage I can only confirm what I presume you already know," he tells the assembled group. "We can quite confidently rule out the major organic pathologies—head injury, dementia, encephalitis, Korsakoff's, and so forth. Epilepsy also seems unlikely given a normal EEG. So we are most likely looking at a psychogenic etiology. And it is well established that nearly all individuals with dissociative symptomology have significant comorbid psychiatric diagnoses, frequently including personality disorders. But I'm afraid it's impossible to say much more than that without a thorough clinical history and exam."

The NHS manager folds his arms. "Which, of course, is precisely what we cannot get, since he will not speak."

"The mutism is a bit of a puzzle," Javad admits. "Aphasia is atypical in dissociative disorders, although it does sometimes present with severe anxiety or posttraumatic stress—rather more commonly in children than adults. There's no apparent evidence of vocal cord damage or paralysis. Of course, one would need to do a scope to see if his voice box has been damaged, and a scan would be necessary to rule out lesions or a tumor in the brain." Without permission, he knows, they could run neither of those tests.

"What about autism?" one of the social workers says.

"It's a possibility, certainly," Javad says. "As I'm sure you know, the resistance to close contact and that sort of flat affect are quite common in individuals on the spectrum."

"But what about the piano playing?" another of the social workers says. "How is that possible if he can't even remember who he is?"

"Musical ability is often preserved in both organic and dissociative forms of amnesia," Javad says.

One of the consultants, a turbaned Sikh, frowns and says, "Quite right."

All they could do was speculate. Perhaps he was yet another illegal immigrant—an asylum seeker who'd jumped off a passing ship. Perhaps he'd been pushed into the sea by ruthless smugglers or the Russian mob. Or perhaps he really was a brilliant pianist who had fled a disastrous performance or some other personal calamity and tried to drown himself in grief.

Javad says, "Are there no reports of anyone fitting his description gone missing?"

The unit manager shakes his head. "Not as of yet."

He had to belong to someone, Javad thinks. Everyone belonged to someone; nobody was truly singular, alone. Eventually someone—a mother, father, sibling, neighbor, lover—would have to notice that he had disappeared.

Around the table, people begin closing their files, gathering cups and papers. The unit manager stands and extends his hand. "This has been quite helpful, Dr. Asghari. Thank you very much indeed."

At home, Amir is hunched over his laptop at the kitchen table, earphones in. Javad touches his shoulder and Amir pulls out one earpiece, tilting his head.

"Grub's on, mate." Javad sets the carrier bag of Chinese takeaway onto the counter. "Clear away your things. Let's eat."

Amir pulls out the earphones and shuts the laptop. There's a sticker of the high-voltage warning sign on the laptop's cover, a yellow triangle outlined in black enclosing a jagged arrow pointing down: DANGER. KEEP OUT. What secrets did he hide in there? Javad thinks of the patient down in Little Brook and what his parents knew, or didn't know, before he disappeared.

"Are you ready for your exams?" Javad pries the lids off the containers and pokes spoons into the food and sets them on the table.

Amir shrugs. "I guess."

"This one's prawns, the other's beef." He spoons some of the prawn lo mein onto his plate and pushes the container over to Amir. "So. I was thinking."

"Thinking?"

"I was thinking that we might go away somewhere for a few days' holiday when term's out. Someplace warmer than it is here."

Amir raises his eyebrows. "A holiday? Are you feeling all right, Baba?"

"I rather fancy Greece."

"I thought you hated sitting on the beach."

"I hear Santorini is very beautiful."

"And we would do what there?"

"Gosh, I dunno. Sleep, read, drink ouzo, eat tzatziki, dandle our feet in the Aegean. That sort of thing."

Amir rolls his eyes. "Oh, go on. Fifty quid you wouldn't even take off your shoes."

Javad spoons some of the beef dish onto his plate. The sauce is rather gloppy. He should have ordered something vegetarian instead. "Come on. You can't turn down an offer of a holiday."

"Who's turning anything down?"

"We don't have to go to Greece."

"Greece sounds great."

"No, really. We can go anywhere you like. Cornwall. The Lake District. The south of France."

"Whatever you like. I don't care."

Javad had once assumed that being a parent would be easier when his son was grown. Now he misses the days when he and Amir did things together, easily, happy in each other's company. For years they'd belonged to a regular set of fathers and sons who played football together on Sunday mornings in the park. The turf was muddy and uneven, with splintery benches along the touchlines littered with kit bags and water bottles and discarded tops. The boys raced up and down the field, decked out in full kit—Barcelona or Manchester United shirts, shin pads, wristbands, fancy boots—the fathers in tracksuit bottoms and rugby shirts leftover from their university days, huffing along behind. Even then Javad's back had not been forgiving of the sporadic punishment, and he'd spend most of the game trying to avoid crashing into other winded fathers or tripping over the small boys swerving around his legs. They didn't know most of the other families—Amir's school was in Caroline's neighborhood—but

Javad looked forward to the feeling of belonging, of being more than just an every-other-weekend dad.

They'd talked to each other back then; at least that's the way Javad remembers it. Walking home from the park in the dimming afternoon, muddy and sore, their weekend together sputtering to an end—as if spurred by the prospect of their impending separation, Amir would start asking questions. Where did water go when it went down the drain? How was it that male snails could lay eggs but roosters couldn't? What did the word *surveillance* mean? He hardly listened to Javad's earnest explanations, rushing onward to the next question as if all he needed was the simple confirmation that an answer did exist.

Javad had become a scientist precisely because of those kinds of childhood questions. As a boy, he'd collected fossils, minerals, butterflies, and bugs. He'd set up a little lab in the cupboard beneath the kitchen stairs, where, to his sisters' horror and his mother's chagrin, he mixed together household chemicals, dismantled small appliances, cut up dead mice and frogs. These were the questions that still fascinated him, even now. What made the eyes see, the muscles move, the nerves react? How did memories form? How did consciousness arise?

Amir eats fast, as if he can't wait to get away. Through the wall comes the faint sound of the piano. The American, Esther. A good-looking woman. That heart-shaped face, that corona of dark hair. There is something about her that reminds him of his sister Darya, the one who stayed in Tehran, the one he hasn't seen in years. A hint of sadness, perhaps, about the eyes.

Amir sets down his fork. "I should probably check with Mum, though. I think she might have mentioned something about going away with her and Niels to some posh place in Spain."

Javad laughs. "Planned? Her?"

"I'm just saying."

"And really, Spain?"

Through the wall, he can hear her playing scales. They ripple up and down the octaves. Major, then minor. A half step up. Major, then minor again. Of course there would be a complication with Caroline. There was always a complication with Caroline. If only she would marry this bloke and get the hell out of Javad's life once and for all. Everything would be easier then.

"I just thought it might be nice," Javad says, "to do something together, the two of us, for once." He sounds more petulant than he means to be.

Amir bends down and picks up his laptop off the floor. "I live here now, Baba, remember? We see each other every day."

"Do we?"

Amir relents. "We'll go somewhere, Baba. Anywhere you like. It will be good to get away."

ESTHER

Coat on, she is standing outside the front door, on her third cigarette of the morning, waiting for the nurse, Zofia, to arrive. The sky is heavy, wind scratched, more like March than May. She is at her limit, coiled tight. She cannot stay in the house a minute longer. What had made her think that she could handle this?

A door slams next door, startling her. It's him, the boy, Amir. He hops down the steps without seeming to notice her and disappears around the far side of the house.

Her stomach kinks. She hasn't seen him since that first April night, a month ago already. Christ.

In a moment he reappears, hauling a rumbling green recycling bin behind him to the street. He's barefoot, wearing cargos and a commando jumper a few sizes too big.

She nods to him as he comes back up the steps. "Is it collection day?"

If he recognizes her, he gives no sign. She can see his resemblance to his father now, up close, although his eyes are even longer-lashed and darker, more intense.

He pauses and gives her a closer look. "Thursday, yep."

She holds her cigarette to the side so the smoke will blow the other way. "I can't seem to keep track of time these days. Thanks."

"Would you like me to pull your bin out for you?"

"Oh, you don't have to do that."

"It's not a problem."

Heat rises in her cheeks. "Well, okay, thanks," she says. She feels foolish. The bin is probably two-thirds empty, anyway.

He bounces back down the steps. The concrete must be cold on his bare feet. He is a bit taller than his father and broader across the shoulders—less wiry, more solidly built. And yet there are still traces of the child in that face that seems too smooth for the dark scruff of bristles along his jaw and chin. This is how boys turn into men, she thinks: like crustaceans, the shell hardening over a vulnerable core. With girls it works the other way around— for all their delicate appearances, they are tougher from the start. How often she had studied the lines of Noah's rounded forehead, the structure of his nose, the soft cheeks and knobby limbs and wondered what he'd look like when he was a man, staring until he looked up and said "What?" and pulled a sour face.

She must be staring at Amir now as well, because as he jogs back up the steps, he shoots her a funny look.

"Thanks so much," she says.

"No worries." The door bangs shut behind him as he goes in.

Her hands are trembling as she lights another cigarette.

Zofia's broad moon-face is as placid as it always seems to be. She comes ambling up the street from the bus stop without any trace of urgency, as if she has nothing else in the world to do, nowhere else to be. She always takes time to chat with Esther's mother, trading anecdotes or jokes in Polish, listening to her mother's complaints and stories with a patience Esther never feels. Zofia helps her mother into the bath, massages her swollen feet, trims her yellowed nails. Esther has read about the Polish migrants struggling to survive in England—scavenging scraps from dumpsters, drinking hand sanitizer, eating rats. Right here, out-side the Finchley Road Underground Station, the migrants lay curled in cardboard cartons, filthy duvets pulled over their heads. What did Zofia think as she passed them on her way here? Com-pared to such suffering, what was one old woman's death?

"Everything is okay?" Zofia says as she comes up the steps.

Esther's gut clenches as anxiety floods back in. "No. Not really. She was up half the night, moaning in pain."

"The pain it is very bad?"

"She'd probably give it a two. But I'd say more like eight."

"Did you give her something?"

"Just Tramadol. One tab at three this morning."

"And nothing else since then?"

Esther shakes her head. She is already in motion, backing away. "I just need to go out for a little while. I won't be long."

Zofia waves her hand as if in benediction. "Everything will be all right."

She is off, walking fast, away, away. She walks without choosing a direction, without caring where she might end up. The wind nee-dles her skin, as if all her nerve endings are exposed. She wants to give up, go home. She has come here to help, but she's not being helpful. She isn't up to it—the worry, the tedium, the pain. What had she imagined? She had thought she could handle anything, had imagined herself calm and reassuring at her mother's bedside, a few last intimate conversations, and then . . . Well. She hadn't wanted to think about that.

The heels of her boots strike a rhythm on the concrete. *Away, away*. Along Adelaide Road, brick walls overhung with leafy bushes front Victorian mansion blocks and Georgian terraces and squinty-windowed modern high-rises. There is a photograph of her standing with her father on a North London street much like this, years back. He stands tall above her in his overcoat and hat.

She has on lace-trimmed ankle socks and patent leather shoes, a terribly serious expression on her face. He looks a little bored. They are holding hands.

In her memory, all that remains of her father are disconnected fragments. Black-rimmed glasses and wingtip shoes. Driving gloves made of unlined calfskin, the knuckles cut out, like the paper snowflakes she made at school. The rosewood scent of his cologne. The ridges along his fingernails, nicotine stained, trimmed straight across. Tufts of hair along the edges of his ears. The stale, smoky whiff of breath when he bent to give her a kiss. His raised voice on the telephone behind closed doors, speaking in a language she couldn't understand.

He was a collector, her father. He acquired the kinds of objects you could hide inside your pocket: stamps, rare coins, Swiss watches, signet rings. Also big, ambitious things: commercial developments, apartment blocks, luxury hotels. Sometimes he would snap his fingers and pluck a five pence coin from behind her ear. When she pried apart his fist to claim it, it was never there. There was something quick and shifting about him, like disappearing ink.

The blocks beat past in her peripheral vision—dark windows and whitewashed steps, black and white like piano keys. She passes the Chalk Farm Underground Station, picks up her pace. *Away, away.*

There is an old sadness when she thinks about her father, a strain across her ribs, long since buried deep. That last day, so long ago, she'd stuck her head out of the taxi window and waved. She had no idea it was the end. She was just thirteen. She didn't know about his troubles with the law, that by then there was already a warrant out for his arrest. She didn't know about the frozen bank accounts or the prison sentence that lay ahead. She didn't know—no one did—about the time bomb ticking inside his chest.

She wishes she could have understood him better. He'd escaped the Nazis, survived the war, built a major property company—created a new, successful life. Why then had he cheated on his taxes, embezzled from his own employees' pension fund? If only she could have known him as an adult, and not just as a child. She might have been able to forgive him his betrayal then.

She crosses the canal. Here in Camden the streets are a cacophony of tattoo and body-piercing parlors, noodle shops, discount shoe stores. Half-price sales. Cash for gold. Electronics shops flaunting gigantic flat-screen TVs, pirated DVDs. She skirts the racks of knockoff handbags, fake designer sunglasses, cheap printed shirts. It is a tattiness particular to London, Esther thinks, although what made it different from, say, Canal Street in New York, she couldn't have said. A woman wearing a burka stands outside a Ladbroke's, jabbering into a mobile phone. Swirls of graffiti cover storefront grates. She passes a 99p Store. A pawnbroker's. A massage parlor. A glass-sided BT phone box, long since obsolete.

She should turn around—she has been walking for nearly an hour, and Zofia will have already gone—but she keeps on walking. Timpani are beating in her ears. She can't go back. Her mother would be better off without her, anyway. In a hospital she would get the nursing care she needs. Esther was no nurse. She was in way over her head. She keeps walking, pulled on by the wind. *Away, away.*

And then, beyond the honking traffic along the Euston Road, a quiet patch of green: St. Pancras parish church. She crosses the road and peers into the leafy churchyard through the iron fence. Four decrepit caryatids are holding up the vestry roof with their stony heads. The caryatids have grim, mannish faces and grimy chitons parted to reveal one round, bare breast. She has always preferred her plaintive Byzantine Madonnas to these tough-girl Greeks.

She turns the corner to the front entrance. A row of Ionic columns flanks tall red doors. LUNCHTIME RECITAL, ENTRY FREE! reads a sandwich board set out at the top of the steps. The performer is a pianist, playing *The Art of Fugue*, by Bach.

Esther steps into the cool dimness of the church. She loves churches, their hush and soar. Angels and apostles cast mottled shadows through stained glass. In the apse, a concert grand piano waits like an offering before the altar, its lid raised like a raven's wing. A smattering of people have settled along the wooden pews: solitary women, old men, here or there a younger person—a graduate student, perhaps, on break from the British Library or University College London, down the street.

Her heels reverberate on the worn flagstones as she makes her way around the perimeter of the sanctuary. She peeks into a dim vestibule at the entrance to the choir loft stairs. A wooden plaque is mounted on the wall, engraved in gold with twelve long columns of names. It's a memorial for the men of the 19th Battalion, St. Pancras Regiment lost in the Great War. She counts to fifty and stops, less than halfway down the first column, still in the *a*'s. *Adamson, Alford, Applethwaite, Ashe.* What did that add up to—a thousand names? Or more? And that was just this regiment. An entire generation of men was lost in that horrific war, the war to end all wars. No, not men—boys. Millions of boys, dead in the bloody mud of Passchendaele, Ypres, the Somme. These days, she thinks, boys are still dying, blown up by IEDs and suicide bombers in Baghdad, Fallujah, Basra, Kandahar. Boys like her Noah, boys like Amir.

She slides into a pew and opens the program. *The Art of Fugue*, the notes explain, was Bach's last, unfinished masterpiece, a virtuoso study of the possibilities of contrapuntal form. The piece is a compilation of fourteen *contrapuncti*, or counterpoints—four simple fugues, three counter-fugues, four double or triple fugues, two mirror fugues and their inversions, and a quadruple fugue—plus four canons, each a different variation on a single theme. Fugues had fallen out of popular favor by the 1740s and were by then considered fusty and archaic, yet still Bach wanted to push the possibilities of the form's constraints and variations as far as they could go. Genius Bach.

The fugue, she reads, is both metaphor and form. Its variations make connections between seemingly unlike things and reveal the ways in which the new is recreated out of the material of the old. It shows us how the present is always in conversation with—in counterpoint with—the past. To Bach, the fugue was both puzzle and enigma, both a reflection of the sublime order as well as the ineffability of the divine. It embodied the flight of the soul toward God.

The pianist, a young Asian woman in a red dress, enters and settles herself on the bench. The opening notes are somber, spare. First the right hand plays alone, then the left joins in. A third voice enters; a fourth begins. The voices intensify, the counterpoint grows more complex. The melody grows syncopated, then inverts; it speeds up, slows down again. Voices chase each other up and down the D minor scale. They call and answer, pull away, close in.

Esther shuts her eyes and stretches out her legs. The wild surge that dragged her here has ebbed, leaving behind a foggy fatigue. Her legs and ankles ache. She gives herself over to the music, unable to follow its complexity. The voices rise and turn, repeat. They fracture, multiply, and split, a kaleidoscope of sound. They gather and release in a cascade of scales.

If her father hadn't died, she thinks. If her parents hadn't escaped. If her parents had never met. If not for all the ifs, she'd have a different story. She'd be a German-speaking central European like her parents and their parents before them, like Johann Sebastian Bach and his twenty children, living in a red-roofed Moravian city or a Prussian town, her life fitted like a nesting bowl inside theirs.

She is neither an immigrant nor a refugee, but she feels like an exile nonetheless. A latter-day wandering Jew. She envies her friends who have genealogies inked into family Bibles, with multi-branching family trees. She doesn't even know her great-grandparents' names, or which forgotten countries they were born in. Moldavia, Galicia, Carpathian Ruthenia? Which of those vanished corners of the Pale?

Gil and his parents and grandparents were New Yorkers through and through. It didn't matter that one of his great-grandfathers had emigrated from Odessa, a grandmother from Berlin. It never would have occurred to Gil not to consider himself American. America had given his family everything they knew. She had loved his parents' chaotic Thanksgiving dinners and interminable seders filled with animated disagreement, their elegant Fifth Avenue apartment and weather-beaten Fire Island cottage, the feeling of security that came from their pedigreed professionalism and wealth. She remembers the first weekend he invited her out to Fire Island to meet his parents. They went down to the beach after everyone else had gone to bed. She lay on the cool sand of the dunes with her head resting in the hollow of his shoulder, looking up at stars she was sure she'd never seen before, and felt the love rush in.

She opens her eyes, hardly aware of the church or how she got here. The pianist's fingers are flying across the keys. The music explodes in climax, draws back to a ripple, whispers, sings. The theme and countertheme return again and again. They are the same each time and yet completely different, just as she is always both herself and not herself in each successive instant, no longer a small girl living in England, no longer a wife or mother, no longer even the same woman she was fifty-seven minutes earlier that very afternoon. She too has circled through the variations and returned to where she started to find that it has changed.

The music stops. The pianist's hands hover above the keys. The strings resound and ring, their vibration rising toward the vaulted ceiling of the church. Everybody holds their breath.

Bach's final, unfinished quadruple fugue breaks off without resolution, without a cadence. There is only silence. A drift.

LONIA

She wakes in darkness, thrashing, her nightdress twisted, the damp sheets sticking to her skin. Pain radiates through her body like a high-pitched drone. She struggles to sit but finds that she cannot. She is dying. She lies back and tries to slow her breath, panic cinching tight across her chest. She is dying. Where is Esther? She is afraid to go back to sleep. *A handful of patience is worth a bushel of brains*, her father used to say. Patience has never been her strength.

Shh, schatzi, her father always said, brushing the hair back from her forehead.

Then the story would begin. *Es war einmal.* Once there was a girl and a boy and their father who lived on Nádražni Street. Then the world collapsed into a heap of bones.

Oh, this worn-out story, unraveling, moth eaten, full of holes.

She sees him now, her brother Hugo, as clearly as if he were standing before her. He is leaning over the table, his jaw shaded with pale stubble, his eyes hard and bright. Light fractures off the chandelier. Their father sighs blue smoke. In Austria the situation is very bad. Jews have been arrested, beaten, fired from their jobs, their property seized. Even here in Moravská Ostrava, the SdP have been demonstrating in the streets. Black- and red-striped party flags fly from all the windows on the Marktplatz. Her father has been writing to business acquaintances and distant relatives in Antwerp, Trondheim, Chicago, Leeds. His middle finger is stained blue with ink.

Hugo talks of olive trees, orange groves, Zionist pioneers. Their father grinds the stub of his cigarette onto his plate.

"And you would do what in Palestine, exactly?"

"Live on a kibbutz," Hugo says. "Work the land."

"You, a farmer? Don't be a fool."

Lonia doesn't want to go anywhere. She likes her room, her school, her friends. The windows of the flat have been thrown open to the sooty August heat. The air that enters is hot as exhaust. Beyond the Vítkovice smokestacks, the sun is red. She has seen photographs of Palestine: dusty streets and Arabs, donkeys, sand, old stones. She doesn't want to leave. She doesn't want to leave her grandparents, her mother's gravesite, her friends. She can't imagine being anywhere but here. She leans her head against her father's shoulder. He lights another cigarette.

"Beneš will not give in to the Reich," he says.

Across the table, Hugo's jaw is set. Lonia knows that look. The door to his bedroom slams.

Hugo and her father argue. The wireless sits between them on the table, a constant drone. Her father expects to be called up. There is talk of evacuating her and Hugo to the countryside. Lonia wonders why men have to fight. Without men there would be no war, her best friend Eva says. Lonia has read about the Amazons, so she knows this isn't true. Still, she is certain women would do things differently. In any case, politics bore her. She is more interested in Hugo's friend Jiri, who loans her books of poetry and brings her wildflowers stuffed in pickle jars.

"The way he looks at you," Eva says. "Watch out!"

"Shut up!"

"I guess he can't get any girls his own age."

In the other room, her father is shouting into the telephone. Her Opa's heart is weak and he has been confined to bed for weeks. She hears the words *doctors*, *money*, *blow over*, *leave*.

Someday, she decides, she will live in a villa like her grandparents', surrounded by climbing roses and lilacs and apricot trees snowing blossoms in the spring. She will have two tall wolfhounds, loads of children, a bright red motorcar. She will wear a hat tipped to a fashionable angle on her head, a fox stole, a diamond ring. In her imagination, the future is like the dioramas in the natural history museum: tiny, perfect, fake.

Hugo brings home copies of *Der Judenstaat* and *Alteneuland*, pamphlets, Hebrew primers. He leaves them strewn about the flat. Lonia and her father step over them, like muddy puddles in the street.

By the time the first snow falls in late December, the borders have snapped shut like traps. The Sudetenland is lost; Beneš has been betrayed. When her grandfather dies, they are not permitted to cross the border to Opava to attend the funeral. Her father finally manages to bring his mother out to live with them, against her will. She spends her days sitting at the window, her eyes watery and unfocused, her speech confused. Barred from practicing law, her father spends the days at home closed in his study, listening to the radio, writing letter after letter to bank officials and immigration authorities. He is growing thinner, brittle, pale as the parchment on which he writes.

Hugo's place at university has been revoked. He manages to find a job in the accounting office at the steelworks in Vítkovice. He rides his bicycle to work, hunched inside his overcoat, zigzagging through the snow. He leaves early in the morning, comes home late. Lonia misses him, as if he has already gone for good.

Lonia walks toward the river through the park where she and Hugo used to play when they were kids. Dirty sludge laps the curbs and seeps through the soles of her boots. Even before the snow stops falling, it is scabbed with soot. A grid of trolley lines scrapes the sky, gray with ash from the coking plants and the steel mills and the deep mines burning coal. Across the river rises the Ema mine dump: a huge, hot heap of slag. The homeless huddle there for warmth.

Everyone is talking about leaving. Somehow Ĵiri has managed to obtain an immigration permit for Palestine. There is wild speculation about the possibility of waiting things out in places Lonia has never heard of: Sumatra, the Dominican Republic, Uganda, Borneo.

No one asks Lonia where she wants to go.

She feels the great wheels grinding all around her, their heavy iron spokes.

It is Hugo's voice she hears now, calling to her from down the street. He is cycling toward her up Nádražni, the tails of his overcoat flapping out behind him like wings. Light snow floats in the nimbus of the streetlamps. He catches up to her at the bottom of the steps, swinging his leg over the seat. He is all angles, her brother, pale skin stretched over long bones. He pulls an aerogram from his pocket.

"Look, a letter came from Ĵiri."

"Are you still going to those meetings?"

"He's living on a kibbutz in the Galilee. He's changing his name to Yigal!"

"It's freezing, Hugo. I'm going in."

His hand is on her arm. This is how it always is between them, this push and pull: his stubborn tug, her giving in.

"I'm going, Lonia. I don't care what Papa says."

She twists her arm away. "And you'll get there how?"

"There are ways."

"You'll just get yourself killed."

The tram comes screeching around the curve, the faces inside blurry at windows fogged with breath. She is seventeen years old; she cannot imagine another life.

She pulls the heavy front door open and holds it as Hugo hauls his bike over the threshold steps and in. Her toes have gone numb with cold. Her father will not let Hugo go, she thinks. Now that her grandmother has come to live with them, her father has let his letter-writing campaign lapse. The doctors have made it clear that her Oma, already vague with grief, will not survive another move. Her father paces back and forth across his study like a big cat in a cage. He sighs blue swirls of smoke. He says, *This too shall pass*, but he doesn't sound convinced.

Lonia trudges up the steep flights of stairs. From the drawer of her dressing table, she takes out the book of Rilke's poems Jiri loaned her, a lovely edition bound in green morocco, stamped with gold. Now she knows she'll never give it back.

The Wehrmacht rolls into Ostrava at dusk on March 13, 1939, a motorcycle cavalcade followed by a rumbling procession of armored cars and tanks and antiaircraft guns. Lonia's father stands over the radio, desperately twisting the dial between snatches of shortwave static from Radio Moscow and the BBC. Out of the windows of the flat, the sun flares red.

Lonia goes into her room and lies down on the bed without bothering to remove her shoes. What would happen now? Would the Germans make a pogrom here as well? Would they smash the windows and beat men in the streets? It was hard to fathom, but of course so many unthinkable things had already come to pass. She does not understand the politics of men, their deals and handshakes and pronouncements. She does not understand why they have to fight.

The cracks in the plaster ceiling look like the boot of Italy. She traces the coastline south from Trieste to Venice, Bologna, Bari, Brindisi. She pictures pastel houses nestled into hillsides, fishing skiffs pulled up on beaches, café tables by the sea. The *Graphic Atlas*, too, is washed in pastel colors: chalky green for Germany, pale yellow for Czechoslovakia, pink for Palestine. Drawn in cross section, scored with lines of longitude, planet Earth is a ball of blue. Now Czechoslovakia was no more. Green over yellow left no trace.

From the other room comes the radio's dull drone, her father's low tones, and Hugo's louder protests. Someone is shouting drunkenly down on the street. Her grandmother is wailing. *Ich will nach Hause!* As if she could just throw wide the windows and fly back home again. If Lonia could, she would sail into the night, out over the red roofs and church steeples, the railway yards and steel mills and mine tailings, the heaps of coke and slag, the telegraph poles and tramways and washing fluttering on backyard lines, out over the border guards and barricades, the soldiers cradling their rifles, over the invisible wall of the frontier.

Lonia blinks and the ceiling cracks morph into the outline of a castle, a tunnel, an underground lake. Where would she go, what would she do, if she had a magic wish?

"Make a wish," Lonia's husband Isaac used to like to say to Esther when she was little. "Close your eyes and wish."

Esther—solid, serious little thing that she was at five or six— would hold her breath and screw her eyes shut tight.

"Stop it, Isaac," Lonia said.

"Are you wishing very hard?" Isaac asked Esther.

She nodded vigorously. Yes, yes, yes.

"Hocus, pocus, filipus!" said Isaac, tapping Esther with a pencil on the head. "Open your eyes!"

Esther opened her eyes and hopped up and down on one foot.

"Let us see if the magic worked," Isaac said. "What did you wish for, then?"

Lonia wanted to kick him. "That's cheating," she hissed.

"A sweet," said Esther, beaming up at him. "A toffee, please."

"Which hand?" Isaac held out his fists.

It was always there, without fail, in whichever hand she picked—a toffee or some wine gums or a Polo mint. Did he carry candy about loose like that, in his pockets, just in case? Lonia could never tell.

He had other tricks as well. He could make a coin go through a solid table. He could levitate, both feet rising a few centimeters off the ground. He could poke a pencil up one nostril and pull it out his ear. *Hocus, pocus, filipus*, he said. It wasn't terribly hard to fool a child, but still.

She never stopped missing him, all these years. But one had to move on. Memory could hold you back. It wasn't necessarily the case, she always felt, that any trauma in your past that you did not expose and come to terms with would fester and haunt you until you did. The pop psychologists didn't necessarily have it right. Memory was no automatic cure. In fact, memory could be a terrible burden—even a kind of disease. Perhaps that's what she is suffering from now, she thinks.

What remains of those shadowed months and weeks leading up to war? Not memories so much as an ostinato, bits of phrases, riffs.

Her grandmother folded in her chair beside the window, high-necked in black, her hair pinned up in tarnished rings.

The noontime whistle from the coking plant splitting the sooty air.

The scratching of her father's pen.

Wurst, kartoffelsalat, schnitzel, sauerbraten, wurst again: what she's learned to make since the cook had to be dismissed. Her father's nightly cognac in a pear-shaped glass. The good Demel chocolates from Vienna now impossible to get.

Phrases from her primer, *Basic English for Czechoslovak Students*: "I am sure to leave to-morrow. We happened to meet in the park. He is likely to arrive by the evening train."

At night, the freight trains' clack and howl.

Rumors like the twilight twittering of birds: that the Rothschilds were negotiating to sell Vítkovice to the Czechs, that troops were massing along the Hungarian frontier, that the chemistry teacher Herr Levinsky was a Soviet spy.

Swastikas cartwheeling from the windows of the buildings around the Central Square, unfurling from the wing mirrors of passing cars.

In the wooden box atop her chest of drawers: A leaf-shaped brooch inlaid with mother-of-pearl. A wafer of mica. An enamel locket containing a photograph of the mother she never knew. A four-leaf clover, pressed. A doll's ceramic head.

Her father, her father: rough-cheeks, smoke breath, the gold rims of his glasses glinting, bending to kiss her goodnight.

Her father is touching her shoulder. "Are you in pain?"

She tries to focus. No, it's not her father. It's her daughter Esther, leaning over her, her dark hair loose, her pale face pinched. The darkness surges and recedes.

"You were crying out. How long have you been awake?"

Lonia struggles to sit up but finds that she cannot.

"You don't have to be a martyr, for god's sake, Mum." A finger slides a tablet between her upper gum and cheek. "Can I get you anything else? Water? Are you hot?"

Lonia manages to shake her head.

Esther sighs and shifts. "I'll sit here with you for a bit. Now that I'm awake."

She is as distant as another planet in the dark. Lonia's eyes drift closed. Behind her eyelids, galaxies swirl blue in space.

THREE

ESTHER

Her mother's friends—the few who remain—come round on Wednesday afternoons to tea. In the old days, they played bridge. Now the old women sit beside her mother on the sofa, stroking her hands, casting sidelong, sagging glances Esther's way. It's the end, their looks say. First her, then us.

Esther sets out a plate of coffee cake and scones, a pot of tea. Her mother sits erect, dressed in her usual cardigan and knit trousers, her pearls around her neck. She has grown visibly thinner in the weeks since Esther arrived in London, as if she is not exactly dying but dematerializing, the atoms of her flesh dissolving into air. She looks like a Hindu ascetic next to Vivian and Myrna and Ruth, with their paunchy arms and floral Marks & Spencer housedresses, their ankles stuffed like bratwurst into rubber-soled orthopedic shoes. Her mother nods, her eyes focused on some distant point, as the other women natter on about their children's and grandchildren's accomplishments, so-and-so's dementia and so-and-so's most recent stroke, the status of their eyesight, their diabetes, their indigestion, the grinding agony of their worn-out knees and hips.

"It's good of you to come over to stay with your Mum," Vivian says, nibbling on a scone. Crumbs gather on the plateau of her ample chest. The other women nod and cluck, sizing up Esther with their puffy, cataract-clouded eyes. They speak about her mother rather than to her, as if she were a child, or already gone.

"She's very fortunate to have you."

"Oh, yes, indeed."

"How long will you be staying, then?" asks Myrna, always the pushy one.

"As long as I'm needed, I guess," Esther says.

Myrna gives her an appraising look. Myrna's daughter Claudia, Esther knows, has recently ditched her husband for an investment banker and snagged herself a four-bedroom flat overlooking Regent's Park and a villa in the south of France. No doubt Myrna is also plotting to fix Esther up with some unappealing, wealthy British Jew.

To change the subject, Esther brings up the matter of the possible leaky pipe. She heard it again, the other night, and it definitely wasn't rain. The old women frown and cock their heads. None of them can hear the sound of dripping, but like her mother, they are in agreement that it must be coming from next door.

Vivian finally notices the crumbs and swipes her hand across her chest. "Who lives there? A doctor, you said?"

"Yes, a neurologist. He's Persian—from Iran."

"Iran," says Myna. "Since the time of Haman, the Persians have been trying to annihilate the Jews. You know the Purim story, don't you, Esther? Of course you do."

"London's overrun with Arabs, isn't it?" Ruth says, scrunching up her lips.

Aryan, not Arab, Esther doesn't say but thinks.

"What's it they're calling it, these days?" says Myrna. "*Londonistan?*"

"Anti-Semitic incidents are at a record high, my Gerry says," adds Ruth.

Vivian sighs. "There's only ever bad news, it seems."

"Gerry's addicted to the news on that computer," Ruth says. "He sits there all day long, glued to the screen, mumbling about the horrid things people write. Switch that bloody thing off, I say. It just fills your brain with hate."

All this hate—it was exhausting. Esther picks up the plates. She no longer knows what to think.

After the ladies leave, Esther's mother complains, as she's always done, about their gossipy small-mindedness and hypochondria and lack of common sense.

Esther says, "Well, they ate up all the coffee cake, at least."

Later, she brings their suppers upstairs on a tray. The visit has worn her mother out. Esther plumps and props the pillows behind her mother's back and sets a bed tray across her lap. Her mother's clavicle protrudes like a wishbone beneath her nightgown's lace-trimmed neck. Through the fine strands of her hair, you can see the mottled pinkness of her scalp. One good gust of wind and she would blow away.

"It's too much," her mother says after a few moments, setting down her fork. The food is hardly touched.

"What is?"

"The food. You always make too much."

"Would you rather have something else?" she says. "I could warm up some consommé, if you prefer."

"I don't know who you imagine you're cooking for, Esther. So much food. It's such a waste."

"I like to cook."

"You never used to cook."

"What are you talking about? I cooked."

"I'm not hungry."

"Just eat a little bit. You need to eat."

Zofia says narcotics kill the appetite, although that doesn't explain why Esther has lost her appetite as well. She prods her salad, forces herself to take another bite. Is it true she never cooked? The busy years of juggling—of packing Noah off to

school and racing to work and back, of coping with the bustle of
the city, the thousand chores of daily life—have resolved into a
blur. Surely she cooked. They couldn't have gone out to eat all
the time.

She takes up the remote and switches on the television, clicks
through the channels. Football. Cricket. Condoleezza Rice.
Saddam Hussein. Something about stricter controls on immigration. Something about a lost pianist, some sort of prodigy. She
pauses, her arm holding the remote outstretched. Apparently suffering from amnesia, he'd turned up on a beach out on the Isle of
Sheppey a few weeks back, dressed in a formal suit, soaking wet.

Her mother clears her throat. "Esther, what are you going to
do?"

"Do?"

"Don't pretend you don't know what I mean."

On TV, the pianist looks as forlorn as a lost child, peeping
out above a blanket with one eye, wild and bright. The National
Missing Persons Helpline has put out an appeal. An 0800 number
flashes onto the screen; already hundreds of people have rung in.
Esther feels a pang of pity. Where had he come from? What had
happened to him? Who could he be? She squints at the screen. He
looks a little bit familiar, she thinks.

Her mother says, "I'm talking to you, Esther. It's been three
years. You must put the past behind you. It's time."

Not yet three years, Esther thinks, not quite. And what were
three years? Three years were nothing. She will not take the bait.

"As your father would have said, water only runs downhill."

Esther picks up her mother's untouched plate. "What does that
even mean?"

"You must put the past behind you," her mother says again. "I
won't be around much longer. You need to move ahead."

"Don't worry about me."

Her mother shuts her eyes. Her eyelids are purple crepe. "I can
feel it going, you know."

"What's that?"

"The energy. It's as if there were a leak."

"The meds do that to you, Mum."

"To tell the truth, darling, it's a relief."

Downstairs in the kitchen, Esther scrapes their uneaten dinners into the bin. Her mother is right. She makes too much food. She cannot seem to manage smaller recipes. The refrigerator shelves are crowded with plastic containers and cling film–covered bowls and plates. The freezer is stuffed with ice cube trays of pesto and bags of cookie dough and quart-sized tubs of consommé. Just the other day she sent Zofia home with an entire batch of pierogi and a loaf of caraway bread.

She should take some of the leftover food to the doctor and his son next door, she thinks. Didn't he say all they ate was take-away?

So much food. It was all going to go to waste.

What the hell, she thinks.

She bends and rummages in the cupboard for a platter. There's plenty of roasted chicken and potato salad and nearly an entire chocolate cake. She is buoyant with the idea. She heaps the platter with food, covers it in foil.

Outside it's nearly dark, the trees and houses flattened into silhouettes against the still-blue springtime sky, like the surreal landscape of a Magritte. Opposite, the dumpster hunches in the shadows, the digging machine finally silenced for the night. Star-lings chatter in the trees. She goes down her steps and up the other side and rings the bell. She hopes it's not too late. She has an urge to leave the plate on the doorstep and run, like a kid playing a Halloween prank.

The boy opens the door. Amir. He's wearing those baggy cargos and a T-shirt that reads *UK Decay*.

She holds out the platter. "This is for you," she says.

"For me?"

"Well, for you and your father. I had a ton left over. I just thought . . ." She is ridiculous, a fool. "He said you guys were always eating takeaway. It's nothing fancy, anyway—just chicken, potato salad. Chocolate cake."

He grins. "Chocolate cake! That's ace." There's a slight gap between his front teeth that makes him look, for a moment, like a little boy.

And all at once her throat is tight and her eyes are overfull and there is a rushing in her ears. She thought she was past this. She was past it. She digs her fingernails into her palms. She will not blink. He is looking at her, waiting. He's a stranger. He's just a kid. What could he possibly understand?

She swallows to suppress the quaver in her voice. "You can just leave the plate over there"—she gestures to her front door— "when you're done."

"Right, yeah. Thanks."

She forces herself to turn and walk, not run, back down the steps and up the other side. She forces herself to give a little wave. But once inside, she turns and presses her forehead to the door and weeps.

Noah died on a Thursday, three years ago, July. Thunderheads billowed in the scorched sky, the air humid and limp. They'd escaped to Connecticut from the city for the summer, that first summer after the world changed, when the leafy hills and clap-board houses and quiet village streets no longer felt quaintly dull but safe. She was already thinking about leaving the city, giving it a dry run, getting the hell out. She'd taken the entire month off work and Gil was commuting up from Manhattan on the week-ends and Noah was hanging around the house, too old for camp, too young to work, sullen and uncommunicative and bored.

They'd had four days of heavy rains and then the heat. Esther sat out on the porch and sipped her coffee and watched the fat bees hovering in the hollyhocks and thyme. From the yellow house the road stretched down the hill and wound its way four miles into town. The maples and pines cast bands of shade across the gravel drive. He had his skateboard, he had his bike. There were hiking trails at Bull's Bridge; there was the waterfall and gorge. There was an ice cream shop and bakery in town, and at Lake Waramaug you could swim. The Ellis boys lived just down the street. All year long he was cooped up in the city. Go on, she said. Get out, go do something. Go. The gravel crunched beneath the wheels of his bike.

She stretched out her legs and listened to the cicadas' drone rise and fall like waves. They had not subscribed to cable; there was no Internet and hardly any TV. The only radio was in the car. She didn't want to hear about the escalating terrorism alerts or reports of Al Qaeda's "dirty" bombs or the rumblings of war against Saddam Hussein. Her mother wanted them to come to London, but she couldn't bear to get on a plane. She didn't want to leave this house, this porch, this chair. To the west, across the hot sky above the Litchfield Hills, contrails ran like lines drawn on a child's Etch A Sketch and slowly frayed.

Now she knows she was looking the wrong way. She was looking at the sky and hills when she should have been looking after her boy. Behind her the screen door screeched and slammed. Did he call goodbye? The moment was only one out of an infinity of other moments. She sipped her coffee, thinking about nothing—about the load of laundry that needed to be put into the dryer, about what to make for dinner, about whether it would rain.

She didn't hear the phone ring. She heard only the click and then the singsong of Noah's voice on the recording—*Hiyya, you've reached the Feinman family. We can't come to the phone right now*—followed by the unfamiliar, official voice and then the heart-stopping words *afraid* and *accident* and *son* and *please*. She ran in and picked up the phone halfway through the sergeant's speech, his voice reverberating through both the handset and the speaker, which continued dumbly to record both of their voices, the policeman's deep and monotone, hers too high and gasping for breath.

The Housatonic was running very high, they said, on account of all the rain. The rocks were slippery, the current swift. The Gaylordsville Fire Department, the Connecticut State Police, the Goshen water rescue and New Milford dive teams were fanned out, searching, below the Bull's Bridge. She stood on the bank by the pullout with the little clutch of kayakers and bystanders and Marcie and Bill Ellis and their two boys and her teeth chattered and her knees shook so hard she almost fell. Someone draped a blanket over her shoulders and she stood and watched the river surging through the gorge. Where did all that water come from? Where did it go? She did not understand it. He knew how to swim. The afternoon was hot and still. Noah's bike was propped against the tree. Static crackled over the squad car radio. Any minute now they would bring him shuffling up the bank, his hair slick and dripping, grinning his goofy orthodontic grin.

"We just waded in a little way," the older Ellis boy said, his pimply face twisted, his big hands flapping at his sides.

His younger brother was staring at his feet. Bill Ellis stepped up and put his arm around the boy. They were encircled by a ring of uniforms and flashing lights. Below the water flowed green and flecked with foam, cool and summery, widening out beyond the rocky gorge. It did not look dangerous. It did not look deep.

"He was right there, I swear to god," the older Ellis boy said. "He was right there, and then he disappeared."

It took the rescue teams over an hour to find him, dead in twenty feet of water, fifteen feet from shore, more than half a mile downstream from where the current must have pulled him in. She was still waiting at the pullout when the call came in. She was not there to see. Later she sat in the waiting room in the New Milford hospital and waited for Gil. She pulled her mind shut like a door. Beneath the fluorescent lights of the windowless room, in the air-conditioned chill, time did not exist. She could see him so very clearly, her boy, stroking through the water, scrambling out onto the bank, resting beneath the overhanging trees.

They buried him in Queens. Gil's grandmother was already buried there, with plots waiting for Gil's parents alongside. The cemetery was right along the flight path to LaGuardia and every few minutes a jet would come roaring low overhead, drowning out the drone of traffic along the Van Wyck and BQE. The rabbi was clean shaven and heavyset with a tall man's torso but too-short legs, barely Esther's height. He looked more like an accountant than a rabbi. He bobbed his head as he said the prayers. He said: *Yitgadal v'yitgadash*. The same old useless words.

Then they bent and threw handfuls of dirt onto the coffin's lid: Gil's parents and brothers and their families, cousins, neighbors, a few of Noah's friends from school. Esther wanted to throw herself in with the clods of dirt, to feel them falling on her body, filling her mouth and eyes and nose, stopping the flow of air. But she couldn't move. She just stood and watched.

The message on the answering machine blinked away in the living room in the yellow house, the red number one on the display a forgotten beacon, until days later when they finally drove up to Connecticut to close up the house and retrieve their things. *You have one new message*, the robotic machine voice said, and Esther pressed the Play button once and then again and again, cutting off before the sergeant's call and her own hysterical response; for there it was, Noah's voice, ringing out into the hollow room, miraculously, impossibly, as if he were right there—*Hiyya, you've reached the Feinman family*—until Gil came up beside her and said, *Don't*, and pulled her hand away and hit Erase.

JAVAD

His PhD student is jiggling her leg up and down, like a sewing machine needle. She has nice legs, Javad can't help but notice, and she knows it, judging by her short skirt and chartreuse tights. Lalitha is from Mumbai. She's one of the newer ones. There's Xiang Li from Beijing, Oscar from Manila, Nahid from Karachi, Wolff-Dieter from Cologne. Plus him. His lab is the bloody United Nations of Queen Square.

Javad's back aches. Too much sitting, too much poring over scans. He reaches around and digs his thumb into the bands of muscles along his spine. He looks out the window onto the filigree of treetops, the brick facades and rooftops across the square, the cloud-smeared sky. He turns back to the computer, clicks through the images on the screen. The gray cerebellar cross sections look like Rorschach inkblots or sliced hardboiled eggs. He tries to focus on the graphs.

"Those are the latest ones, there," Lalitha says, pointing.

"Interpreting deactivation can be quite tricky, as you know," he says, looking up.

The jiggling stops. "But the data does support the inhibition hypothesis."

"Maybe. I'm not sure."

Javad always has to remind himself that these students were

very young. They wanted results, answers, proof—not murk and ambiguity and fumbling in the dark. They didn't like to make mistakes. Who did?

His mobile phone vibrates in his pocket. On it are three un-answered messages from news reporters enquiring about that patient he examined down at Little Brook a fortnight back. Ever since the bulletin went out on the Missing Persons Helpline, the story has exploded in the news around the world. The "Piano Man," the *Mail on Sunday* dubbed him—a silly moniker, as if he were the hero of a romantic movie. Now he's an "enigmatic prodigy," a "silent genius." Everybody wants the mystery to be solved. Everybody wants him to be saved.

Lalitha re-crosses her chartreuse legs and starts jiggling again. "Do you think we're on the wrong track, then?"

"Have another look at Spence's study comparing hysterical and feigned paralysis. Also Halligan's work. PET may offer a better approach than fMRI, in the end."

He sees her flinch. He understands. Her parents back in Mumbai probably had a line of prospective husbands queued up in the wings. And here she was, wrestling with identifying a neurological basis for conversion hysteria. He thinks again of the patient down in Kent. Amnesia could be a manifestation of conversion disorder. It could also quite easily be faked. And as studies like Lalitha's would eventually show, it probably made little difference to the brain.

A fugue is a fugue is a fugue, he thinks nonsensically. There was something he couldn't quite put his finger on about that bloke.

"A new set of PET scans will take weeks," she says.

He tries to put on his jolly voice. "That's how it goes, I'm afraid."

Lalitha looks peeved. "I'll try."

"Carry on, then," he says. "Until next week." Some days he feels less like a research supervisor than a psychiatrist.

He rings Caroline as he leaves the Institute. They are replacing the carpet in the corridor and the floor is littered with rubbery curls of torn-up carpet, glue guns, tool belts, putty knives. He picks his way around the mess. The subflooring looks flayed. He has put off ringing her all day.

The phone bleats and bleats. Finally, she picks up. "What do you want?" she says.

He pushes open the doors and steps onto the street. He always forgets about caller ID. "My solicitor, Charles, tells me he got a letter from you the other day."

Caroline says, "You owe me. Don't pretend you don't know that." There is the sound of something scraping, a chair being pushed back. The bang of a door.

"He's nineteen years old," he says. "In case you forgot. Child maintenance has stopped."

"I'm not talking about child maintenance and you know it."

At the entrance to Queen Square, a very old man is pushing an even older-looking woman in a wheelchair. An oxygen tank is propped next to her on the seat. The old man stops and hobbles around to tuck the blanket more closely around the old woman's legs. It is an intimate gesture, tender and sad. That will never be them, Javad thinks.

"Look, I've arranged a meeting for us with Charles," he says, turning the corner. "We can discuss it then. Wednesday morning. Ten o'clock."

"Javad, leave it. There's no point."

"The point," he says, "is that if you want to reopen this stupid bloody conversation, you'd better come along next Wednesday."

"Let me be perfectly clear," Caroline replies. "I'm not discussing it."

She sounded quite lucid today, he had to admit. Maybe she hadn't started drinking yet. "The circumstances have changed," he says.

"Nothing has changed, Javad. And I'm not getting married again, if that's what you're hoping for."

Anger, hot as ever, rises in his cheeks. The situation was intolerable. She was no longer the self-styled single mother/starving artist she pretended to be. But even though she was now living with her new Swedish dotcom millionaire, or whatever the hell he was, and even though she contributed absolutely nothing, and never had done, to the expense of raising their son, and even though she's always been completely useless as a mother—despite *all* that, he had to continue to pay her a ridiculous amount of money and keep on doing so until one or both of them were dead. It simply wasn't right.

"Look," he says, "I'm not debating this over the telephone. We'll discuss it with Charles like two civilized human beings."

"What is it that you don't understand, Javad? I am not discussing it."

He crosses the road to Russell Square, walking fast, not looking, nearly bumping into a fellow with blond dreadlocks and a T-shirt that reads *Butcher Blair*. Probably one of the SOAS kids. Javad wonders if Amir is at the library, studying for his exams. It's just over there, at the far corner of the square. He wishes he could talk to Caroline the way a normal couple would talk about their son. But what would he say? *I don't know him anymore at all.* The thought jabs like a finger at his chest.

"I've got to go," Caroline says. "Just send the bloody check."

"Write it down—Wednesday at ten," he says and flips his phone shut.

He knows she won't turn up, knows that even if he took the matter to the courts, it's unlikely that he'd win. But he cannot leave it be.

Let go, his physio always said when he went in to see her with his lumbar spine in knots. She had wonderful hands, his physio, strong as a man's. It was a strange and powerful thing, a stranger's touch. Touch healed. Infants failed to thrive, even died, if they weren't held. He misses it. *The laying on of hands.*

It has been twenty-three years since that Sunday morning he arrived home after an all-night shift at the hospital and found her, an utter stranger, sleeping in his bed. Curled on her side, his sheets wrapped around her, like caterpillar in a cocoon. A head of bleached-blond hair. White shoulders moving softly with each breath. He'd blinked, then tiptoed out and shut the door.

His flatmate, Kurosh, was leaning against the kitchen counter, bleary eyed and disheveled, making toast. The place was littered with dirty plates and empty cans filled with cigarette ends. It stank of smoke and beer. Kurosh was stumbling his way through his final year of medical school. He came from one of the wealthiest families in Tehran. Now his parents lived in a three-room flat in Paris, refugees.

"And who, might I ask, is the girl?"

Kurosh shrugged. Eamon had brought her, he thought. Or it might have been those blokes from the John Radcliffe who'd popped down to London for the night.

"And?"

The toast popped up. "Maybe she missed her train."

When Javad went back into the bedroom, the girl stretched like a cat and blinked.

"You do realize you are in my bed," he said.

She smiled and yawned. There was a slight gap between her two front teeth.

"It's a very nice bed."

He'd never met anyone like Caroline before. She could fit everything she owned in the boot of an antique Morris Minor and seemed to have no interest in remaining in one place. With her hippie mother, she'd lived on a canal boat along the Jericho Canal in Oxford; in a caravan in Wales; on an island in the Firth of Clyde. She had a degree in painting from The Slade. She was Javad's photographic negative: all blond hair and milky skin against his swarthy lank. When she looked at him, he felt filled with light.

Love flooded the caudate brainstem with dopamine, like cocaine.

Naked, she took the headphones of her Walkman and pressed them to his ears. The music flowed into his eardrums like a wave. Sade's "Smooth Operator," that sexy 1980s kitsch.

He sent a letter to his mother from their weekend honeymoon in Cornwall, which was all the time he could get off from work. He enclosed a snapshot of the two of them, taken with the camera on self-timer, his arm crooked around her neck, hood up, posing on a rain-soaked cliff.

By the time Amir was born, three years later, things had already changed. The baby lay between them, his black head latched to Caroline's blue-veined breast: a bond, a wedge. Pushed to the far edge of the mattress, Javad lay sleepless in the dark. He stretched out his arm but couldn't reach.

Who are you? she'd shouted, not long before he left. She wore the baby strapped in a carrier to her chest, and when he flapped his arms and she waved hers they looked like the four-armed goddess of destruction, Kali.

She said, *I don't know you anymore at all.*

At the sound of traffic, Javad looks up. To his right rise the Ionic columns and tall red doors of St. Pancras parish church. Ahead, late afternoon gridlock chokes the Euston Road. For a moment, he feels dizzy. The city pulses all around him. A helicopter is vibrating overhead; trains rumble underground; cars and people stream past like synapses across basal ganglia, like a time-lapse photograph of lights. It was a mystery how two people ever came together. Life flung you out like an elemental particle, colliding and dividing, spinning into space.

At home, Javad stands at the kitchen counter, considering the platter. It has been sitting there since the week before. Amir had said he would return it, but of course he has not done so yet. He runs his fingertip along the embossed gilt rim. It belonged to the American, or rather, to her mother. He will take it back.

Esther opens the door after the third ring, a dishtowel in her hands. She is even prettier than he remembered, although the delicate skin beneath her eyes looks slightly bruised, as if she hasn't slept.

"I hope I'm not disturbing you," he says.

"No, of course not. Not at all."

"I just wanted to bring this back," he says, handing her the platter. "And to thank you. It was very kind of you to think of us. The food was delicious."

"No problem. It was my pleasure."

"That cake! I had to arm wrestle Amir for a piece."

She smiles. "Honestly, you could eat here every day of the week and we'd still have food left over. I don't know what my problem is. I keep forgetting that my mother hardly eats."

"How is she doing?"

Her face tightens. "Hanging in there. Thanks for asking."

"Will you be staying on for a while longer, then?"

"Oh, I'm here for the duration, I'm afraid."

Her eyes meet his. She pushes her hair back out of her face. "Would you like to come in for a moment and have a drink?"

He has the unexpected sensation of compression in his chest. "That would be lovely," he says. The air between them is charged with energy, like light.

Her side of the house is the exact mirror image of his, with the sitting room and kitchen off to the right instead of to the left of the stairs. It feels familiar yet strange, like a place encountered in a dream. He follows her into the kitchen, where she pulls out two glasses and a bottle of white wine and sets a wedge of cheese and a handful of crackers on a plate.

"You'll have a glass of wine, right?" She hesitates. "Or don't you drink?"

"Oh, no, wine would be very nice indeed."

She hands him the plate and picks up the bottle and the glasses in one hand. "Shall we go outside? It's not too chilly out tonight."

They step out back into the garden. The evening light is soft. He sits on the bench and she pulls up a chair.

She pulls out the cork and pours the wine. "Cheers," she says, handing him a glass. "To neighbors."

"To neighbors."

She gestures to the backs of their conjoined houses. "Have you ever read that children's book where these kids crawl through the attics of a block of London terrace houses and meet a magician? I've always wondered if our attics connect."

He follows her gaze. "I should have thought that would be against fire regulations."

A look of disappointment crosses her face. "You're probably right," she says.

She crosses her legs, leans back in the chair. She is wearing a white blouse, faded jeans. Her body has the contours of early middle age, softness over an armature of bone. She turns her wine glass in her hands. She has long fingers, unvarnished nails—a pianist's hands, he thinks. No ring.

The conversation turns to work. She asks him about his research, nodding as he natters on about the new study on memory retrieval and inhibition that they're getting ready to launch. Then she tells him about her job at the museum, her voice growing animated as she describes the painstaking work of conservation, the challenges of scraping away or dissolving centuries-old paint and varnish, infilling rotten wood, repairing tears and cracks in ancient artifacts. It pleases him to learn that conservators used optical imaging technology, just like neuroscientists. Only where he saw cerebellar neurons lighting up in bursts of neon color, she saw hidden Madonnas and forgotten saints.

He leans forward and cuts a slice of cheese. "Byzantine art? Lots of golden icons, as I seem to recollect."

She takes a sip of wine. "I'm a chemist by training, not an art historian. But I've always been fascinated by the Byzantine Empire. It was the crossroads of Greek and Roman and early Christian and Slavic and Islamic cultures—a true East meets West. And as for icons, beyond the various technical challenges, I've just always loved their purity, I guess. The icon maker is typically anonymous, almost beside the point. I like the way the artwork—the object, not the artist—is the most important thing."

"My ex-wife is a painter. I rather think she'd disagree."

Her eyebrows arch. "When you make a piece of art, you cast it off like a bottle thrown into the sea. What *you* think about it, what *you* intended for it, is pretty much irrelevant in the end."

"As with children."

She gives him an odd glance. "Yes, I guess that's right."

"Like mine, at any rate. He's an utter mystery to me."

She lifts her arms and twists her hair up off her neck. He is conscious of the pale skin of her neck and the loose curve of her breasts beneath the thin fabric of her shirt.

"Is he out of school now for the summer?"

"Soon. He's just got to sit his first-year exams."

"What's he studying again?"

He sighs. "Middle Eastern Studies. Islamic History."

"You don't sound too enthused."

"I'm a scientist. I've got no clue what one does with such a degree. And I don't think he does, either."

"But that's what kids that age are supposed to do, right? Find themselves? Explore their identity?"

He pushes up his glasses, rubs the bridge of his nose. "His mother's English. He's lived in London his whole life. He's never been anywhere near the Middle East."

"Maybe that's the point."

Is it? He leans forward. "I'll tell you something. The last time I came back into the country, last March, I got held up at immigration control at Gatwick for nearly two hours. No explanation, nothing. Two hours. They took me into an interrogation room. 'Where are you from? Are you Muslim? Are you observant? Why do you live here?' I've lived here for twenty-five bloody years. You don't really get it until you've felt them glaring at you as if you had a bomb stuffed down your trousers." He exhales hard, takes a drink of wine. "Sorry. I didn't mean to rant."

"That's all right." She has pulled one of her feet up on the edge of the chair and is resting her chin on her knee. "And what about you?"

"What about me?"

"Are you? Observant?"

"Oh, yes, quite. A devout atheist."

She smiles and lifts her glass. "I'll drink to that."

"Cheers," he says. He is thinking of Amir with his feet up on the headboard, reading the Qur'an. Maybe he was just exploring his identity. Maybe she was right.

Afterward at the door, as he is leaving, he leans in and kisses her. He doesn't think, just does it. First on the cheek, then, gently, on the lips. His hand on the back of her neck. Her body, yielding, against his. So long since he has felt this.

ESTHER

"So you're not going back to the States?" Across the table, Phil's bushy eyebrows arch over the green rims of his eyeglasses.

"I'm just kind of feeling things out right now," Esther says. "You know."

She has called Phil, her former colleague at the Cloisters, on an impulse. She has been in London for six weeks already, and her mother is still alive, the flame of life still burning like the miracle oil in the menorah restored by the Maccabees. Her mother's words—*it's time*—have been ringing in her ears since the other night. Maybe she is right.

Like everything else in London these days, even rumpled Phil has acquired a sheen of postmillennial prosperity. He's wearing little rectangular glasses with green titanium rims. His bald head shines as if it has been waxed. Once they would have gone to the pub for a ploughman's and a pint. Now he's taken her to one of those trendy Japanese noodle shops that have cropped up all over London, with long tables covered in butcher paper, waiters juggling fragrant bowls of curry and ramen and soba noodle soup. She lifts her spoon and slurps.

"We might have some freelance work for you down the road a bit," he says. "Though private practice would likely be your best bet."

"Cleaning old ladies' worthless heirlooms?"

"Everyone's outsourcing these days. Including us. Budgets are tight."

"I understand."

"I'll put some feelers out. You never know."

"I'd appreciate it."

She hates groveling, elbowing her way back into the game. Maybe she should just be done with it, the whole museum scene, the rivalries and infighting between curators and conservators, the day-to-day tedium of the lab. It was different in the days when she first knew Phil, back in the early 1980s, when she was still in graduate school and he was a postdoc just arrived in the States. They'd worked together one summer, side by side in the new East Seventy-Eighth Street lab, eyes squeezed up to the Zeiss magnifier or hunched over the work table, scalpels and swabs in hand. They drank street-vendor coffee in blue Greek-lettered paper cups and smoked, stubbing out their butts in the coffee dregs. One of Phil's tapes was always playing on a boom box—Lene Lovich or Philip Glass or The Police, music that, even now, brings back the smells of acetone and ethanol, hot wax and paint.

The project was a badly damaged late Byzantine panel painting of a Madonna and child—an Orthodox icon of the Virgin *Glykophilousa*, Mother of God of Loving Kindness, the "sweet-kissing" mother and child. When it first arrived in the lab, the panel was nearly completely black, the original image overpainted and covered in a coat of filthy oil, the plank warped and spongy with insect holes and rot. You could just barely make out the faint curve of the lips, an eye, and the thin hint of a nose, all no more than traces of shadow against the blackened ground. The child wasn't visible at all.

The tiresome, nerve-wracking, painstaking work of cleaning and repair had taken weeks. Details emerged in slow motion, lines and textures and shades of color growing gradually distinct: the edge of an outstretched finger, a fold of drapery, the crease of an eyelid, the gold points of a star. Esther had imagined the long-forgotten craftsman (a pious old Cypriot: wiry, weather beaten, missing teeth) whose hands had first appraised this white mahogany plank, whose eyes had gauged the proportions, who had channeled divinity into these lines and shapes. It was as if her own hands—retracing the contours he'd drawn, retouching the tempera he'd mixed—were reaching back in time and meeting his.

By the end of that summer, they'd uncovered the figures of the Virgin and her child. The Virgin's wine-red cloak was bordered in gold filigree and stamped with stars, her halo burnished gold against an ochre ground. She gazed out in unblinking sadness, her head tilted toward the stiffly mannish child in her arms, her cheek pressed to his forehead, his little hand reaching up to touch her chin. Knowledge of the Passion already written in her pain.

Phil, a biochemist, was interested in polarized light microscopy, infrared reflectography and the microchemical investigation of the cinnabar and lead white pigments in the ancient paint. His was a labor of fact-finding, of generating hypotheses and assembling proof. He was interested in the revelations of science, not the divine. Christ was not her god, either, but the work filled her with a kind of reverence all the same. It was miraculous. The survival of the material thing through such a vast expanse of time. What remained.

"Do you ever miss New York?" she asks Phil now.

He slurps his noodles and looks up. "Can't say that I do, not really. The bagels, perhaps—H&H, was it? But then, I'm not really a nostalgic person."

"I didn't ask if you were nostalgic."

"Are you?" His rectangular glasses glint.

"Nostalgic? No."

But she is lying and they both know it, although it's not the city that she is nostalgic for so much as the person she was back then, back there in the lab with Phil, at twenty-three. Wandering on her lunch break through the echoing galleries of the Frick or the Met; waiting on the sweltering subway platform for the screech of the graffiti-tattooed train; walking home along the edge of Central Park as the rush-hour traffic crept past, honking, with doormen stepping out from beneath the awnings and blowing their whistles and waving their white-gloved hands at cabs, while the shadows of the apartment buildings stretched long across the pavement in the early evening light. She misses that vibration she felt every time she came back to the city from out of town and saw that net of lights stretched out across Manhattan and New Jersey and the Bronx and Queens, the midtown skyscrapers rising like jeweled stalagmites out of the darkness, heroic, grand.

It was what the Buddhists called *māyā*, she understands. *Not-that*. An illusion. None of it was real.

Philip signals for the bill—two fingers lifted, eyebrows raised. Like the hand gesture of blessing in an icon, she thinks. He's been doodling on the tablecloth. Little triangles like hazard signs. The world is full of symbols she no longer understands.

They kiss goodbye outside the restaurant. Phil smells of the lab, a faint chemical tinge of ethanol and glue. He crosses the street to the museum, then turns and waves.

She meanders north, vaguely in the direction of the Tube. The afternoon is warm and breezy. She takes off her jacket, slings it over her shoulder, picks up her pace. She feels irritated with herself. Why had she imagined Phil would help? Down a side street, she glimpses the BT Tower, studded with rings of satellite dishes, like the minaret of a futuristic mosque. Who is she fooling? Better just to walk away.

Gray stone facades line both sides of Gower Street. Red double-decker busses squeal. Cyclists weave among the cars. A small sign posted next to a door says ANATOMY. She imagines skeletons hanging on demonstration hooks, cadavers stiff on gurneys underneath white sheets. Or bodies half-dissected, slit from groin to sternum, flayed. There would be white walls and sinks and worktables, scalpels and microscopes, X-ray machines. Like a conservation lab, she thinks. There were many ways to peel back the skin.

She has nearly reached the Euston Road when she sees him. He is standing on the median strip, waiting to cross the street, facing her but looking the other way. He's wearing saggy jeans, a black T-shirt, earphone wires hanging at his neck.

It's him. Amir.

Her heart spasms in her chest. Seven million people in this city and it's him. How could it be? What were the odds? How easily might she have arrived a minute earlier or later, have chosen a different route! Again she feels the electric shock of that that first, late, jetlagged night. Only this time, he doesn't look her way.

The light turns red. The signal bleeps. He crosses, turns toward the hospital, carries on. She waits a beat and then moves forward too.

She couldn't have said what made her do it. She might have been thinking that they must be going in the same direction, heading home. She might have been imagining she'd catch up and touch him on the arm and he would turn and smile, revealing that little gap between his teeth. She might have been thinking of Javad and that kiss she doesn't know what to do with, that's been pricking at her since the other evening like a splinter just beneath the skin.

Or maybe it's a sign.

She follows him past the sweeping green-glass entrance of the University College Hospital, past the row of ambulances parked in front. Two medics step out in front of her, wheeling a trolley, and she loses sight of him. She swerves around them, picks up her pace. His head bobs back into sight.

She follows him across the street and into the Warren Street Underground Station, fumbling for her wallet, feeding her card into the turnstile, pushing through. Escalators rumble deep into the tunnels. She steps onto the first escalator, pausing a few feet above him and standing to the right, holding the rail. This is one of the deep Underground stations. The rail lines here run ten stories below the level of the street.

She follows him off the first set of escalators and onto the next. The tiled walls gleam greenish yellow in the dirty fluorescent light. The heat of the day has collected in the tunnels and the air smells of stale urine, moldy, dank. At the bottom, he turns left toward the platform and she follows. She glances up. The sign says: NORTHBOUND VICTORIA LINE.

She waits on the narrow platform behind a group of noisy French schoolchildren clustered around their guide. She squints at the map posted on the wall. The Victoria line stops at King's Cross, Highbury & Islington, Finsbury Park, Seven Sisters, Tottenham Hale. Not Finchley Road. Though you can change at King's Cross for the Jubilee line, she thinks.

Farther along the platform, Amir is fiddling with his iPod, his head pulsing to the silent beat. Bright orange panels in the pattern of a maze back the benches built into the tunnel walls. Mazes like the minotaur's labyrinth. Theseus following Ariadne's string. Another sign? Suspended above the tracks, a CCTV camera points its hooded eye.

Soon the rails begin to click and ring. With a dank, hot breath of wind, the train roars in. Amir steps into a carriage and she boards the same car at the other end. Amir takes a seat with his back to her. She sits near the door. The doors slide shut. The train jerks forward with a hydraulic hiss.

This is a Victoria line train to Walthamstow Central, a recorded female voice intones, plummy as a newsreader's. Long gone the Cockney drawl. The train jolts into the tunnel. Her ears pop. It is dim inside the car and hot.

As a toddler, Noah had loved to stand up on the subway seat and watch the world blur past. She would hang on to the waistband of his diaper as the carriage rocked and swayed. As the train entered the tunnel, his little voice would rise above the engine's roar: *Mummy, Mummy, look*. She'd turn to look, but the only thing that she could see was the reflection of their faces doubled in the scratched and dirty glass.

At King's Cross, Amir doesn't stand up. He is not heading home, then. Her stomach twists. If he sees her, what would she say? She has no excuses now.

A tall man wearing the long white tunic and crocheted skull-cap of a Muslim cleric takes a seat across the aisle from her. He has an untrimmed beard and dark Semitic features, like a Hasidic Jew. Isaac and Ishmael, she thinks. He sets a large, rectangular black case, like a doctor's bag, between his feet. He keeps his eyes downcast, twisting a kara bracelet around his wrist. The other passengers flick quick glances toward him and away: suspicion's covert flare.

With a long screeching sound, the train accelerates, and her heartbeat accelerates too. Everyone was paranoid these days, of course, and for all her liberal politics, she was just as paranoid as the rest. It was one thing to express outrage over racial profiling and quite another to sit across a subway carriage from a Muslim cleric carrying a suspicious-looking case. What could be in there? Medical supplies? Religious documents? Legal briefs?

The cleric twists his bracelet around his wrist. *I'm watching you*, she thinks. But if he made a suspicious move, what would she do? Would she have the guts to pull the emergency cord, to scream?

This is a Victoria line train to Walthamstow Central, the female voice on the recording says. *The next station is Finsbury Park. Doors will open on the left-hand side. Change for the Piccadilly line and National Rail Services.*

The train begins to slow with a descending squeal. Amir stands and moves to the door. The cleric bends forward and picks up his case.

The doors open and Esther steps off the train. *Finsbury Park*. What was Amir doing here?

She follows the crowd of passengers off the narrow platform, scanning for Amir. But he has vanished. Beyond the platform, tunnels stretch in both directions. She chooses the one signposted SEVEN SISTERS ROAD.

Outside the station, she turns in place. Elevated train tracks stretch above the street. Along the rusty stanchions, someone has spray-painted *TOX 03*. She is a long way from the tony streets of Bloomsbury and Hampstead. There is a Halal House, a Muslim bookshop. A woman wearing a burka is walking toward her, tugging an enormous suitcase on wheels. There's no sign of Amir.

Finsbury Park.

What was she doing here? She must be losing her mind.

A black taxi is idling at the curb. She runs toward it. The driver lowers the window.

"Home," she says. "Just take me home, please."

LONIA

Time has a different rhythm now. Days and nights bleed together as she drifts in and out of sleep. Her daughter appears and disappears, brings food, clears it away again. The rim of brightness at the borders of the curtains sharpens and then fades. Time dilates and contracts.

In the stillness of the afternoons, or late at night, the sound of the piano rises through the floorboards, the joists and crossbeams ringing with the vibration of the old Blüthner's strings. The notes like fractals, a filigree of counterpoint.

Rilke's great tree of sound.

O Orpheus singt! O hoher Baum im Ohr!

Music for the beginning and the end of time.

She does not believe in, does not imagine, angels. But she feels the cogwheels turning, great steel-black gears like those that drove the engines of the winding machines that raised the ore and lowered workers into the deep Ostrava mines.

The voices in the fugue call and answer, circle and repeat. Ripples expand outward in concentric rings.

In her dreams, or memory, music is playing, slow and lugubrious: a dirge. They are gathered around the radio, Lonia and her father and Hugo, listening to a broadcast of *Má Vlast*, the windows of the flat thrown open to the dirty summer breeze. They lean in toward the radio, toward the miracle of it, the Czech Philharmonic playing Smetana's defiant lament for their betrayed and vanquished nation, crushed beneath the German fist. They can't believe that the Germans have permitted the broadcast to go on the air.

Her father wipes the corners of his eyes. "There is hope."

"Are you mad?" Hugo snorts. "No."

It has been decided. They are to leave. Their father is worried that Hugo, with his secret meetings and leftist leanings, could be drafted or arrested or worse. Their father's letter-writing campaign to find a sponsor overseas has failed, but in Kraków there are cousins on her mother's side with whom they can stay until the situation settles down or an emigration opportunity opens up. Since the Poles annexed the area around Tešin in March, the border is right there, on the east side of Ostrava, and Kraków is less than two hundred kilometers beyond that. Lonia is to go with Hugo. Best for both of them to be safe.

It will only be for a little while, her father promises, at most a couple of weeks. The Russians and the French will surely stop Hitler if he tries to grab Poland too. Even Hugo agrees that the Bolsheviks, unlike that pansy Chamberlain, should at least have the guts to try.

Meanwhile, swastikas are flying from the windows along every street. Jewish businesses are being confiscated by the state. Whispered rumors flap their wings: Jews beaten by the Brownshirts, Jews sent to forced labor camps in the Sudetenland, Jews rounded up and shot. Nearly every night, they hear the fire engines clanging. All six synagogues in Ostrava have been torched.

Hugo approaches as she's washing up from dinner. Lonia pulls a gold-rimmed plate out of the sudsy water and rubs it with the rag. It is her mother's wedding china, Moser's best from Prague. Goodbye, plate, she thinks. She is saying goodbye to everything, each goodbye a little benediction, one item at a time. Goodbye, sink. Goodbye glass. Goodbye, old life, goodbye.

"Are you ready?" Hugo says.

She rinses the plate under the tap and hands it to him, nodding toward the tea towel hanging on its little hook.

"You dry," she says.

She is not ready. How could she be ready? She does not want to leave. How will her father and grandmother manage without them? She remembers, when she was a very little girl, shutting her eyes and imagining that the whole world had disappeared. She feels that way now, as if none of this will continue to exist when she's not here.

"I was wondering, Hugo—"

"What?"

"Perhaps Frau Becker could come up to help with the cooking and cleaning a few days a week?"

His eyes narrow. She knows that look.

"You can't say a word to anyone."

"I'm just—"

"He's a grown man, Lonia. He'll manage fine."

She pulls the last dinner plate from the soapy water and rubs the gold rim with her thumb. It is embossed with a delicate pattern of flowering vines. It reminds her of her grandfather's prize roses, her grandmother's beans and peas. She wonders who is tending to the garden now. Goodbye, roses. Goodbye, peas.

She reaches into the murky water and pulls the plug. The dishwater is suctioned down the drain, leaving a scum of soap suds and food dregs. She takes a breath.

"Hugo—"

"What?"

"Never mind."

"What?"

"Hugo—if we get caught, what will—"

"We won't get caught. Everything is arranged."

In the *Graphic Atlas*, Poland is yellow; Palestine is pink. Hugo's plan, Lonia knows, is to make his way south to Trieste or Split and on to Palestine by sea. Lonia could come back to this shithole if she wants, Hugo says, but not him.

Goodbye map, she thinks.

She has never been anywhere but here. When she is someplace else, who will she be?

The "taxi" arrives to pick them up at half past five in the morning. The black Škoda idles at the curb as they rush to say goodbye. Her father presses a little leather pouch into her hand—her mother's diamond ring. He pulls her close and grips her tight. Her heart twists. His cheek is rough against her face. He says, *God bless*.

The driver's arm is sticking out the rolled-down window, a cigarette between his fingers burning down to ash. It is raining lightly; the sky is low and gray. Hugo climbs in the front and she slides in the back. The car lurches away.

At the main gates of the colliery, the watchman nods to the driver and waves them in. Everything has been arranged. Money has changed hands.

It is one of the smaller drift mines near Tešin. Half of the mine property is now on the Polish side. Three months ago, they could have simply walked across what is now the border along the forest trail. Train tracks stretch pas the colliery into the forest through an infantry of old-growth lodge pole pines. Their trunks stand as straight as sentries in the mist.

The colliery is strangely peaceful in the early Sunday morning stillness, the machines silenced, as if enchanted, frozen in time. The scaffold of the winding tower and the old steam plant chimney rise like the steeples of some infernal church. Loaded hoppers wait alongside the rails, heaped with lump coal, cube coal, nut and rice coal, bits of broken stone. Three men are standing in the shadow of the tipple. Two of them are young and look like brothers, redheads, doughy-skinned and stocky, strong. The third man, the guide, is older, smaller, wiry, stooped. He has a miner's dirt-seamed hands and a sled dog's eyes, the pale blue of ice. Slavic eyes, Lonia's father would have said. They nod, shake hands. It is a matter of money, not generosity, she understands.

The four of them follow the guide around great heaps of slag and shale to the entrance of the mine. Train tracks disappear into the black mouth of the adit. A mantrip sits at the opening, ready for the next shift, its little flatbed engine and green wagons like a child's toy, out of scale, a joke. They skirt the train and follow the guide into the mine.

It is so dark inside the tunnel that she cannot tell at first whether her eyes are open or shut. She never knew there could be such complete darkness—that darkness could have substance, texture, mass. She reaches for Hugo's belt and shuffles her feet along the uneven ground between the tracks, blind. Her body feels weightless, immaterial, as if it has dissolved into atoms, spinning in outer space.

She has never really considered before what lay beneath the ground, here in Ostrava, this land of mines. Even the visible evidence—the steel headgear towers, the squat brick plant buildings crisscrossed by chutes, the smokestacks exhaling crooked plumes of smoke, the industrial geometry laced with tiny lights at night—has never signified anything other than the familiar contours of the city's skyline. But now she is deep inside it, swallowed up like Jonah in the belly of the whale. Over their heads sit tons of rock and dirt, roots and decomposing plants and bones, which, over the millennia, will be transformed into hard seams of anthracite—black gold. The tunnel air is choked with dust. It has a fiery smell. She can taste it, feel the grit of it between her teeth. She pulls her shirt up over her mouth and nose, trying not to cough. It is difficult to breathe.

Once they are safely clear of the entrance, the guide switches on his miner's lamp, and the redhead brothers pull out electric torches. She and Hugo have no light. She keeps her grip on Hugo's belt, running the fingers of her other hand along the tunnel wall. Rough rock, then a timber post, then rock again. There are many ways to die inside a coal mine, she knows: cave-ins, rockfalls, explosions, floods. The darkness squeezes her lungs tight. She stumbles and nearly falls. Ahead, the guide's lamp and the brothers' torches flicker like distant stars.

They walk on and on, deeper into the mine. They pass indecipherable pieces of machinery, bundles of dirt-clogged tools hanging on wire loops, heavy canvas curtains, wooden doors. In just a few hours it would all be back in motion: the conveyor belt rumbling, compressors bellowing, a racket of coal tubs jolting along the tracks, the coal cutter grinding at the face. Hundreds of hunched men with blackened faces and dirt-seamed hands. Her mouth is dry. She licks her lips and then regrets it, her tongue now acrid with dust.

Finally, they pause and the guide sets down his lamp. They have come to a junction where the adit splits. That way to the face, the guide says, gesturing to the left. The other way to a second, disused exit, now on the Polish side. Not far now. In the clouded light, she can make out a low-roofed trench, the muddy ground, walls timbered with wooden beams. One of the red-haired brothers pulls out a flask and passes it around, and she takes a sip and chokes, the schnapps trailing a hot flame through her chest.

"You work here long?" Hugo asks the guide.

The man frowns, nods.

"Since the age of sixteen," he says. "My brothers and my father and his father and his brothers too."

"It's a tough life," one of the redheads says.

The guide gives a short laugh, like a bark. "It's a living, that's all I can say."

It is only another kilometer or so to the opening of the adit, but it is the longest distance she has ever traveled. Space has contracted into blackness. Time has wound down to a stop. Somewhere, in another universe, her father is still standing in a doorway, raising his hand, his face wet with tears, his glasses glinting in the early light.

Finally, the darkness thins and the tunnel opens out into a wider, higher space. They pause at a niche cut into the rock—a shrine to Saint Barbara, the miners' patron saint. Offerings of miners' tokens and coins lie in the coal dust at a plaster icon's feet. The guide bows his head and mumbles a prayer, crosses himself. The saint looks out at them with her placid, indifferent gaze. Lonia whispers a silent thank you. So what if Jews did not believe in saints?

Outside they squint into the stab of daylight. The shuttered colliery grounds are quiet on this side, too. It is still a Sunday morning in 1939.

What was a border, anyway? The forest here was the same forest as on the other side. The trees the same stark lodge pole pines. The air damp with the same misting summer rain.

In Lonia's dream, she's falling. The pavement cracks and buckles, the cobblestones break and drop into the void beneath the street—a sinkhole, a mineshaft—into which she's falling, somersaulting, head over heels, weightless, wind whooshing through her skin, released from gravity. Her skirt flips up; her limbs fly out; her fingers scrape the rocky tunnel walls. Far above her, the blue eye of daylight winks shut. She can feel it loose inside her chest, her wild heart.

She jerks awake, gasping for breath, her nightgown damp with sweat.

Through the floorboards the Blüthner is still singing.

O Orpheus sings. O great tree of sound. O fugue-song of escape.

FOUR

AMIR

Mole is down below, Bigsby overhead. Long tiers of cat ladders stretch down the steel-clad access shaft like a spinal column encircled by skeletal steel ribs. The shaft is a derelict cathedral, a missile silo, a space ship. The thrum of traffic overhead has long since faded. Now there's just the reverberation of exhaust fans and every movement's metallic ping. The air smells dank and burny. Underground air, trapped.

They are three boys in black hoodies, trainers, and dirty jeans, climbing down into an uncharted tunnel beneath the Thames. The tunnel stretches from Pimlico to Battersea, if Mole is right. It's not marked on any map.

They've already traversed a strange, bright, orange-lit tunnel, hot and dry, lined with enormous pipes. Steam pipes for district heating, Mole said. Mole was the tunnel rat, an engineer. This expedition had taken weeks of trolling for information on the Internet and endless nights of recon before they finally settled on a plan. Bigsby had been all for infiltrating the Pimlico Accumulator instead, but Mole wasn't too keen on climbing a forty-one-meter heating tower in plain view of anyone looking out a window in the Churchill Estates. (It's a gigantic fucking pressure cooker, Biggs," he said.) Of course, as it turned out, the tunnel entry wasn't any less exposed, the manhole right there on the Embankment for anyone driving past to see. They had to wait until nearly 2:00 a.m., crouched behind a low brick wall, until a gap in the traffic opened long enough for them to pop the cover and drop in.

Their torch beams strafe the chamber's walls. The shaft is streaked with rust and smears of white—bat guano or lime. Shadows flare. Amir lowers himself another rung, steps onto a rest landing, shrugs off his rucksack, and pulls out his camera. He braces himself against the rail and shoots. There's not much light.

A muddy trainer dangles above his head. "Stop faffin' about down there."

"Piss off, Biggs."

He fires off a string of shots, shoves the camera into his pack.

At the bottom of the shaft, two gigantic steam pipes stretch into the tunnel. Two equally enormous pipes hang overhead. The pipes are sticky with black insulating gunk and hot. Straddling the narrow trench of filthy standing water that has collected between the pipes, Mole leads the way. Bigsby follows; Amir takes up the rear. Their trainers squelch. Their torch beams twitch. There's the *pling* of water dripping, a scrabbling sound that had better not be rats. They are beneath the river, beneath the Thames, twenty feet of water coursing overhead.

The first Thames tunnel was dug at Rotherhithe between 1825 and 1843, Mole says. Incredibly enough, trains still run through it, between Dalston Junction and Croydon, on the East London line. Amir has been on that train often enough; he'd never have guessed the tunnel was so old. The tunnel builders had to do the digging by hand with spades back then, inching along the iron framework of Brunel's famous tunneling shield, fetid river water spraying over them. Their oil lamps exploded if they hit a pocket of methane gas. Workers routinely passed out after a couple of hours underground, and then they hauled them up and sent down a fresh crew. Men died of dysentery or fever or drowned when the river broke through, as it not infrequently did.

This tunnel was probably dug in the 1920s, Mole says. Amir

swings his torch upward, illuminating a spot where a few support beams have been welded to brace a dent in the tunnel wall. If the tunnel ruptured, they'd be swept away in an avalanche of water, their bones pulverized, their lungs crushed. They'd be buried beneath tons of muddy silt and sand. No one would ever find them. No one even knew that they were here.

He has always been drawn to secret, ruined places: to the filthy coal chute in the cellar, to the attic crawl space, stuffed with yellow insulation, to the graffiti-strafed path beneath the railway bridge with its urine reek. As a child, he used to like to climb inside the armoire or wedge himself beneath the bed. Hidden on the window seat, cloaked in the curtains, he'd read Lewis, Tolkien, Rowling, Anthony, Peake. The books opened onto other universes, parallel realities, cracks and gaps in time. In hidden places, you transformed.

Now Bigsby says things like, *Transgression is an essential precondition of resistance to the carceral system of modern society.* When Bigsby talks like an academic in his Yorkshire accent, it cracks Amir up.

He met Bigsby right off at SOAS, in Welcome Week. He'd done his obligatory tour of the Fresher's Fair, dodging the gauntlet of arms waving him into the Brazilian jiu-jitsu society, the *Spirit* newspaper, the Palestinian solidarity society, the Stop the War coalition, the cricket club. He'd ended up hunched over a pint at the student union, alone. Bigsby had sidled up beside him—tall, lantern jawed, thin lipped, his head a nest of curls—and held out his hand.

"John Biggs."

Bigsby came from up north, from West Yorkshire, outside Leeds. He was in his second year, studying anthropology. He was into ethnography, sci-fi, semiotics, UrbEx, climbing, multiplayer video games.

"*Urb*-what?" Amir said.

"Urban exploration. Infiltration. Ghost hunting. Call it what ye like."

"And what exactly do you . . . infiltrate?"

Bigsby's lips twisted into a smile. "Abandoned buildings," he said. "Storm drains, utility tunnels, conduits, tower cranes."

He reached into his bag, pulled out a laptop, and clicked on photographs: gaping tunnels, grime-encrusted machinery, vast seas of twinkling lights.

"Where's all this, then?"

"All around, if ye know where to look."

"Yeah, right."

"I'm not fooling. Behind all those 'no access' signs. Raight beneath yer feet."

Amir leaned in closer. The pictures showed crumbling brickwork, train tracks stretching into darkness, dust motes floating in beams of torchlight. Sewer pipes a man could walk through without ducking. Smashed windows. Concrete walls. Stairwells cordoned off with caution tape.

"Is it dangerous?"

"Only if yer an idiot."

"Ever get caught?"

"Nay. They'll just rap yer knuckles for trespassing, anyhow, so long as ye don't have owt that could be taken for a weapon or a tool for vandalism—no knives or lighters or spray paint, none o' that."

"So where are you going next?"

Bigsby tipped back the last of his pint and grinned. "Guess ye'll just have to coom along and see."

Now, up ahead, Mole is squinting up a narrow brick-clad shaft cut into the top of the tunnel wall. They all come to a stop.

"Switch off a sec," Mole says.

They turn off their torches and everything goes black. They crane their necks, following Mole's gaze. Far above, Amir can see the faintest will-o'-the-wisp of light.

"What the fuck is that?" Bigsby says.

"It's the moon, you wanker," says Mole. "We've done it. Crossed to the other side."

Amir holds his camera up and keeps the shutter open to catch the pallid streak.

From that point on, the tunnel is newer, cleaner, the pipes better insulated, the cylinder clad in dry concrete. It dead-ends at another exit shaft lined with tiers of hooped metal ladders. Again, they climb the cat ladders to the highest landing. Just above them is the manhole cover, which opens, if they have reckoned right, to the streets of Battersea, beneath the Chelsea bridge.

They sit down on the metal grate of the top landing, dangling their legs over the abyss. Bigsby pulls out a flask. "Here's to us!" He whoops. "To an epic journey!"

The whisky burns. They've done it. Scored a first in an uncharted tunnel. Walked right beneath the Thames.

"Is the Battersea power station right above us?" Amir asks.

"Yep," Mole says.

"Did you ever get in there?"

"Once. Got into the control room and then climbed up onto the roof."

"I really want to do that." Amir leans over the rail, holding the camera at arm's length, the dark drop doubled on the screen.

"It was fucking awesome," says Mole.

"Aye, it's a classic," Bigsby agrees.

"I heard they're going to rip the whole thing down soon, though," Mole says, spitting. "They're going to make it over into a leisure complex—luxury flats, a sports center, all that shit."

Bigsby shakes his head. "That's fucked up."

"That's what everybody wants, isn't it?" Mole says. "A fancy flat and a fancy car and big fancy bank account to pay for all of it."

"Not me," Amir says.

"Yeah, right. Just give it a couple of years," Mole says, waving the flask. "All this will be nothing but a rosy memory of your misspent youth."

"Go on," Bitsby says.

"You'll see. You'll be sitting at a fucking desk, in a fucking suit and tie, just like the rest of them."

"Oh, and ye won't be?"

"Piss off, Biggs."

They pass the flask. Bigsby stands up, unzips. Piss splatters into the void below like rain.

Amir pulls out his camera and scrolls through the shots taken earlier that night: the hot orange tunnel, the tiers of metal ladders, the guano-smeared shaft, the gigantic gunky pipes. Mole and Bigsby grin out at him. Their faces are nothing but spots of light, photons in a digital stream. Already none of it seems real.

He remembers once, when he was little, a game of hide-and-seek. They were down in Richmond, he and his mum, at a party thrown by some of her friends. He remembers lawns like great green football pitches, enormous houses, spreading trees. The grownups were pouring drinks, waving their hands—*go on, go outside and play*. He followed the group of children around the back.

He didn't know the other kids. One of the boys cocked his head at him and said, "Are you a Paki?" And when he didn't answer, "Are you adopted, then?"

Ready, steady, go! the seeker shouted and they scattered. He ran around the far side of the house to where the lawn ended and the woods began and scrambled up a low-branched tree. He could hear the seeker counting off, slowly at first, then rushing to the end. Then there was just a tingling silence, broken only by the seeker's panting breath as he ran by, oblivious, beneath the tree.

Amir gripped his branch between his legs and waited. His blood beat inside his ears. He was not a Paki. He was not adopted. He hated the lot of them. He wished them dead.

The sky turned pink, then navy. The light dimmed. All he'd have to do was spread his arms, he thought, and he could fly, broad-winged as a hawk, out above the rooftops and back gardens to the river and onward to the open sea.

Squirrels scrambled in the upper branches; a dove cooed somewhere in the leaves. He didn't hear the other children yelling *ollie ollie oxen free*, or the grownups calling them in for supper, his mum frantically shouting his name. He doesn't know how long he stayed there in the darkness, doesn't remember skinning his knees and shins climbing down the tree. He remembers only the anger in his mother's voice when he finally came straggling in, and her fierce and furious embrace.

After an expedition, back at university, everything—the Victorian brick buildings, the modern glass and concrete blocks, the library, the lecture halls with their projectors and screens and rows of chairs—seems touched by the proximity of decay. He notices the cracks, the scuffs and nicks, the watermarks left by a leak, the peeling paint. He nods to the cleaner, leaning on his broom; to the workman slipping into a supply closet; to the old Bangladeshi woman dragging a cart behind her, emptying the bins. The other students and faculty members rush obliviously past. The great machine rumbles on, pulling them in its wake.

Amir crams in with the other first-years around a table in the student bar. They set down pints of beer and plates of greasy chips.

"Did you lot see this?" Sayyid pulls out a copy of *The Guardian*, the pages folded back. He reads, "'The union has failed to provide an adequate response to concerns about allegations of anti-Semitic activity on Britain's campuses, chiefly at the School of Oriental and African Studies.'"

Tawfiq grimaces. "They should be writing about all the anti-*Islamic* activity on Britain's campuses instead," he says.

Ian grabs a handful of chips. "No joke."

"The Jewish students go whining to the authorities and it's national fucking news," Sayyid says, shaking his head. "I read Nassim's article in the *Spirit*. This is not a matter of anti-Semitism. This is about those colonialist Zionist fucks who continue to occupy our land!"

Amir looks down at the wet rings left by his glass along the table-top. They have opinions on everything, the others: the situation at Guantanamo, the Gaza tunnels, the new anti-terror legislation, the proliferation of CCTV cameras, the arguments justifying or condemning suicide attacks. Amir admires their passionate, sure-footed politics. They knew exactly who they were; they were willing to take a stand. He feels as if they have opened a secret door to a new world that until now has been completely hidden from his view. He can't talk about anything that matters with his parents. His father would just go off on another lecture about the ayatollahs and the dangers of religious fundamentalism, as if it were still 1979 in Iran. And his mum, well. She doesn't think about anything but herself.

From across the table, Miranda catches his eye and smiles. She's always smiling. Her eyes are dark and thick lashed, outlined heavily in black.

Sayyid's voice grows louder. "Nassim told me he's been getting death threats from the American Jews. Death threats for a sodding article! They're worse than Hitler!"

Ian nods. "Haven't they heard about free speech?"

"People will defend free speech all right when the attacks are directed against *us*," Tawfiq says. "But don't try speaking out against the Israeli terrorists. Oh no."

Is-ra-ee-li, Tawfiq says, with the proper accent on the third syllable. He is fluent in Arabic, even though he grew up here. Amir wishes he spoke Arabic. He doesn't even speak Farsi. It is hard going, starting so late.

Miranda is still smiling at him. She leans a little closer. "So what do you think?" she says.

"Me?"

"Yeah, you."

"About what?"

"You ready for that last exam?"

"I don't know. I guess."

"We're having one final study session. My place, tomorrow afternoon. Will you come along?"

He has been to a few of these so-called study sessions at Miranda's flat up in Finsbury Park. Not much studying has gotten done, so far, at least. Mostly they sit about and laugh and drink.

"Tomorrow?"

"Yes. Just bring along some study aids. Your choice: booze or sweets."

Amir runs a finger along the condensation on his glass. "Maybe?"

"Come on," she says. She touches his arm. Even her eyes are smiling. "Say yes."

ESTHER

It is hot. Not yet the end of May and already it's a sweltering ninety degrees Fahrenheit in central London, the hottest day in May in more than fifty years. So hot that three trains get stuck in an Underground tunnel south of Baker Street, trapping the passengers for hours. So hot that for ninety minutes even Big Ben, stalwart survivor of the Blitz, refuses to tick.

"It's global warming," Esther says, fanning her mother with a magazine. The bedroom is stifling. The windows are wide open, but no air is moving out or in. The room smells of illness, medicinal and oversweet.

"Nonsense," her mother says. She sits propped against the pillows, a damp towel rolled around her neck. A cooking show is on TV. A plump young man with a goatee is talking about pork bellies, gesturing at a pink and white side of flesh laid out on a metal tray. Were pork bellies actually bellies? Esther has never kept kosher, but there was still something disgusting about the thought of eating the stomach of a pig.

"This is why they invented air conditioning, Mum," she says. "Don't you even own a fan?" She hands her mother a glass of water and watches as she drinks. Apparently the elderly lose the ability to sweat. Hydration, Zofia has told her, is the most important thing.

Her mother gestures vaguely. "There should be one about somewhere. Have a look in the basement. There might be one down there."

Dank trapped air breathes out the cellar door. Esther tugs the string for light and makes her way down the narrow wooden stairs. It's cooler down here, at least. Old suitcases hunch beneath a sheet. She prods a rack of dusty garment bags that reek of naphthalene. A carrier bag crammed with mildewed shoes, another stuffed with handbags. A sewing machine.

Ancient artifacts. Some are hers, it seems. From a metal crate, she pulls out an algebra textbook, a French grammar, a couple of old paperbacks—*The Great Gatsby*, *Oliver Twist*. She riffles through the yellowed pages of the Dickens. Her name, *Esther Fagin*, is penned in loopy girlish cursive on the inside cover of the book. Of all the things to have saved. She has always hated the way people look at her when they hear her surname. "Fagin?" they said. "Really? Like Fagin the crook in *Oliver Twist?*" She tosses the book back into the box.

She finally locates the fan, a table unit with rust-flecked blades inside a wire cage, over in a corner, covered with a yellowed pillowcase. She picks it up, gathers the frayed cord into a loop. The basement will have to be cleaned out. The whole house will have to be cleaned out, packed up, sorted, sold. It was overwhelming. She will keep only the piano, she decides. The piano and her mother's pearls. That was it. No more fetishizing material things.

She trudges back upstairs, carrying the fan. Her mother has dozed off, her mouth agape. Esther sets the fan on the seat of a chair and plugs it in. It oscillates slowly, with a rusty creak. It won't cool things off much, but at least it makes the hot air circulate.

On TV, the cooking show has ended and the news is on. They are talking about the Piano Man again. Good lord. Have they still not been able to identify him? She hears the words: *not the French busker . . . back to square one . . . shrouded in mystery again*. The calls and emails to the Missing Persons Helpline have continued to pour in. How could a person stay lost like that, she wonders, hidden in plain sight? What was he trying to flee? She clicks off the TV.

From the photograph over on the dresser, her father shoots her a forbidding look. *Fagin the Jew*. Not the leader of a ring of child pickpockets, but equally a thief. What had made him do it? Arrogance? Or greed?

"He was a survivor," her mother always said, tapping her temple with a fingertip. "You have got to understand the mentality. He knew how to find ways of doing things that others said could not be done."

Esther knows the story—knows, at least, that somehow, just before the Germans invaded Poland and the war began, he managed to get hold of all the required papers—passports, tickets, exit permits, entrance visas—and sail with her mother to safety across the sea.

But clearly he'd found ways of doing other things, as well. The trouble was not only his financial dealings, but also his alleged connections to the Eastern bloc. There were rumors that he'd been a bit too friendly with a Soviet diplomat in London, that he'd been in contact with KGB officers in Kraków and in Prague, that he'd funneled money to Moscow through accounts in Swiss and Israeli banks. Some suspected he was a double agent, working for the Mossad.

Esther's mother said simply that he'd been seeking information on members of their families who were lost during the war. That the money sent to Moscow was intended to help Soviet Jews who wanted to escape. It was the height of the Cold War, after all. Of course the authorities would be suspicious of a Russian-speaking Eastern European Jew.

She stood by him no matter what, her mother.

"He saved my life," she said.

In the Jewish cemetery at Willesden, Esther's father's head-stone is engraved in gold. At the bottom of the headstone is a Hebrew acronym: *tav, nun, tzadee, bet, hey.* "May his soul be bound up in the bond of life," the saying went. She has always wondered why Jews pray for bondage after death and not release. Half of the headstone is still blank. She glances over at her mother. Her chest rises and falls with the even, shallow breath of sleep. It would not be much longer now.

Esther grabs her cigarettes and lighter and steps outside into the garden. The heat presses like a weight. The air is muffled, de-pleted. Even the birds have been silenced by the heat. In the dis-tance there is the low rumble of what she hopes is thunder. If only it would rain.

The grass is overgrown and snarled with weeds. Her mother would not be pleased. Heavy purple blossoms drip from the wis-teria that twines along the wall. It needs to be pruned. Above her rise the secret backs of houses, a patchwork of windows and mis-matched brick. How many others have lived here before her? It seems impossible that after her mother is gone, after she is gone, all this will still be here.

She taps a cigarette out of the pack and flicks the lighter, breathes in. It isn't fair, she thinks, that bricks and buildings, even weeds, should all persist, but not one boy. Her boy. Her son. A noose cinches around her throat, the old familiar grip of grief.

For a fleeting moment, in the awful, breathless grip of yearn-ing, she feels that he's not dead but simply somewhere else. At any given instant, after all, there are only two conditions: *here* and *not-here*. *Fort-da*, she thinks, remembering her Freud. Here, gone. If someone is *not-here*, what difference does it make, really, whether they are alive or dead? The only difference is the way you think about the loss, the permanence of the thing. The past—

history, time slipping from one moment to the next—is *not-here* in the same way as well. It is gone but can be called back, re-called, at any time—in story, in language, as an imaginative act. So you could say, in some way, that her son is still alive, only *not-here*. It is a conditional tense existence: the past unreal.

The thought floods her with relief. It doesn't matter that she can't go into his room and touch his model planes or stare up at the stick-on stars on the ceiling. He is close—closer than she has felt him to be in years. She was not losing him. He was near.

She glances up at the back windows of the house. She squints but can't see in. It is hard to believe that Noah would have been nearly nineteen now, nearly the same age as Amir. She was always adding and subtracting, running the numbers, to hold that empty place. What would he be doing on this hot May morning? He wouldn't be here in London with her, surely, waiting for his grandmother to pass away. She would have insisted he stay home, hang out, have fun. Maybe he would have a summer job. Maybe he'd be out on Fire Island or hanging out with friends. Maybe there would be a girl. She has often tried to conjure for him a girlfriend, someone spunky and clever and sweet. She pictures him lanky, in baggy jeans and a loose T-shirt, dark eyed, intense.

She has not seen Amir since that afternoon she followed him onto the Tube. She can hardly remember why she went after him the way she did—she must have been half-mad. She thinks of the white-robed, bearded cleric seated across from her that day on the Tube, how he'd kept his eyes downcast, twisting that metal band around his wrist, as everybody, herself included, shot him suspicious looks. He was probably a perfectly nice fellow, she thinks, feeling a flush of shame.

She grinds her cigarette under her heel and tosses the butt into the dead leaves. She hasn't heard from Javad, either, since the night they kissed. She feels a hollow pang of disappointment mixed with guilt. She has not kissed another man since she married Gil. But everything had now begun to shift.

That week only Ruth comes round for tea. Myrna is off at some posh Algarve resort with Claudia and her kids, and Vivian is "taking the cure" at a Slovak spa. ("Trying to slim down, more like," her mother said.) The heat, thank god, has ebbed. Esther helps her mother downstairs to the sofa, and Ruth settles in beside her, nibbling on a slice of lemon tart.

Ruth does nearly all the talking. She goes on about the awful weather, about her grandchildren and their various engagements and new babies and impressive jobs and university degrees. Then she starts in on the latest incident—the British university boycott of Israeli academics—that has made her husband, Gerry, apoplectic with outrage.

"The British universities are the worst," says Ruth. "Hotbeds of anti-Semitism, the lot. They're breeding grounds for Islamic radicals, Gerry says."

"Protesting the Israeli occupation isn't necessarily anti-Semitic, is it?" Esther says.

Ruth regards her as if she is repeating an elementary lesson to a child. "Anti-Semitism is like a virus, Gerry says. It may mutate and take new forms, but it will never go away."

Esther reaches for the teapot. "Would you like a bit more tea?" She should know better than to argue politics with Ruth.

"That would be lovely, please," Ruth says, holding out her cup. "Gerry's got cousins over in Tel Aviv, you know. During the Gulf War, one of Saddam's Scud missiles landed on the street right outside their flat. Gerry's cousins were down in the basement shelter, gas masks on, frightened out of their wits." She slurps her tea. "They survived the camps for this!

One person was killed and eighty-four injured. Right on a residential street."

Esther has never been to Israel. If truth be told, it is not a place she has ever felt much desire to see. When she thinks of Israel, she pictures bulldozers and checkpoints, Israeli soldiers firing on little skinny boys throwing stones. She thinks, too, of burnt-out cafés and busses blown up by suicide bombers, flag-draped Hamas fighters jubilantly shooting AK-47s in the streets. Hatred bred only more hate.

Esther's mother rouses herself. "My brother Hugo believed that Israel—Palestine, as it was then, under the British Mandate—was the only possible homeland for the Jews."

Ruth shakes her head. "It's not an easy life over there, I can tell you that."

A husk of questions catches in Esther's throat. But her mother's eyes are focused somewhere far away. Her mother almost never spoke about her brother. Esther knows only that he died in Europe, in the war. Esther picks up the plates and carries them into the kitchen. They have never been close, she supposes, in the way of other mothers and daughters. There was always a certain distance to her mother, a margin of reserve. It was a European quality, perhaps, or maybe she was simply of a different generation, a different world. She was not given to displays of physical affection; they rarely hugged or touched. She was certainly nothing like the American mothers of Esther's high school friends in Boston, with their frosted hair and wood-paneled station wagons and weekly doubles matches at the country club, the mothers who bought their daughters bell-bottom jeans and Vaccaro turtlenecks from Settebello in Harvard Square, who encouraged them to go on dates and knew which boys were bad news and which were not. With Esther's mother, there were no tell-all snuggles over unrequited crushes or broken hearts. Esther would never have dreamed of telling her mother about the high school dances that ended up in guilty make-out sessions beneath the bleachers; the nights spent fumbling with hooks and zippers on basement couches or the slippery backseats of someone's father's car; or in later years, the wrenching breakups and stupid pregnancy scares, the reckless college flings.

Only for that first year or so after they left England, in that first drafty rented house in Newton, could you have called them close. For months, Esther woke in panic, her heart thudding, dread wrenching at her chest. Her mother's bedroom was at the far end of a long, dark hall. Shadows fingered the walls. The dim light above the stairs gleamed like a wolf. Nearly paralyzed with fear, she'd force herself to sprint the shadowed gauntlet to her mother's room and crawl into her bed. The sheets were chilly in her father's vacant spot. She'd wriggle toward the softness of her mother's body and wait for her mother to reach across and pull her in.

Eventually she got used to it, of course, like you get used to anything. The two of them at the dinner table in the too-big house filled with someone else's things. The enormous supermarkets and cars. The hard *r's* and flat vowels. The kids at school who looked at her funny and said, "Where are you *from?*"

What could she do? She lost her accent. She slept in her own bed. She pulled away.

She bumps into Javad the following afternoon, out on the street. She has just made a quick trip to Waitrose, and he looks like he's been to the gym. He's wearing athletic shorts and a red soccer jersey that reads *Vodafone* across the chest. They embrace and then just stand there awkwardly, the kiss hanging in the air between them, sharp and glittery as a trinket or a shard of glass.

"I hope I didn't offend you, the other evening," he says. "With my, er—impulsiveness."

She feels a goofy smile spread across her face. "Offended? Oh, I'm not offended."

"That's good. I wanted to ring you, but I didn't have your number. I don't even know your surname, in point of fact, so I couldn't look it up. I've been meaning to stop by."

She feels a wash of relief. "You could have just rapped on the wall," she says. "You know—Morse code."

He laughs. "I'll give that a go next time."

She likes his laugh. It twinges deep inside her, a vestige of desire, like sensation in a phantom limb.

She looks at his shirt. "So do you play soccer?"

"Football, do you mean?"

"Sorry, football. Right."

"Nah, I've got a bad back. I'm just another over-the-hill Man U fan like all the rest."

The sky is white. It smells like rain. She shifts her weight.

He pushes up his glasses and rubs the bridge of his nose. "I was wondering. Would you like to get together one of these evenings, perhaps, for dinner or a drink?"

Yes, she would. Very much indeed.

He takes her out the following week to a Persian place on West End Lane, where he orders for them both in Farsi: Mirza Ghasemi and Ghormez Sabzi, fragrant with fenugreek and limes. They go out again, a few days later, for beer and burgers in the garden of a local pub. Talk flows easily. He tells her about neurology, neuro-imaging studies, and something that sounds like *ephemeri* and the prefrontal cortex. She nods as if she understands. What a thing, to glimpse the workings of the brain! She tells him about leaving London for Boston; he tells her about coming to London from Tehran. They talk about their fathers, both of whom died, too young, in jail. Their lives are mirror images, Esther thinks. The thought gives her a thrill.

Still she hasn't mentioned Noah. She knows she should tell him—she must. She will. Only there are no words for what she has to say. Music is better. Words just get in the way.

Above all, she doesn't want his pity. She doesn't want to hear him say the thoughtless things that people always say. *I can't imagine anything worse than losing a kid. God doesn't give you anything you can't handle. I know how you feel.* She knows that once she tells him everything will change.

She stops into the Vodafone shop on the Finchley Road and buys an inexpensive cell phone. His is the only number she programs in. They take to talking at night, after her mother has gone to sleep. She presses the handset to her ear. It is warm, as if it were a living thing. His voice resonates inside the secret chamber of her eardrum, gentle and deep.

May has given way to June. The world is wide awake. The birds are up and chattering in the gray dawn at five in the morning; there's still a wash of daylight in the western sky past ten at night. It is strawberries-and-cream weather, sunbathing in the park weather, Pimm's weather, croquet weather, cruising through the locks weather, the season of fancy hats and college balls, opera at Glyndebourne, cricket test matches, and Royal Ascot and Wimbledon and Henley after that. She does not want to be anywhere but here. It is June in London and the roses are in full bloom and the trees and grass are lush and green. She sits outside on the front steps, smoking, her blood pulsing through her heart, the sun warm against her skin, and for the first time in three years, or maybe in forever, she feels alive.

JAVAD

At the Institute, things are quiet. Only Xiang Li is always puttering about, his hair looking as if he just woke up. Javad squints at his computer screen, scrolling through the latest fMRI scans. Red and yellow blotches mark the images like a radar map of an approaching storm. They show the neural activity in a patient with retrograde amnesia. There are clear signs of activation in the dorsolateral prefrontal cortex and decreased activity in the hippocampus, as one would expect. Something is inhibiting memories from being retrieved—but what? Did the activation of the DLPFC cause the amnesia, or did the amnesia, caused by something else, simply activate the DLPFC? The human mind is notoriously bad at distinguishing correlation from causation. Every action spins a web of consequences that are impossible to predict.

He finds Xiang Li in the staff room, assembling his usual peculiar midmorning snack of dried shredded pork and soy butter on a slab of white bread. The coffee in the pot is cold. It has probably been sitting there all week. Javad opens the fridge. No milk.

"You go on holiday soon?" Li says, his mouth full.

Javad shrugs. "I'm not sure yet." He pours out the dregs and dumps the grounds into the bin, rinses out the pot, starts afresh. Since the end of term, Amir has been coming and going at all hours. Days pass where they hardly see each other at all, Amir rising long after Javad has left for work, slipping home after he's gone to bed. The only signs of his son are the dirty dishes left on the kitchen table, the grimy ring around the bathtub, the clods of mud along the stairs.

"How about you?" he asks Li. "Will you be taking some time off?"

Li makes a face. "Nah. Too much work."

The coffee maker burbles and hisses. Rumor has it that Li naps beneath his desk. It looks rather as if he spends nights there as well.

"Did you finish recruiting the volunteers?"

"We have nine as of now. Nine right-handed men."

"Well done."

Li shakes more dried pork onto his bread. "We need at least five or six more, I think."

"Yes. There are always a few who get claustrophobic in the tube and refuse to carry on."

Javad picks up a coffee cup and frowns at the brown stains. It would be an important study—an investigation into the neural differences between lying and telling the truth. Deception was poorly understood from a neurobiological point of view, and the timing was excellent, funding-wise. There was a great deal of interest in brain imaging these days. Even the anti-terrorism folks over at MI5 were nattering on about how MRI scanning would soon make the lie detector test obsolete.

If only it were that simple. Just the other day, Little Brook had rung up about their mute amnesiac to follow up on the possibility of doing a scan. Still they had no clue as to who he was. First had come reports that he was a Czech drummer from an 1980s tribute band. Then the British tabloids dug up a possible link to an amnesiac last seen in Canada; Italian TV networks detected a resemblance to a man filmed at an instrument fair in Rimini, testing out a baby grand. People likened him to the tormented pianist, David Helfgott, in the movie *Shine*. But now even the tabloids seemed to be getting tired of the story after so many weeks of speculation and no breaks. It was as if he'd disappeared all over again. Probably that was what he'd wanted from the start.

Javad thinks of the young man's cowering affect, that glimmer of intelligence in his cagey eyes. The answers were all right there, of course, buried in the circuitry of neurons, in the obscure communicative chemistry of the brain. But how to decode them? They still didn't know how to tell deception from delusion, malingering from a psychotic break. You could scan his gray matter until grass grew beneath your feet, and it wouldn't tell you a bloody thing.

When she rings, she just says *hey*. Her voice is as soft as an embrace.

Amir is sitting at the kitchen table, tapping away on his laptop, earphones in. Up close you could hear the whump of bass.

"Hey." Javad presses the phone to one ear and a finger to the other and moves into the sitting room. She's just there, on the opposite side of the wall, less than a meter away. "Come over," he says.

This is the little game they play. He will ask and she'll refuse. He guesses it suits them both, for now at least.

"I can't. It's late."

"Just for half an hour. One glass of wine."

"I really can't."

"I'm sure she'll be all right. You won't be far away."

"I'm sorry." There is a rustling, a shift. Her breath, amplified through the phone, approaches and recedes like waves.

"You're a good daughter," he says.

"I'm not, really. I haven't been, anyway."

"I'm sure that's not the case."

"You don't know." A silence. Then she says, "She begged me to come back to England. She had nobody in the world but me. But I wouldn't do it. I didn't do it. All these years, I stayed away."

"You had your life to live."

"That's true. I did." She pauses. "But I was angry, too."

"Angry about what?"

"Oh, I don't know. Everything. Angry that she wanted me to be with her. Angry that she didn't try harder to keep me close. Angry that she took us away from my father. Angry that he screwed up. Angry that he died. Angry at her for defending him, as if that could make up for what he did."

"You don't seem like an angry person to me."

"You don't know me very well, I guess."

He leans against their shared wall. Maybe not yet, he thinks.

"Is your son home?" she asks.

"He is, actually, for once."

"That's nice."

Javad glances over into the kitchen. Amir is tapping away at the laptop, nodding to the beat. "I suppose. As usual, he's been glued to his computer all night."

"All the kids are these days, aren't they?"

"So it seems. But as he's quick to remind me, I'm usually stuck to a screen as well." He presses against the wall as if he could touch her through it. "Are you sure you won't come over? You can meet him properly."

She sighs. "I really can't."

"All right," he says. "Another time, then."

In the kitchen, Amir pulls out an earphone and says, "Who was that?"

"A friend."

Amir raises an eyebrow.

Javad fills a glass with water from the tap. "Someone you don't know."

"And you say I never tell you anything."

"Well, you don't."

"Neither do you."

He leans back against the counter. Fair enough. Behind the unshaven face before him he can still make out the little boy. The long-lashed, trusting eyes. The gap-toothed grin. The feathery heft of him at four or five—the way he'd coil his legs tight around Javad's body and wrap his arms around his neck. He'd begged and begged, back then, *Why can't I come and live with you?*

"It was that American from next door, wasn't it?" Amir says. "The one who brought over that chocolate cake?"

Javad's stomach does an involuntary flip. "Yes."

"Aha!"

"There you have it."

Amir tips back in his chair and smirks. "Do you fancy her?"

"She's just a friend."

Amir rolls his eyes.

"What? It's true."

Amir's expression shifts. "She's a bit of an odd one, isn't she?"

"Why do you say that?"

A shrug. "I don't know. She just seems a little weird. Also, she smokes. I've seen her a couple of times, puffing away, out front. Even in the middle of the night."

"Lots of people smoke."

Amir makes a face. "Baba, I can't *believe* you'd snog somebody who smokes."

He feels his cheeks go red in spite of himself. "Who says anybody's snogging?"

"Whatever," Amir says.

He has always been cautious with women around Amir. He's had girlfriends, of course, but he always felt things had to be quite serious before he'd introduce them to Amir. Not like Caroline with her endless stream of men. Only Alison came close—he nearly proposed to her, once upon a time, back when Amir was maybe nine or ten. They used to meet up at weekends—in London when Amir was at Caroline's, or in Oxford when her ex-husband had the kids. She was clever and funny, a lecturer in musicology, and he liked their lazy lie-ins on Sunday mornings, their long walks to the pub out in Port Meadow or through Hampstead Heath, the concerts and lectures and recitals that she was always organizing for them. But eventually it had become apparent that distance suited them better than proximity, that their intimacy depended on a buffer zone of space. He would not move there; she would not move here. And in the end, he supposed, he couldn't picture her as a mother, or her two redheaded daughters as sisters, to Amir.

And now? Could he imagine it?

He sets his glass down in the sink. Amir has returned to the laptop. *Weird.* What was that about? Was that really what Amir thought? Did it matter? Amir was no longer a child. He was an adult, or nearly, leading his own life. As Javad must lead his.

In the light of the gooseneck lamp, he stretches out on the sofa with *The Guardian.* Flash flooding up in Yorkshire, suicide bombings in Palestine and Iraq. The doors to the garden are open to the June night. It is too late now for the piano; next door, Esther is probably asleep. He hears it in his head instead, the blue halftones of Bach.

He inhales the night air: humid, earthy, green. In the shady garden of the house on Hesabi Street, there was a shallow pool that turned green as glass in the summer heat. Around it, his mother kept coleus and geraniums in clay pots. They had two turtles, too—Xerxes and Artaxerxes, impossible to tell apart—that he fed lettuce leaves and celery stalks. He remembers how they lumbered, oddly agile, on their stubby legs; the green-brown patchwork of their shells, their armored underbellies, the precise chewing movements of their small, sharp beaks. Turtles were long-lived creatures. Perhaps they were there still. His sister Darya was still living in the house. She and her husband, the dentist, had two daughters, already grown. The dentist was bearded, devout; the women blackbirds in chador. He has not seen his sister in nearly thirty years.

Sometimes it amazes him that he is here in London, that this is where his life has led. How easily it could have gone a different way. For a long time, he had assumed that one day he'd go back to Iran. The mullahs would grow old, the regime would change, the sanctions would be lifted, the war with Iraq would end. He has never thought of himself as an immigrant. *One day.* For years it seemed to hover just there, just out of reach. Yet somehow, almost without being aware of it, he had veered off course, the distance growing with each passing year. Of course, he could be in Tehran tonight, at least in theory. It was nothing—a six-and-a-half-hour flight. He could take a taxi straight from the airport to Hesabi Street and ring the bell. *Khodaye man, peeshi!* Darya would gasp. *Good God, it's you!*

Javad was the youngest of three children, the long-awaited or accidental boy. His sisters, six and eight years older, called him *peeshi*, little cat. They dressed him up in their skirts and scarves, let him try on their lipstick and clomp around in their high heels. He lay on his stomach on the floor and watched them turn before the mirror, Darya in a miniskirt, Shirin fussing with her hair. He remembers the smells of hairspray and nail polish and cheap jasmine perfume, the 1970s hits on LPs stacked on the spindle of the record player in its suitcase, open on the floor: Giti Pashaei, Googoosh.

He'd sneak up on them and make them scream, or eavesdrop on their conversations from his hiding spot beneath the bed. *Peeshi!* they'd screech and reach down and pull his hair. Their world—the world of girls—was an exotic realm. He was the court jester, eunuch, spy. A receptacle for information he couldn't fully understand.

By the time he turned twelve, both Shirin and Darya were already studying at university. His skin was still smooth, his voice unchanged. He was obsessed, in those days, with taking things apart: transistor radios, broken watches, clocks. In the cupboard beneath the kitchen stairs, the wooden crate that served as his workbench was littered with tiny gears and springs. He rigged two magnifying glasses and a flashlight to a headband, which gave him the aspect of a strange, gigantic bug. He scrabbled about, an awkward, dreamy child, alone in the garden or on the flat roof from which you could look down upon the orange taxis and red double-decker busses stuttering through the traffic lights along Pahlavi Street, or see in the distance the Alborz mountains, brown and crenellated in the summer, white with snow in the winter. At Abe Ali there was a ski resort. He imagined himself sailing down those distant peaks like the Shah and his family and their jet-set friends, as if on wings.

At what point did he become aware that Darya had a secret? And that her secret was a man? Hidden beneath the bed as she and Shirin whispered, he listened, antennae up, attuned to her tone of voice—a new note of urgency or fear. They'd met at university, she confided to Shirin. He was a graduate student, a geophysicist. He came from Isfahan. He had long hair and played the tanbur and the guitar. He took her up to the observatory and showed her how to look through the solar telescope at the dark flares on the surface of the sun. It looked, she said, like a giant orange rotten fruit. Afterward, they kissed. *French kissed*, she whispered. Shirin said, Ooh, look out!

Oh, *peeshi*, you little sneak, Darya said afterward, ruffling his dusty hair, when he crawled out from beneath the bed. Don't you say a word, you hear?

He didn't intend to betray her. He didn't know, then, that words could be launched like missiles, impossible to call back. He couldn't have foreseen the consequences that stretched far beyond his twelve-year-old horizon, out of sight. He couldn't have known that in just a few short years, they'd all be scattered: he in London, Shirin in L.A., Darya and his mother sequestered behind the veil. Their father imprisoned in Evin.

It was an August evening. The sun was dropping to the west

beyond the skyline, the foothills of the Alborz washed in golden pink. He was outside in the garden with his father. The turtles nibbled on the half shell of a rotten quince. His father paced around the glass-green pool, puffing on his pipe. He was a methodical, precise man, an engineer. He was a supporter of the Shah, a fan of modernization, though a traditionalist at heart. He wanted education for his daughters, but he did not approve of dating; he did not believe that marriage should be a child's choice. All he had to do was to give a little tug and out it came, Darya's secret, unspooling like a thread. Afterward, he called her into his study and shut the door. Ear pressed to wood, Javad listened. He remembers, or thinks he remembers, the words *inappropriate* and *Jew* and *shame*. He remembers, afterward, Darya's tight face, her red-rimmed eyes half-hidden by her hair.

He hadn't meant to betray her. What if he had held his tongue? What if she'd gone off with her long-haired Isfahani geophysicist instead of marrying the man their father picked? What would her life have been like then?

On the hottest nights of summer, they slept up on the roof. He remembers, that August, waking in the strange, still darkness of the early hours of the morning, unable to fall back to sleep. Darya lay nearby, curled the other way. The air had cooled and the thin cloud layer had cleared and the sky was filled with stars. It felt as if gravity had been reversed, as if he were looking down onto a valley pricked with lights, instead of the other way around. Never before had he felt so alone. He watched as one star fell and then another, streaks of white against the void. Meteors. He had read about Comet Swift-Tuttle's gaseous tail, about the constellation Perseus and its nebulae and galaxies, about its brightest star Mirfak. Now the constellations were dying, the stars detaching themselves from the order of the heavens, succumbing to the pull of gravity, freefalling through space. The stars dropped all around him. They traced white arcs across the sky and disappeared.

ESTHER

Toward the end of June, the heat comes back, another record-setting, tarmac-melting wave. The TV weather map is dotted with glaring yellow suns and bright red heat index alerts. Public health officials urge the elderly not to leave their homes, warning of the dangers of the heat. In Hyde Park, bikini-clad girls sprawl on lawn chairs and leap through the fountains, as if they're at the beach.

Her mother is irritable. She is itchy, she is hot, her mouth is dry, her muscles ache. Esther brings her cold drinks and ice chips in a cup. She wraps damp towels around her neck and feet.

It's too hot to cook, too hot to eat. Esther considers cucumber soup, cold poached salmon, an arugula salad, then gives up and just makes scrambled eggs. Her mother takes a few bites and pushes the plate away. They flip through trashy magazines. Splayed across the floor, the titles almost form a sentence: *Tatler*, *Cosmo*, *Yours*, *OK!* They can laugh together about Russell Crowe's tantrums and Camilla's hideous wedding hat, at least.

But her mother can't get comfortable. Her back hurts, her neck hurts. She wants to sit up, she wants to lie down, she can't catch her breath. Esther repositions the fan, then unplugs it and moves it to the sitting room and helps her mother down the stairs onto the sofa. It's a little cooler there, at least. She props and re-props the pillows, brings her another drink.

Half an hour later, she finds her mother struggling to stand; now she wants to go back upstairs; now she's got to pee. Esther grasps her around the waist and half lifts, half drags her up. It is a good thing her mother has lost so much weight. She frets and frowns, slaps at Esther's hands, pulls her arm away. Every time Esther leaves the room, she calls again for help.

A different nurse arrives in the afternoon. Zofia is on holiday, it seems. Esther misses Zofia. This English nurse has lanky hair and pasty, blemished skin. She has an annoying habit of tilting her voice upward into a question at the end of every phrase.

The nurse wraps the blood pressure cuff around her mother's arm and pumps, her lips moving as she counts. "One hundred over sixty," she says to Esther. "It's a bit low. She could be dehydrated?"

"I don't know," Esther says. "She pees. She drinks."

Her mother's eyes are glassy. She fingers her strand of pearls like prayer beads. "Take me downstairs," she rasps. "I can't breathe up here."

"Oh my god," Esther says. "Not again."

The nurse pulls the stethoscope out of her ears. "Her heart rate is a little fast, perhaps? She seems rather anxious. It could be the heat?"

"She's like this all the time now. She's never comfortable. I can't leave her alone for a minute."

"It's terminal agitation," the nurse says, as if agitation, not the cancer, were the incurable disease. "It's not uncommon at the end?"

"You'd know better than me."

"For god's sake," her mother cries. "Why won't anybody listen to me?"

"You can increase the morphine dosage, if you like," the nurse says. "It just depends on how alert you want her to be?"

Esther isn't really listening. The euphemisms wash over her: *comfortable, pain management, terminal agitation, final days.*

Her mother's voice is higher, strained. "I can't breathe!"

"Come on," Esther says to the nurse. "Help me take her down-stairs, at least."

The heat worsens at the weekend. On Sunday it tops out at 91.4 degrees Fahrenheit in central London, yet another record peak. The air is thick and still. The kitchen smells like something is rotting in the bin. What would be normal summer weather in New York is unbearable here. Esther debates checking into a hotel. But half the hotels in London lack air conditioning too.

The on-call hospice nurse is patient on the phone. Does she have pain that's not well managed? When was her last bowel movement? Is she breathing effectively? Has her medication dosage recently been changed?

Esther twists the telephone cord around her left hand. "I don't know what to do."

"You can give her two milligrams of lorazepam to ease the anxiety."

"As well as the morphine?"

"That's correct."

Esther's hands tremble as she pops the yellow pill from the blister pack. Maybe *she* should take the tranquilizer instead. *Mother's little helper.* Right.

Esther sits on the edge of the chair at the side of the bed and fans her mother with a magazine. Sunk against the pillows, her mother's head looks as small as a child's. The bedside table is crowded with pill organizers and tissue boxes and blister packs of pills. The untouched food is still sitting there as well: congealed eggs, stale toast.

What was a good death? Was there such a thing?

Was it a suffocation of pillows? An oblivion of drugs? A hunger strike?

Esther checks her phone. The screen is blank.

The root of all suffering is desire, the Buddha said. *Oh, Javad*, she thinks.

She takes a deep breath and holds it, counting the seconds, the way she used to at the swimming pool when she was a kid, sinking to the bottom at the deep end, looking up at the bubbles roiling overhead, pressure building in her chest, a dizzy creep. This time she doesn't even make it to fifty before her lungs release. The body always wins out in the end.

Downstairs, she takes out the letter she started writing Gil a few days back. Her handwriting slants across the page. *Dear Gil.* It seems so archaic, handwriting a letter, an outmoded thing, like garter belts or linen handkerchiefs. How hard she'd worked, once, on shaping those little capped *a*'s and two-looped *g*'s! Now her hand aches from the unaccustomed act. But it's better than talking on the phone. They haven't spoken in the last few weeks. Still, she wonders to whom she's really writing. Whom she's trying to convince.

She knows exactly how Gil will press his lips together when he reads the letter. How he'll fold the pages and slide them back inside the envelope with its tidy slit, the way he'll leave it on the table in the foyer beneath the gilt-framed mirror they bought together at that little antique shop on Bleecker Street, years ago. She can see the dark bristle of his hair, the half-moon pouches beneath his eyes, his smoothly shaven cheeks, his well-cut suit and silk tie. She knows exactly how he'll slide off his shoes, hang up his jacket, pour himself a glass of red wine. Settle into the study. Answer emails. Redline a brief. He moves forward, steady as a clock, one tick at a time.

That steadiness was what she'd wanted, of course. She wanted to be anchored in the granite bedrock of Manhattan, to be inscribed within Gil's world, that thirty-block circumference of Central Park. If you connected the dots from the Fifth Avenue apartment he grew up in, across to Columbia, down the Upper

West Side to their apartment, and over to his law firm's offices at Forty-Ninth and Lex, you'd trace the ring. Even when he was out on Fire Island or in Connecticut, Gil never really left the city. He'd sip his coffee, cross his legs, fold back the *Times* with a subway rider's practiced flick.

How could he do it, day after day, retracing those same paths they'd walked together for over twenty years? How could he stay in that apartment, with Noah's room still there behind that never-opened door? The old grief spiders in her chest. Gil will never leave the city. She can't go back. Maybe it just came down to that.

Again her mother is calling, crying out. Gasping for breath.

Esther takes the stairs two at a time, her heart hammering, her mind a static buzz of fear. Oh god, what now? Was this it?

Her mother is clawing at the sheets. Her chest is heaving. She cannot breathe.

Esther's fingers tremble as she dials. The hospice line rings and rings.

This nurse insists, in an overly cheerful tone of voice, on calling Esther "love." You can increase the dose of morphine, love. No, love, nurses don't make house calls out of hours. Ring 999, love, if you feel that you can't cope. Sometimes hospital is for the best.

Her mother is wailing like a child. "I want to go home!" she cries.

Esther is quivering, adrenaline firing her limbs. She will not send her mother to the hospital. She promised she would not. She gave her word. But neither will she stand by and watch her suffocate to death.

She is not thinking, just moving. She runs down the stairs and out the door and down the steps and up the other side. It is already after ten, still hot. The midsummer sky is streaked with the last vestiges of light. The clouds have turned as purple as a bruise. The rubbish bins, pulled out to the curbside for collection, reek. She presses the bell, hopping up and down in agitation, then presses it again.

He opens the door with a look of such happy surprise that she almost feels ashamed. "Esther!" he says.

"It's my mother," she says. "Please."

He is wearing linen trousers and a short-sleeved shirt. His smile fades. He gives her a puzzled look. "Is everything okay?"

"Can you just come with me? I need your help." She is shaking. "Hurry, please!"

"Yes, of course." He bends to slide on his loafers, moving slowly—too slowly, she thinks.

"Please, please, hurry please. She can't breathe."

Straightening, he says, "You do understand that I'm a scientist—a researcher—not a clinician?"

His eyes are warm and kind. He had to help her. He was a bloody doctor, for god's sake.

"You went to medical school, didn't you?" she says.

It is all she can do not to run. He follows a few steps behind.

Please, she thinks, as she rushes up the stairs. *Please don't let her die. Not yet. Please.*

But her mother is not dead. She is still moaning, her chest rising and falling, her hands pressed against her chest. "I can't breathe. I can't breathe!"

Esther waits, jittering with fear, as Javad steps into the bathroom to wash his hands. She clenches her fists as she listens to the water run.

For fuck's sake, hurry up, she thinks.

Javad takes the chair by the side of the bed and shifts one of her mother's arms onto his lap. "If you can speak, then you're still breathing," he tells her mother, his fingers on her wrist. His voice is capable and calm. "Just try to relax now. Everything's going to be all right."

"Who is he?" Her mother swivels her head. Her eyes are wild. "What's he doing here? Where have you taken me?"

"He's a friend, Mum. He's a doctor. He's here to help."

"I want to go home!"

"Hush, Mum."

He looks up at Esther calmly, and she takes a deeper breath. "Did they give you an oxygen tank, perhaps?"

"Of course." Esther runs and fetches the emergency kit supplied by hospice, the oxygen tank and the liquid morphine and the oral syringe. "There's also this. Her last dose was at six."

"Aha." He pushes up his glasses and squints at the instructions, then squirts the morphine between her mother's lips. She blinks at him and swallows.

"Well done," he says.

He takes up the oxygen canister, attempts to screw on the regulator, turns it around, tries it again the other way. "Bloody hell, I haven't touched one of these things in twenty years," he says. He looks up, his lips turned up in that half smile. "Now you can see why I chose research." Javad places the plastic mask over her mother's nose and mouth and gently loops the elastic over her ears. He adjusts the gauge.

Esther watches him work, her arms crossed over her chest. She is still shaking, her heart hammering in her chest. Why couldn't she have done these things herself?

The sound of ragged breathing fills the room, a mechanical wheeze and hiss. Esther crosses her fingers and waits. Slowly, the heaving of her mother's chest subsides. Slowly, the panic in her eyes begins to ease.

Esther lets her clenched arms release. "Is she going to be all right?"

"For the time being, I should think so. She should feel more comfortable in a bit." Javad steps around the bed to where she's standing. He wipes the perspiration off his forehead with the back of his hand. "Crikey, this heat."

"I just—" she falters. "I couldn't—"

"It's all right."

"I'm really sorry I dragged you over here so late."

"Please, don't apologize. It's not that late." Again that half smile. "Besides, I've been wanting to get together. I just didn't know this is what it would take."

She tries to smile. She listens to the sound of hissing. So this is what it's come down to: air in, air out. Air moving over the esophagus, across the diaphragm, into the lungs and out. It sounds like breaking waves. How many more breaths would she take?

Tears prick Esther's eyes. She tries hard not to blink. "This isn't the way I thought it would be."

"What did you expect?"

"I don't know. Not this."

He pushes up his glasses and rubs the bridge of his nose. He is taking in the room: the heavy furniture, the rusty fan oscillating on the chair, the framed photographs arrayed along the chest of drawers, the smells of medicine and impending death.

"You don't just lose a person when they die," he says. "You lose your history, too. That's the hardest thing. When there's no one left to share your memories, it feels as if they don't exist. At least, that's the way it was for me."

"I thought I'd be ready. My father passed a long time ago. But I'm not."

He gestures to the framed portrait of her parents. "Is that him? Your father?"

"Yes."

He walks over to the photograph and picks it up. "He had a very strong face."

"That's one way of putting it."

He sets the photo down and picks up a different frame. She draws in her breath. It's the picture of Noah at his bar mitzvah, rocked back on his heels from the weight of the Torah in his arms, Gil and her on either side. The three of them, a family. Noah had just read from Parshat Noach, of course—the story of the Flood. It was November, the cusp of the new millennium, Y2K, all that apocalyptic fuss. She is smiling in the photograph, proud, oblivious to all that lay ahead.

She can see the questions reflected in Javad's eyes. Her words are ringing in her ears. Her stupid lie. *No husband, no kids.*

There is a pause. There's always a pause. A pause like a weight.

"He died three years ago," she said. "It was an accident. He was fifteen."

"I'm so sorry," he says.

"I should have told you," she says. "I know. It's just that—"

"It's all right."

"I'm sorry."

"Shh."

This time, he doesn't kiss her. He just puts his arms around her and holds her, his lips against her hair, her wet face pressed to his chest.

LONIA

She floats along a morphine river, lucid stretches syncopated by tidal waves of pain. There is the sound of breaking waves. People come and go, give her pills and medication, and rub her bloated feet. Her body drifts away.

The morphine river carries her to Kraków. It is June. Every day the midsummer sun rises in a sky as blue and bright as water. The banks of the Wisła are green, and beneath the red rooftops and cupolas of the Wawel Castle, leaves flutter like handkerchiefs in the breeze. Couples stroll along the promenade, jackets off, sleeves rolled up, arm in arm or holding hands. Low-slung barges chug slowly past. It is long past ten before the sun turns red and drops into the river like a flaming coal.

Lonia wants to go home. She misses her father, her bed, her things, the familiar sounds and smells. Their mother's distant cousins are elderly and stooped, humorless, devout. They speak Yiddish inflected with a Polish accent that Lonia can barely understand. They smell of boiled cabbage and decaying teeth. The old man mumbles the blessings through his untidy beard, swaying as he prays. They give Hugo a daybed in the study and Lonia a narrow bedroom and a pile of a grown-up daughter's cast-off clothes. Hugo gives them the letter their father has sent along containing money and an expression of his thanks. The old man nods and tucks the envelope away.

Hugo and Lonia spend their days in a hall near the town center where refugees are given free meals and tea. People from relief organizations are working to help them obtain transit visas, entrance visas, ships' passage, immigration guarantees. Hugo befriends a group of Zionists, members of the Hanoar Hatzioni youth group. They sit around smoking and drinking tea, pontificating about the Jewish homeland, spinning out utopian dreams. Every few days, a list of names of those who have been granted immigration permits is posted on the notice board beside the door. Until then, they're stuck in limbo. There is nothing to do but wait.

At first Lonia stays close to Hugo in the refugee hall, but after a few days she begins wandering out along the cobbled streets of Kazimierz. The quarter is crowded with black-hatted religious Jews, flat-capped boys, and babushkas hunched over tubs of flowers and barrels full of grains. She meanders through the colonnade along the Market Square, pigeons scattering at her feet. She buys an *obwarzanek* from a cart and eats it on a bench below the Grunwald monument, King Jagiello triumphant above her on his giant horse, the Teutonic knight sprawled at the base of the pedestal beneath the horse, his dead arm dangling off the ledge.

War with Germany, which everyone says is coming, seems impossibly far away. Wars were fought in trenches, in the mountains, among men. Her father had served as a lieutenant in the Kaiser's army when he was young. He wore a high cap and riding boots and carried a regimental sword. She gazes up into the blue. It is such a pure blue it makes her eyes ache. Why did there have to be war in a world like this?

And then there is Isaac. Isaac, who changes everything.

She is in the refugee hall, dim in the afternoon heat, sipping tea from a stained glass, half listening to Hugo and his newfound

Zionist friends. They are droning on about Jabotinsky and Boro-
chov and Trumpeldor, the same old boring talk. Soon they'd
move on to the even more thrilling topic of communal farming,
these city kids who couldn't tell a turnip from a tomato, God help
them, their hand-rolled cigarettes stinking up the air. And then
something shifts. She feels his gaze before she even sees him—a
focused intensity boring into her from across the room, where he
is leaning against a pillar, staring at her. He stares without blinking. It is a shameless, demanding, proprietary gaze. It dares her to
be the first to look away.

She looks away. Then back. Blood rises in her cheeks. Inside
her gut, a knot pulls tight. It feels like resistance, but she is already
giving in.

Even Hugo notices, turns around, then laughs. The others
look over, squint. Who the hell is he? Someone says he's from
Subcarpathia; someone else says, no, from Łódź. Another one of
them rubs together his thumb and fingers and says, "That fellow's
got connections, if you know what I mean." Hugo elbows her,
jokingly. "Maybe you should get to know him, then," he says.

She walks over to the samovar to refill her glass of tea. She
does not look at him, but she can feel him move her way. He steps
up to her as she straightens, her glass hot in her hand, and his
shoulder brushes hers.

"Tell me your name."

"Why are you staring at me? Didn't anyone teach you it's rude
to stare?"

His arrogance almost makes him handsome, she thinks, even
though she knows that Eva, on whom she has always relied in all
matters regarding boys, would probably disagree. He has a high
forehead with thick eyebrows and a fleshy nose—a Talmudic
face, like an Old Testament prophet, although he is probably not
much older than Hugo—and a way of standing that makes him
look taller than he is. He closes his hand around her forearm and
grasps it tight.

"I just want to say that you are the most beautiful girl I've ever seen."

She laughs, in spite of herself, and pulls her hand away. "Oh please."

"You don't believe me?"

"Don't you have *any* manners?"

"Why is it impolite to say what I think?"

"Is this how you always pick up girls? With lies?"

He does not smile. "I never lie," he says.

A group of old ladies is pushing to get through to the samovar. Lonia steps aside and Isaac follows.

"Meet me here this evening," he says. "We'll go for a walk, get to know each other. All right?"

Lonia glances back across the room at Hugo. He has swiveled around in his chair to watch. They are probably all laughing at her now. Who cares? No one has ever talked to her this way before.

"All right," she says. "Tonight." She turns away, her heart flapping like wings.

The moon is rising out of the Wisła, a fat planet, huge and gold. The breeze is cool. She's wearing his jacket, her hands lost inside the sleeves.

"Paris or Venice?" he says.

They are playing a game, although it well might be a test. With Isaac, it's hard to say.

"Paris," she says. "Although I wouldn't really know, I've never been anywhere but here."

"Good choice."

She smiles self-consciously at his approval. "Bridge or chess?" she says.

"That's easy. Chess. Swimming or ice skating?"

"I don't know how to swim."

"A pity! I'll have to teach you. Your go."

"Sachertorte or apfelstrudel?"

"Rigó Jancsi."

"Answer the question!"

"But Rigó Jancsi is so delicious . . . all those layers of chocolate and—"

"You have to play by the rules! It's your game!"

"Okay, fine. Sachertorte. Bach or Chopin?"

"Bach."

"No way. You're a Chopin girl, I can tell."

"Oh, you think so, do you?"

"I know so."

"Well, you're wrong."

"No, I'm not. It's your turn, go."

"What's the point, if you know everything already?"

He laughs and puts his arm around her shoulders. He smells like smoke and musk. The earth has sprung its orbit. The huge gold moon is floating upward like a balloon.

"I like you, Lonia," he says. "I like you very much indeed."

On midsummer's night, Noc Kupały, there are bonfires by the river. They wander through the crowds of celebrants gathered along the embankment by the Wawel Castle. There is the sound of drunken singing, of someone playing a guitar. Lights flicker at the water's edge where candles float inside wildflower wreaths. The sky is still a rich, deep blue, although it's long past ten.

Hugo has come along with them tonight, along with a couple of his Hanoar Hatzioni friends. She walks behind them with Isaac, hand in hand. Groups of young people are standing around bonfires, clapping and cheering as couples leap over the flames. It was an old midsummer's ritual: the lovers' leap. If you did it holding hands, it meant you'd never separate.

"Come on, jump with me," Isaac says.

He interlaces his fingers with hers and squeezes tight.

"No way."

"I won't let go, I promise."

Lonia shakes her head. They stop and watch as a girl in a white dress breaks out of the circle of onlookers and runs solo toward the fire pit, her dress billowing as she leaps. One quick prance and she has made it. There are cheers and someone yells, "Go find yourself a man!"

"I'll never let go," Isaac whispers. "You'll never get away from me."

His words twinge along her spine. A promise or a threat? Who is this man she met just last week? He seems to come from nowhere, he has no family, and he speaks five languages without an accent, like a spy. She rubs her fingertips along the ridgeline of his knuckles, the metacarpal bones. She does not want him to let go.

"Last year we were dancing on the banks of the Oder," one of the Hanoar fellows is saying.

"Next year in Jerusalem," says Hugo.

"*B'ezrat hashem*," says one of the girls. She's one of the religious ones, always in long sleeves and stockings, even in the heat.

"Better make it this year," Isaac says. "Hitler will make a grab for Poland, and it won't be long. I wouldn't count on making it to Jerusalem if I were you."

"Your parents should have named you Jeremiah," the Hanoar fellow says. "The prophet of doom!"

"You should listen to me, then."

Isaac doesn't need to remind them that no entrance permits to Palestine have been granted in weeks. Just the other day, the Brits announced that from now on they will deduct any illegal immigration numbers from the official quota, which is already only a fraction of what it was before the White Paper came out three months back.

Isaac is not a Zionist. He's a *makher*, as her father would have

said, a pragmatist, not a zealot: a fixer, a finagler, a maker of connections, a greaser of skids. Money and connections matter above
all, he says.

Lonia is sick of the talk and the waiting, the speculation. It was
pointless. They are no better off here in Kraków than they were
at home. Dressed in borrowed clothes, eating donated food, all
they do is wait and talk, talk and wait. All they could do is hope
their names show up on the visa list posted by the door. It was like
Isaac's game, only you didn't get a choice—you went wherever
you were sent. Sweden, Borneo, Shanghai, New York.

Home was barely two hundred kilometers away, on the other
side of an imaginary line. Her father was still sitting in his study,
listening to the radio, his glasses reflective in the light. Nothing
had changed except that she and Hugo are not there but here. She
understands that if war breaks out they might send Hugo off to
fight, or give him trouble because of his left-wing politics, but
she's only a girl. Why would anybody bother with her? Why
couldn't she go home? None of it made sense.

Isaac steers her down the sloping grass toward the river's
edge, where a group of girls are launching candlelit garlands into
the stream. It's another lover's legend—that your future husband
will be the one to catch your wreath. There is a splash and a yell
as a young man plunges into the water, fully clothed. Isaac puts
his hand around her waist and draws her tight.

"Tell your brother he'd better not count on getting to Palestine."

"Go on. *You* try telling him that."

"You must make other plans, in any case. Time is running
out."

"He's my *brother*. I'm not going anywhere without him."

It's always been this way: Hugo and his big ideas, Lonia tagging
along behind. They have come to this place together. They escaped
together through the underworld of the mine. Now they only had
each other. She would do whatever he did, go wherever he went.

Isaac twists her arms behind her back and pulls her close. His tongue flicks against hers, urgent, quick. Her heart's on fire. *Leap*, his kiss says, *leap*.

All around them, everything is burning. Fireworks boom and pop, and sprays of sparks cascade across the sky. Bonfires blaze along the embankment, orange flames shooting up into the night. Candlelit wreaths bob and flicker along the river like tiny stars. Then there is a gust of wind, and a few of them go dark.

She opens her eyes to find her husband Isaac sitting on the chair across the room, his legs crossed, smoking a cigar.

"Put that stinking thing out," she tells him, waving her hand. "I can't breathe."

"You did what you had to do," Isaac says. He is talking about her brother. "Don't eat your heart out."

"That's what you always say," she says.

"There is nothing you could have done to help."

"You don't know that."

"But I do."

Oh Isaac, you old fool, she thinks. How she has missed him, all these years.

He tips his head back, breathes out smoke in a blue stream. "I did try to find him. I sent money. I even kissed the hairy ass of that stinking Svetnikov."

"I know. You shouldn't have done."

He places a gold one-pound coin on the back of his forearm, then flips his arm forward, catching the coin in his hand. He opens his fist and holds it out for her to see. His palm is empty. The coin has disappeared.

FIVE

JAVAD

His mobile rings on Monday evening just as he is getting home from work. *Esther* is the first thing he thinks. He hopes her mother hasn't taken a turn for the worse since the previous night, though he knows that she won't last long in any case. It would be merciful if it were quick.

He shoves the front door open with his hip, sets down his brief-case, fumbles in his pocket for his phone. He flips it open, squints at the screen.

Not Esther but his ex. Shit.

"Thank god," says Caroline. Her voice a rush. "Let me speak to Amir."

The house is silent. He calls Amir's name once, then again for good measure, and waits.

"Try him on his mobile," he says to Caroline. "He's not home."

"I did. It went straight to answerphone. Where is he, then?"

"I haven't got the foggiest. I just walked in the door." He bends to collect the post scattered across the floor.

"Look, J, I've had a bit of an accident, I'm afraid. I've tripped and hurt my ankle." Her voice is furred. Alcohol or shock? "Broken it, I should think."

"Jesus, Caroline."

"Bad luck, isn't it?"

"How much have you had to drink?"

"Do me a favor for once, Javad. Okay? Don't start."

"Look, if you're truly hurt, you should be ringing 999, not me."

"They'd have to break down the bloody door. I'll never make it down the stairs to let them in. I can't move an inch."

"Where's what's-his-face? Your Swedish bloke?"

"Niels. He's Dutch, not Swedish. He's out of town, in any case."

"That is a pity."

"Look, I really need your help. Please!"

"And what do you need me to do?"

"Just come round and help me sort out a taxi to A&E. You can let yourself in. Amir's got a set of keys."

"I told you. He's not here."

"Go and have a look in his room—I'm sure they're there. They're big old clunky things. He keeps them clipped to one of those climbing rings, what do you call them. Try the top of his chest of drawers or the pockets of his jeans."

He doubts if he'll even be able to find the chest of drawers in that mess. This is the last thing he needs. "It really would be a whole lot easier if you'd just call the police."

"J, I'm in agony." She is crying now. "Can't you just do one thing for me?"

After all these years, he thinks, will it never end? They're like fellow convicts on a chain gang, shackled for life.

He opens Amir's door and switches on the light. Even though it has cooled off a bit, the room is still stifling from the weekend's pent-up heat. The floor is a wreck of clothing—trainers, hoodies, socks, T-shirts, one mud-caked boot, a pair of cargo trousers. The bed floats above it like a raft, the duvet twisted with the sheets, the pillows squeezed. A pair of jeans is looped over the footboard. He picks his way across the mess and feels inside the pockets. No keys.

The desk is covered in books and papers, the laptop, a digital camera, computer cables, a dirty plate, a Mars bar wrapper, a half-full mug of tea covered with a curdled skin of milk, a half-unfolded map. Javad picks up one of the books: *The Adventures of Ibn Battuta: A Muslim Traveler of the Fourteenth Century*. And another: *Muslim Travelers: Pilgrimage, Migration, and the Religious Imagination*. He sets the books back, turns to the laptop. DANGER, KEEP OUT warns the sticker. He shouldn't snoop, but curiosity gets the better of him. He flips up the lid.

The screen blinks and lights. The desktop is dotted with blue folders. He clicks on one of them and a grid of photographs opens: Dim shots of what looks like old machinery, rusty pipes. Brick walls topped with curls of barbed wire, manhole covers. A nighttime cityscape shot from a great height—necklaces of tiny lights. He closes the folder and clicks on another, finds more of the same. Two boys leaning against a graffiti-covered wall. He looks closer but recognizes neither of them. What had he expected? Naked girls?

He feels a twinge along his spine and whirls around, but it's just the cat. It mewls and arches its back. He shuts the laptop and steps back. The keys, the keys.

He picks up a chunky paperback from the bedside table. A swirl of blue and white Arabic calligraphy adorns the cover. The Qur'an. He pulls out a flyer tucked inside it as a bookmark. *Muslims United Against Oppression*, the boldface header reads. It's a call to join a protest march against the new anti-terror legislation, held a few weeks back. Did Amir march? Why doesn't Javad know anything?

Amir has propped one of Caroline's art pieces against the wall, unframed, the canvas and staples showing at the edges. It's one of her latest "memory map" collages. He steps closer. There's something that looks like part of a depth chart of the English Channel, a ripped postcard from a seaside holiday village, a black-and-white photograph of small boy running on a beach. His back is to the camera, arms flailing, shoulder blades sharp. Javad steps closer, squats down to see. Was it Amir?

It was. It was Margate, he remembers; he was there. The trip was Caroline's idea. They were separated, the divorce not official yet. Amir wanted him to come, she'd said. She'd put the child on the phone. That piping voice. That eager breath. *Baba, Baba, please.* He'd felt something rise up in his throat then at the sound of his son's voice. Something like fear.

Margate was tatty, seamy, cold, and dank. Caroline adored it, the kitsch of the Shell Grotto and the arcades, the tacky tearooms, the pubs that reeked of grease and piss. Amir kicked and wriggled, threw tantrums, slipped out of one's hands and ran away. Caroline wandered off, her camera slung around her neck. Javad chased after Amir. He looked so little, now, in that photo, with those slender limbs and jutting elbows, racing off along the strand.

The photograph has been ripped and scratched with a sharp object, streaked with slashes of black paint. The contour map is a mass of squiggly concentric lines—rather like cerebral gyri and sulci, he thinks. Javad can't fathom what prompted her to do it. He cannot understand what's become of the woman who was once his wife.

He straightens up too quickly, feeling the strain across his lower back. The keys are on top of the chest of drawers, clipped to a carabiner, right where she said they'd be. It annoys him that she was right. He shoves them in his pocket, switches off the light.

"A nice clean break by the looks of it," the consultant says, clipping the X-ray to the light box. He's a fix-you-right-up-in-no-time sort of bloke, an aging athlete by the looks of him, all sinew and grit. He palpates Caroline's foot and she howls like an injured cat. Already her ankle is blotched red and purple and so swollen that the bones have disappeared.

He looks up over his glasses. "What was it you said you did?"

"Tripped," Caroline says lightly. "Silly heels."

And a fifth of vodka, Javad thinks. She's lucky she didn't break her bloody neck.

Javad crosses his legs and shifts on the plastic chair. They've been here nearly two hours already, bypassed by a shooting victim rushed in on a trolley, the waiting room filled up with a gang of brown-skinned boys in droopy jeans and chains, followed by the police. The sergeant had stopped and eyed him and Javad shook his head. *Not mine, mate.* Caroline kept her eyes closed, lips drawn. The last time they were in a hospital together, he thinks, was when she gave birth to Amir.

"We'll have to keep it splinted until the swelling goes down," the consultant says. "Keep it elevated, stay off it. You'll want to come back in to see the orthopedist to have it set in a few days' time. I shouldn't think it will require surgery or pins."

"Crikey, I should hope not," Caroline says. Her bleached-blond hair is cropped short and needs to be touched up at the roots.

"In the meantime, here's something for the pain." The dcoctor pecks with two fingers at a keyboard. A printer whirs. "A little pampering would be in order, I should think," he says to Javad and winks, handing him the slip.

Javad pockets the prescription and turns away. "Right."

In the taxi, Caroline rummages in her purse. "Have you got your mobile? I must have left mine at home. See if you can get hold of Amir now."

"Why?"

"How am I to manage? He'll have to come and stay with me for a bit. Until I'm back on my feet. On both feet, that is."

"When does what's-his-face get back?"

"His name is Niels, I told you. Not for another week. He's over in Beijing."

"What's he doing in Beijing?"

"Look, just pass me the phone."

The taxi lurches and he braces himself on the hanging strap. "We're going away on holiday soon, you know, me and Amir."

"Oh, you are, are you? That's a laugh. You've never taken him on holiday in your bloody life."

"Well, I am now."

"I guess you'll just have to postpone the trip."

He feels as peeved as if he actually had booked the holiday. "What about your mother? Can't she come to stay?"

"*My* mother? Right."

She reaches for the phone but he holds it away, out of reach, like kids playing piggy in the middle.

She edges forward on the seat and raps on the partition. "Driver, can you stop, please, at a chemist? There should be a Boots coming up in a couple of traffic lights."

"No, carry on, don't stop," Javad calls to the driver; then to Caroline he says, "You're not filling that prescription."

"Give it to me."

"You can take some paracetemol if your ankle hurts. You can't mix opioids with alcohol."

"Just give it to me, Javad. It's mine."

"For Christ's sake, Caroline."

"I'm in agony!"

"You'll survive."

She shakes her head. "You think you're so clever. You know everything, don't you?" A short laugh. "God. People never change."

And what does he know? He turns away. He knows nothing. She is right.

Out of the window of the taxi, the North London streets blur past. The stubborn sky still light.

He's lying on the sitting room floor, head propped on a book, knees bent, doing the exercises for his back. The windows are open to a passing storm, fat raindrops pelting the roof and street. Thunder rumbles. The front door bangs.

"Baba?"

"In here." Javad reaches for his glasses and lifts his head. Wet trainers, ripped jeans. "How is she doing?"

"All right." Amir sits down on the sofa. "She's pretty hopeless on crutches, though."

Javad rolls to his side and sits up. He's eye level with his son's knees. Two bony kneecaps poke through the shredded jeans. "Mind the leather. You're dripping wet."

"It's pretty funny," Amir says. "You should see her trying to get to the loo."

"She'd better take care she doesn't break the other leg."

Amir is fiddling with the carabiner clipped to his keys. "Why do you always have to be that way?"

"What way?"

A shadow flicks across his son's face. "She doesn't drink *that* much, you know."

"If you say so."

Amir gives him a hostile look. "I say so."

"Fine, then."

The rain is sheeting off the eaves, turning the window into an opaque screen. Javad glances over at his collection of optical instruments arrayed on the bookshelves: the praxinoscope on its wooden stand, the Norrenberg polariscope, the Gilbert pocket telescope, the antique surgical loupe. He has never lost a child's fascination with the world viewed through an optic lens, with the way a mirror, a light, and a spinning disk could make a row of static pictures jump to life. All perception produced not by the eye but by the brain. *Deceptions of the senses are truths of perception*, the great Purkinje said. An image of the world is not the world. Things are never what they seem.

He says, "How long do you think you'll stay over there?"

"I don't know. Why?"

"Just wondering when you'll be home, that's all."

A shrug. "I don't know. Until Niels gets back, I guess. I came home to get some things." More fiddling with the carabiner. "By the way." He looks up. "She says you owe her money. Is that true?"

Not this again. Not dragging in the kid. Bile rises in his chest. "I don't owe her anything."

The boy raises his palms. *Innocent.* "I'm just telling you what she said."

"And I'm just telling *you* to tell *her* to bugger off."

Amir stands up, leaving a wet smear across the sofa's leather seat. "Jesus. Forget it."

He is at a disadvantage, here on the floor, his son standing over him like the victor in a fight. From this vantage point, Amir seems very far away. "I'm sick of her manipulations is all," Javad explains.

"And I'm sick of *your* manipulations. All right?"

"That's not fair."

"It's not?"

"I'm not the one who's manipulating you."

His son's face darkens. "Oh yeah, right, sorry. Just—*How much has she been drinking, Amir? Tell her she's full of shit, Amir. How much longer are you staying over there, Amir? When are you coming back, Amir?*"

"When you live with someone, it's common courtesy to let them know when you'll be around."

"Right, then. Whatever. I won't be around."

The door slams so hard the floorboards shake. There is a stomping on the stairs, and then, upstairs, the bedroom door slams as well.

ESTHER

Tuesday morning and Zofia's back. She adjusts the oxygen apparatus, reviews the medications. Her smooth moon-face, her capable hands, are a relief.

It is the twenty-first of June, the summer solstice. They watch the midsummer celebrations on TV: Bonfires at Land's End. A sunrise gathering at Stonehenge. The sun rises above the great stone monoliths. The sky is silver, the sun a platinum disc. There were those who said that at midsummer, the membrane that separates this world from the next grows porous, frayed. It is easy for a soul to slip away.

"You missed all the excitement," Esther says to Zofia. "I came this close to calling an ambulance the other night." She pinches together her forefinger and thumb to demonstrate.

"We will arrange for a Marie Curie nurse to come and stay at night," Zofia says. "You have nothing to worry. It will be good—give you a break."

Esther nods, obedient as a child. She likes the British way Zofia pronounces the name, with flat vowels and the accent on the first syllable: *Marry Curey*. It seems a different person from the very French "Madame Curie" she'd read about in a children's biography—a fierce iron-haired creature, dressed in black, holding up a radio-active test tube. These hospice nurses wore light blue uniforms with daffodil pins in the lapels.

Together she and Zofia bathe her mother, change the sheets, settle her back in bed. Her mother is calmer now, sedated, her eyes puffy and vague. She parts her dry lips as if she's about to speak, but all that comes out is a whispery groan.

"What's that?" Esther says, but her mother does not respond.

She is speaking another language, maybe. She has so many stored inside her, vestigial, disused: English, German, Czech, Polish, some Russian, a little French. Or perhaps she is speaking in tongues.

"The other day she kept saying she wanted to go home," Esther tells Zofia. "I don't think she even knows where she is half the time. She told me she could see my father, too, sitting over there in the corner of the room."

"It is quite normal," Zofia says.

Normal? How strange. Esther leans across the bed and kisses her mother's papery cheek, strokes her milkweed hair. People slipped away, no matter what you did. A quick rap on a taxi window, a screen door's screech and slam, and they were gone.

Again—a muted whisper.

"Did you catch that?" she asks Zofia, but Zofia shakes her head.

Esther takes her mother's hand and strokes the knotted knuckles, the twisted veins, the yellowed paper skin. "I love you too," she whispers back, although she has no idea if that is what her mother meant at all.

The telephone rings later in the afternoon. It's Gil. They haven't talked in weeks. The words she has laid out so carefully in her letter—the letter still unfinished, tucked inside a book on top of her mother's desk—have flown away. Useless words. She can hear her own breath, amplified in the receiver. Breath reconstituted as bits of binary code, traveling at the speed of light.

"I just wanted to see how things are going," he says.

"She won't last much longer, according to the nurse." She twines the phone cord around her wrist.

"She's a fighter."

"Yes."

The familiarity of Gil's voice annoys her: the slightly overlong pauses, the gruff *uh-huhs*. The lawyerly way he finally clears his throat and says, "So are you coming back?"

"Don't start, Gil." She twists the phone cord tight. "Not now."

"I need to know."

"Really? Do you? My mother is dying, for Christ's sake."

"Esther, please."

"What do you want me to say?"

"It's a very simple question."

"No, it's not." She feels as if she should be crying, but instead everything inside her has gone tight.

He clears his throat again. "I'm not going to beg."

"I know."

A pause. "This is it, Esther. Do you understand? I hope you've thought this over carefully."

She says nothing. She twists the phone cord around her wrist the other way. "I'm sorry," she says finally. "I really am."

His voice is tight. "Look, you take care of yourself, all right?"

And beneath the strain and gruffness in his voice there is the sound of words shattering into shards of light, and she understands that she has been released.

Jane, the Marie Curie nurse, is a godsend. She wears her long hair in a high twist. Bangs frame a warm, soft face. She has two grown children, she tells Esther, and two huge Newfoundlands that she dotes on like the grandchildren her sons (one gay, the other "a ladies' man") seem unlikely to produce. She is to arrive at nine each evening and stay all night. Esther would like to hug her. Actually, Esther would like to throw her arms around Jane's legs and kiss her feet.

Esther feels cheered up enough to make a carrot-ginger soup and bake a few baguettes. She gives one loaf to Jane, freezes the rest. Her mother takes only a few spoons of applesauce or ice cream these days. The metabolism slows, the nurses have assured her. She's getting all she needs.

In a burst of newfound energy, Esther dusts the sitting room, washes the bathroom floors, sweeps the stairs. Then she begins the work of emptying out drawers and filling bags with her mother's clothes, coats and sweaters, shoes. There is so much stuff. What to get rid of? What to keep? Everything seems saturated with nostalgia: the mantel clock, the enameled colander hanging on its kitchen hook, the afghan folded over the back of the sofa, the porcelain figurines and cups, the books. But what exactly is she nostalgic for? It's hard to say.

She sorts through her mother's jewelry, setting aside a strand of Polish amber to give to Zofia, a pretty Venetian glass bead bracelet for Jane. She flips through the recipe cards she finds stuffed into a kitchen drawer. Some are in German: *Lammrippchen, Leberknödel, Rigó Jancsi*. A few are annotated with spidery handwritten comments. On a strawberry shortcake: *Made for Noah, London, June 1993—lovely!* On a recipe for chocolate mousse: *Keep cool but do not freeze!*

At the back of the desk she finds an old file folder of legal documents pertaining to her father. Inquiries and summonses, indictments, appeals. *Tax evasion. Misappropriation of funds.* The worm of suspicion swivels its ugly head. What was the truth? There was no way of knowing. She slips the file back.

From another drawer, she pulls out a stack of photographs. Snapshots from the sixties, by the look of her mother's bob and sleeveless sheath. There's one of her parents in formal dress, picnicking on what looks like the great lawn at Glyndebourne, holding up champagne flutes. There's one of her father sitting on a chilly-looking beach. He is thin legged, hairy chested, wearing a floppy hat. Another photograph—older, smaller, black and white with deckled edges—shows an angular young man in a heavy overcoat, gripping the handlebars of a bicycle. On the back, somebody has inked *Mährisch Ostrau 1938*. It's not her father. Who then? She sighs and puts the photos back.

The packet of letters is tucked at the back of the same drawer, bound with a corroded rubber band. The envelopes are made out to an address in Kraków, Poland. They are unstamped, never mailed. She unfolds the thin sheets. She recognizes her mother's familiar slanting cursive. *Mein lieber Hugo*, the salutation reads. Hugo, her brother, lost in the war.

It is strange, the way these traces of the past resurface, like the vestiges of an underpainting beneath a well-known oil, or ancient roads revealed in photographs taken from the air. She looks down at the sixty-year-old letters in her hand. Too bad her German stinks.

She calls Javad from her bedroom, late. "Hey," she says.

His voice is low and rough. Perhaps he'd been asleep. Something has shifted between them since the other night. Everything has changed, but not in the way she'd feared. Something has loosened, opened up.

She tells him about her mother's disorientation and bad dreams. He tells her about his quarrel with Amir. He hasn't heard from him all week.

She undresses as they talk. In the mirror above her chest of drawers, she considers the sharp ridgeline of her clavicle, the looser skin along her neck. Her skin is freckled and pale. She's lost weight.

"Maybe he just needs a little space," she says, cradling the phone against her shoulder. "He'll come around, I'm sure."

Would Noah, too, have been a sullen stranger at nineteen?

Had she been that way as well? The summer after her first year in college, she'd stayed on in the city, working a catering job, subletting an apartment with a bunch of friends. Her mother had already moved back to London by then. Did she mind that Esther didn't join her? Esther has no memories of her mother from that summer, as if she didn't even exist.

She slides one arm out of her blouse, switches the phone to her other hand, then slides the other arm out, letting the blouse drop onto the floor. She reaches back and unhooks her bra and shakes it off as well. Her nipples tighten, bare.

"All I get from him are evasive answers," Javad says.

In the mirror—her throat, shoulders, ribcage, breasts. The skin along her abdomen is still faintly puckered from pregnancy long ago. Oh, her middle-aged body. A little saggy, but not bad still.

She says, "Maybe he's got a girlfriend."

"Not bloody likely. Half the time he looks as if he just climbed out from under a rock!"

"Maybe girls like scruffy. You don't know."

"Maybe you're right."

But there are a lot of things he doesn't know about his son, she thinks. He doesn't know about him sneaking in that first cold April night. He doesn't know about Finsbury Park. She thinks of the boy's eyes, so like an icon's. She remembers that complicit look.

"It will all work out," she says. "Just give him time."

She slides her nightgown over her head, holding out the phone as she wiggles her hands through the arm holes. When she brings it back to her ear, Javad is saying something about the adolescent brain. Hormones, the limbic system, the frontal lobe, judgment. Recklessness and risk.

She wonders if he'll ask her to come over. He is being careful with her now, she thinks. Who can blame him? She's one big complication: her mother is dying, her son is dead. And now that Jane is here, if he asks, will she say yes?

She gets into bed. The sheets are cold against her skin. Oh, her body. How long has it been since anyone touched her besides Gil? How long since even him?

From the first, she and Gil had turned away from each other in their grief. At night, he went to bed without her, and she lay alone in Noah's room, searching for consolation in the glow-in-the-dark stars. They sidled past each other in the kitchen, in the hall. They blamed each other. They blamed themselves. Friends asked how they were doing. Get counseling, everybody said.

And they did. They tried. They sat side by side on leather armchairs in the therapist's Upper East Side consulting room. The therapist crossed his legs, revealing a hairy band of skin between his trousers and his socks. There was a framed reproduction of Kandinsky's color study hanging above the therapist's head, colorful concentric circles like a target at a shooting range. Gil spoke formally, as if he were in court. Esther just sat there, feeling nothing, oblivious to the tears slipping down her cheeks.

The therapist handed her a box of Kleenex. "It must be intolerable, the prospect of losing another person that you love," he suggested.

Esther shook her head. What was he talking about? That wasn't it at all.

On the afternoon of their last session, she stood by Gil in the November drizzle at the corner of Seventh-Eighth and Madison, waiting for a cab. "I'm sorry," she said. He put his arms around her and kissed her. "I'm sorry too," he said. His eyes were shiny and hard. Any passerby would have thought they were in love. But she knew it was the end. She couldn't feel anything at all.

After she hangs up, she lies in bed, unable to sleep. She moves her hand down to touch herself, but she is dry. She has hardened. She has turned to stone. There is a disease that causes the skin to thicken with collagen into a scabrous hide that stretches taut across the joints and bones, the face becoming a keloid mask. Eventually, the internal organs too grow rigid, stiff. She pictures the inside of her body as a cave, glittering with pyrite and mica veins: the liver obsidian, pink marble lungs, a jasper spleen, a granite heart. *Ossified*. That's how she feels.

She should just get up and go next door, she thinks, but she's too old for recklessness. You were reckless when you were young because you didn't know better. You just went for it without thinking. Opened yourself up, unzipped your skin.

Just once, she'd hooked up with a stranger. Reckless, yes. She was a few years out of college, on the shuttle, flying back from Boston to LaGuardia on the last flight of the night. Boarding, she'd caught his eye as he passed her going down the aisle. He was very good looking, with thick hair and gray eyes and finely cut features—pretty, almost, as a girl. She felt his good looks like a punch, a shock of raw desire. He took a seat a couple of rows behind her. She swiveled around, pretending to be looking for someone else, caught his eye, turned back. After a little while, she turned around again.

He came up to her after they landed, inside the terminal, alongside the long rack of free magazines. He wore a navy blazer, jeans, expensive-looking leather shoes. He might have been a banker or an attorney. She smiled at him and he smiled back. He was so good looking. She asked him if he'd like to share a cab into the city. He said sure.

They pushed through the terminal doors to the taxi rank. This was how girls ended up dismembered, she thought—strangled, raped, and dumped behind a rock in Central Park and left for dead. She was not reckless. She triple-locked her apartment door, didn't do drugs or bungee jump or even ski. One by one, the yellow cabs pulled up and sped away. He opened the cab door for her and she slid across the lumpy seat. He climbed in after her and leaned toward the Plexiglas partition and told the driver, Ninety-

Sixth and Third, and she nodded, even though she lived nowhere near there. Not an axe murderer, she told herself. Although of course there was no way to tell. The taxi veered around a bend. Their legs and shoulders touched.

His building was a brand-new high rise on the northern edge of Yorkville, a steel and glass cylinder that rose above the squat prewar apartment buildings and dingy ground-floor storefronts and the projects. His high-floor windows faced east. Through the darkness, she could see the East River splitting around the tip of Randall's Island, the Triborough's lit-up span, the twinkling expanse of Queens. It felt as if they were still on the plane. He put his arms around her and pulled her to him. She opened her lips to his.

After it was over, he apologized. What for? She ran a finger along his forearm. The hair was gold and fine. The way he said it—*Are you okay?* As if he thought he'd hurt her. But he was no axe murderer, and she wasn't hurt in the least. The whole thing had been her doing from the start.

But she was no longer flying. Whatever it was that she had wanted, it wasn't here in the apartment on Ninety-Sixth Street. It was like that time in sixth grade when she'd nicked—the word "clipped" comes back to her, long-lost Boston slang—a Chap Stick from the drugstore on a dare. It felt hot, there in the pocket of her sweatshirt, as if it might burn a hole. She'd dropped it in a dumpster on the way home.

He was beautiful, naked beside her like a golden idol. She felt a wash of guilt, or shame. She got out of bed and dressed.

Now she wonders why she fled. What did it matter, any of it, in the end? There was such beauty in the way two bodies touched.

A few nights later, the doorbell rings. Jane is already there— it's late.

"Enough with the bloody phone," Javad says. He has on his

leather jacket, his lips curved in a smile. "Come on. Come for a walk with me instead."

She pulls on a cardigan, gives the Marie Curie nurse her phone number, makes sure the ringer on her mobile is turned up loud. "I won't be long," she promises.

"Don't you worry about a thing," says Jane.

It's a chilly evening, damp. The sky is indigo, smudged with darker clouds. They wander up and down the streets of South Hampstead—Swiss Cottage, Belsize Park. Curving streets of redbrick terraces, whitewashed mansion blocks, flowering trees and tidy hedges, the occasional incongruous modern block.

It's the Fourth of July, she realizes. An ordinary Monday here. Back home, there would be fireworks, crowds gathering in the streets, bottle rockets shooting off, children twirling sparklers in the air. In the year of the millennium, they'd watched the fireworks display from the rooftop of their building. Sprays and wheels of color shot up over the Hudson beyond the rooftops to the west. *Rat-a-tat* pops and thudding booms. Esther's mother hated fireworks. She always said that they reminded her of the Blitz.

"What do you hear from Amir?" she asks.

"Not a word."

"I'm sorry."

He turns up his palms. "What can I do?"

They pass a little playground—a rocking duck on a spring base, a sandbox, metal swings, a slide. She remembers pushing Noah, for hours it seemed, on the swings. Her palm against his little spine, touching and releasing. *Again, again*, he said. Up he flew and back.

Javad gives her a sideways look. "Will you be putting the house on the market, then?"

For a moment she doesn't understand.

"Property values won't keep on going up forever," he says. "It's a good time to sell, I should think."

"Actually, I've been thinking I might stay."

He slows and turns. "Stay on? Here in London?"

It is the first time she has said the words out loud. "For a while, anyway." Saying it aloud makes it feel real.

"You don't need to get back, then?"

"There's nothing for me there."

"Nothing?"

"This is all just—a lot." She shrugs. "I need some time."

He puts his arm around her shoulder and draws her in. Softly, he says, "I'd like it if you stayed."

She leans her head against his shoulder. He smells of aftershave and musk. "I'm a basket case," she says. "I'm warning you. My life's a mess."

"Esther, Esther," he says in a singsong. He presses his lips into her hair.

"Trust me, I'm a basket case."

"I think that you're just fine."

They meander down one street and up another. Through the occasional lit window, she catches a glimpse of the blue flicker of a TV; a row of bud vases on a windowsill, each containing a single miniature red rose; a harp's curved neck and scroll. The secret interiors of other people's lives.

By the time they loop back to their own block, her feet ache. It is late. At the bottom of their steps, he puts both arms around her and draws her in. His lips are warm and wet. The universe has narrowed to a single point. There is nothing in the world right now that she wants more than this.

AMIR

It is not difficult to flee. He stuffs some clothes into his rucksack, silences his phone. He deletes his father's texts unread. His parents each assume he's with the other. Sod them both, he thinks.

Most nights he stays at Bigsby's. They hang around playing World of Warcraft, smoking weed, and watching their favorite DVDs: *28 Days Later*, *The Zone*, *Mad Max*. The best bits are the settings: blighted wastelands, derelict buildings, radioactive skies. His hard drive is full of photographs of places just like these, only his photographs are real.

They argue over where to explore next. Bigsby wants to have a poke around Millennium Mills down in the Docklands, but for weeks now, Mole has been drawing up a hit list of "ghost stations" in the Tube. He's been collecting maps and diagrams and photographs of disused tunnels, platforms, branch lines, tracks. He sprawls on Bigsby's sofa, munching on crisps, his laptop propped on his skinny thighs. "Right then," he says. "Down Street. Aldwych. Belsize Park. Mark Lane. King's Cross. Have your pick."

"Has anyone got into any of them yet?" Amir asks.

"You can hire the Aldwych booking hall for fancy parties, for fuck's sake," Mole says.

"Martin," Amir says. "People like *us*."

Stoned, Bigsby gets all philosophical. "The *raight* question," he says, cracking a Foster's, "is not has anyone got in, but why more haven't even tried?"

Mole shrugs. "There's rumors."

"I'll tell ye why," Bigsby continues. "Because it's not possible. It's a panopticon out there."

Mole rolls his eyes. "A what? Speak bloody English."

"Bentham," Bigsby says. "The power of surveillance." He mimes pressing the shutter of a camera. "Smile, yer on CCTV!"

"That's why you got to be a ninja, Biggs," Mole says.

"And never mind the live rails, the zero-clearance tunnels, station workers, locked doors, cleaners, mice, transport police. They won't just rap yer knuckles and send ye packing, either. Ye'll go raight to jail."

"You shouldn't smoke, Biggs, it makes you paranoid," Amir says, and even Bigsby laughs, but they know that what he says is true.

The fuse has been lit all the same. He can feel it crackling in the air. It's all right there, waiting for them, right beneath their feet.

Come study with me, Miranda texts.

Since the night of that last revision party back in May, that has been their little joke. That night, Ian showed up with a fifth of vodka and Miranda's flatmate handed round a batch of chocolate biscuits laced with weed, and the study session soon degenerated into a loud and inebriated argument over 9/11 and the Mossad conspiracy, with Miranda uselessly attempting to shift the conversation back to the Muslim *umma* and their exam. And then, somehow, it was two in the morning and Amir and Miranda were lying on her bed, her shirt pushed up, her breasts cupped in his hands.

"I like studying with you," she said, smiling, coming up for air.

She was always smiling.

He likes her smile. He's never had a proper girlfriend before, and he's not certain if Miranda counts exactly as a girlfriend now, seeing as they haven't done much, really, other than have sex. He likes the secrecy of it, the dark kernel of it lodged behind his breastbone, the silent understanding of two bodies that words can never match.

Some days he stops at the Costa's on the Seven Sisters Road where Miranda works now that term is out. He sits outside and reads the paper or just watches the people coming in and out of Finsbury Park Station over the road. When he goes inside to order, sometimes he'll pretend he doesn't know her. He'll put on a fake posh accent and say, "A flat white and a toastie, please, Miss." The other barista just rolls her eyes and says, "Yo, Miranda. Your toy boy's here." But Miranda just smiles and shakes the frothed milk back and forth as she pours it over the espresso to form a swirly heart.

Other days, he wanders through the park, watching the lawn bowlers and the duffers on the tennis courts, or lies out on the grass beneath a tree, looking up at the leaves, his earphones in, his iPod cranked up high. He's lived in London his whole life, but this is a whole other world: gritty, dirty, real. It's like that storm drain or manhole you've walked over a thousand times but never noticed until you knew where to look. Everything is multiple. It is strange. Even his own face, reflected in the bathroom mirror, seems a doppelganger of his former self.

The Finsbury Park mosque is not far from Miranda's flat, just a few blocks from the Tube. It's a newish redbrick building with bright green window trim—an odd primary-school touch. The concrete minaret along the side could be mistaken for a lift shaft, but sometimes you can hear the call to prayer from the street: *Allahu Akbar, Allahu Akbar.* Even though it has been ages since the police raided the mosque and arrested the former imam and his jihadi radicals, the street out front is still cordoned off with traffic cones and caution tape. A CCTV camera keeps watch beneath the streetlamp across. Most days there's a policeman stationed there as well, pacing up and down along the spiked brick wall.

A couple of weeks ago, for the first time, he went in. He slipped off his shoes and stood among the other men and tried to follow as they raised their hands in reverence, crossed them in supplication, and bowed their heads and knelt, prostrate, touching their foreheads to the ground.

Their voices rose as one: *Subhaana rabbiyal-a'laa.* Glory is to my Lord, the Most High.

Something twisted inside him then, a kind of longing for something for which he had no name.

They decide to start with King's Cross on the theory that it will be easier to get into a cut-and-cover station than the deep Underground. Even so, it takes a while to find a way in. Bigsby is tempted by the Gothic clock tower of the old Midland Grand, cordoned off for renovations, but Mole urges them on. They scout the concourse of the main King's Cross Station, mugging alongside the tourists for an obligatory PLATFORM 9 ¾ photo op. They suss out the Thameslink platforms, the Underground ticket halls, the warren of tunnels running underneath.

The disused Metropolitan line platform they're searching for is one of the oldest bits of the Underground, Mole says, built way back in 1863. Two high-explosive bombs dropped here and killed a man during the Blitz. The old Met line station house, closed since then, is easy enough to locate. It's around the back of the main station, a blank white building wedged between a Royal Pizza parlor and a dodgy payday lender's shop. The metal fire door—handle-less, locked—is signposted KEEP CLEAR—EXIT FROM EMERGENCY ESCAPE ROUTE—THESE DOORS ARE ALARMED. There's no way in from there.

But down a narrow, brick-paved side street, looking down from a narrow bridge onto an exposed stretch of track, they spot the disused platform. They lean over the railing, gazing down. It's nothing but a weedy patch of concrete in the shadow of a high retaining wall. Trains run past it all day long, as they have done since 1941—for more than sixty years. It is right there, for anyone to see. It's just a different kind of seeing, like walking into a dark room on a bright, sunny day and letting your eyes adjust to the lack of light.

Bigsby is all for abseiling straight onto the platform from the bridge, but the drop looks dangerous and there are windows and CCTV cameras everywhere they look. They note the locations of the cameras, the security systems, the fire exit stairs. Somewhere, there's got to be a crack.

It's Amir's idea to follow the graffiti tags, and sure enough, good old Tox leads them straight in. Two nights later they are back, dressed in dark hoodies and trainers, armed with cameras, stoked on adrenaline. Warnings rumble through their heads like freights: Lights mean workers. Dark tracks are live. Rail trespass carries an automatic fine of one thousand quid.

Breathing hard, dry-mouthed, hearts gunning in their chests, they drop down and wait. The disused platform is lit up bright as day. Above them is the bridge they were standing on the other day. Just street noises overhead. Amir pulls out his camera and fires off a bunch of shots. Everything's in sharp focus, clear, hard edged. The rails flash in the sodium glare.

Moving out of the light, they climb a flight of stairs to a cross-over passage and find themselves in a long corridor that has the musty smell and feeling of a catacomb or tomb. The walls are scabby with rust, the ceiling draped with old wires and cables and rusty pipes. The corridor is bricked up at the end, but a sign posted on the wall still states: KING'S CROSS 200M. NUMBER OF STEPS TO EXIT: 44.

Mole says, "Always so helpful, they are, the T.A."

An abandoned place remembers, Bigsby always says. They might be the first people to have set foot here since the Blitz.

Amir takes out his camera and documents their finds. Retaining wall. Escape tunnels. Alarmed doors. Tracks. The camera flashes. He works fast. Getting in is the challenge. Sticking around is just asking to get caught.

They are right out in the glare, back on the open platform, when it happens. The vibration comes before the sound, a faint humming along the rails. Deep in the dark recess of the tunnel, a red eye blinks.

"Fuck," Bigsby says.

Mole dashes for the thin line of shadows behind the platform pillars and they tuck in behind him, pressing their backs against the wall, and wait.

"Don't move," Mole hisses.

Amir holds his breath.

A shuddering fills the narrow space, the thrum of diesel, and then with a spray of light out of the tunnel comes a blue train like a slit-eyed monster, a work train, thundering along the tracks.

And then with a gust of stale and gritty breath it's passed, snaking across the open stretch of track and into the black mouth of the far tunnel, taillights blinking, the engine noise subsiding like an ebbing wave.

They exhale, doubled over, gasping, almost laughing, surrendering to relief.

Bigsby exhales hard. "That was a heart attack."

"You should see the look on your face!" Amir says. "It's brilliant."

"Fuck off," Bigsby says.

Everything is vibrating, everything is sharp and hard and clear. The lights along the tracks are shining extra bright. They are utterly, intensely alive.

Twenty minutes later they are out, surfacing like divers rising from a wreck, breathing their private prayers of thanks to the patron gods of exploration for bringing them back from the world of the dead. They've peeled back the layers of history; they've turned back time.

Zombies move along the main concourse of the King's Cross Station, mobile phones and iPods playing static in their zombie ears. Their zombie eyes are dead. They take no notice of the three boys in black hoodies and jeans. Late-night zombie cleaners follow, obliviously sweeping, dragging rubbish carts behind.

Only the CCTV cameras watch with their all-seeing eyes.

LONIA

Time has pooled, the way a river eddies along the bank, out of the flowing stream. Time ripples outward, decoupled from the turning of the earth, the diurnal movement of the sun. All that's left are fragments. The membrane is frayed.

There's no more pain, no more fear. She has given in to the dull oblivion of morphine, its weightless dissolving warmth. She floats above her body, hardly aware of the pumping labor of her failing heart and lungs. She leaves it to the ministrations of the women who turn and prod and wipe, whispering as they come and go. Only her dreams are vivid. Only the past is real.

The women whisper by the samovar in the refugee hall; the men shake open the daily papers, smoke from their cigarettes rising in the air. War, everybody says, is very near. Arms are being smuggled into Danzig. Fortifications are going up along the German frontier. The Polish army is calling up its men. What happened to Czechoslovakia, everybody is saying, cannot be permitted to happen here.

Letters arrive from their father every couple of days. *Meine liebsten Kinder*, he writes, his cursive elegant, his updates bland. Lonia pictures his ink-smudged fingers, his glass of cognac, his cigarette smoldering in the ashtray to a tail of ash. Seated at the kitchen table, she contemplates the nib of her pen, the blank stationery page. Her replies are just as bland. She does not mention Hugo's Zionist friends, their talk of blockades and bribes. She does not mention Isaac: his yeshiva bocher face, the thrilling flicker of his tongue, his demanding gaze.

Isaac comes and goes, disappearing without warning, reappearing a few days later, offering no explanation for where he's been. Rumors ripple through the hall. Some say that he's an anarchist. Others say he is a spy. Lonia believes the stories he has told her: that his parents died when he was a child, that he was raised by an aunt and uncle in the hills of Subcarpathian Rus, that he studied in Berlin. The details—of the Ruthenian peasants gathering for the crush, of riding the U-Bahn across the Oberbaumbrücke—give his stories the ring of truth whether they are true or not.

In the afternoons, they walk together along the streets of Kazimierz. The flat stone facades along Krakowska Street are gray. The cobblestones are gray. Gray clouds spit summer rain. At the Third Bridge crossing, Lonia stops and leans over the iron balustrade. A whippy wind is blowing hard ridges in the water. The Wisła, too, is gray, the color of concrete.

"Poland is finished," Isaac says. "We are in the worst place one could be."

"That's thinking positively," Lonia says.

The river slides beneath them, moving fast today. The ducks paddle close to the muddy bank, out of the stream. From here, the river flowed north to Warszawa and from there all the way to Danzig and the open sea.

"I want you to come with me," Isaac says.

"Come with you where?"

"We'll see."

"And how, exactly, do you propose we get to wherever this is? Perhaps you have a flying carpet? Or maybe you'll just snap your fingers and entrance permits will magically appear?"

He gives her a sideways smile. His eyes are dark and hard. "You just have to trust me."

"Easy for you to say. You don't have a brother or a father. You're not leaving anyone behind."

"Go to Palestine with Hugo, then, if that's the way you feel."

She sighs. "We haven't got papers yet. You know that."

He takes her hand, interlacing his fingers with hers, rubbing his thumb along her metacarpal bones. Her hand feels very small in his.

"Come with me, Lonia."

"I just want to go home."

She tries to pull her hand back, but he tightens his grip. "I have a contact," he says. "He says he can get us visas to England."

"Oh he does, does he?"

He makes a wry face. "There is only one problem."

"Only one? What's that?"

"I'm afraid I had to tell him we were married."

She laughs. Married!

"The point is there's a chance. It's just a matter of money."

"Oh! Of course it is. I see." She pauses. "And what about Hugo?"

"I'll try, Lonia, but it will be difficult. I can't promise anything."

From here she can't see the embankment where they walked at midsummer amid the flaming bonfires and flickering wreaths. It seems like months have passed, not just weeks. Time no longer seems to function in the ordinary way. A blink ago she was a schoolgirl in Moravská Ostrava. A hundred years ago, she kissed her father goodbye.

Back at the flat, she pulls out from underneath the mattress the leather pouch her father gave her that contains her mother's diamond ring. She slides it onto the third finger of her left hand. It is too big. She holds her hand out. The diamond is shot through with spears of light. *Married*, she thinks. She's almost eighteen.

Outside the open window of her bedroom, a bird is singing: a few melodious trills followed by a rapid sequence of chirps and clicks. A nightingale, she thinks. She can hear the old woman doing something in the kitchen, banging pans. She turns back to the window. The romantics had it wrong; you could hardly call it singing, this noise the nightingale makes. It whistles, chatters, makes a squeaky sound like kisses blown through puckered lips.

She slides her mother's ring off her finger and tucks it back into the leather pouch. Should she let Isaac sell the ring? She imagines it tucked inside the crease of Isaac's jacket pocket, in the fat fist of a black market dealer, on the plump white finger of some Polish bride. *Please forgive me, Mama*, she thinks.

She imagines her long-dead mother looking down from wherever it is the angels dwell, her dark hair fanned out behind her, her white arms raised. Her mother's angel eyes are fierce.

Go, her mother says.

A stirring ripples through the refugee hall. Chairs scrape back; there is movement toward the door. A knot of people forms before the notice board on the wall. The list of immigration permits is going up. Once again the roulette wheel has been spun.

Bored, Lonia turns the pages of one of the illustrated weeklies. The pages are filled with advertisements for fortune-tellers, palm readers, mediums, spiritualists. Could a clairvoyant tell her what the future held?

One of the Hanoar Hatzioni girls, the religious one, squints at Lonia as she returns from checking the notice board. The girl is wearing a dowdy long-sleeved beige plaid dress with an oversized white collar, her hair tied back in childish plaits.

"Any luck?" Lonia says.

The girl shakes her head.

"Still hoping to get to Palestine?" Lonia asks.

"The British aren't issuing any more entrance permits. You know that."

"My brother says there are still ways to get there."

The girl glances across the room. "It doesn't matter. The Zionists want able-bodied workers who can build the country, farm the land. They have no use for old people or small children."

Lonia follows the girl's gaze to a nearby table where a woman wearing a headscarf is bouncing a baby on her lap. She is surrounded by half a dozen older children—little boys with curling *payes*, girls in ill-fitting dresses cut from the same bolt of ugly plaid. The father was probably at shul. He'd better be praying very hard, Lonia thinks.

"Families should stick together," the girl says, sticking out her chin. "That's the most important thing."

Back at the flat, Lonia and Hugo quarrel. They are in the study, whispering, the old cousins already gone to sleep. Hugo crosses his arms over his chest.

"Are you going to listen to him or to me?"

Why was everything an impossible choice? *Paris or Venice? Swimming or skating? Bach or Chopin?*

"I'm just telling you what he said."

"What, that Hitler's going to make a grab for Danzig? That the Jews are finished here? That's news? I've been saying the same exact thing since before Austria fell!"

"You could make a lot of money as a psychic, you know. I hear it's all the rage."

"Shut up, Lonia. What the hell do you know?"

"I don't know anything, clearly."

"Then you could listen to me for once. Not some *shvitzer* you just met."

"I am listening. It just sounds dangerous to me."

Hugo turns away. He has not succeeded in getting immigration permits to Palestine. But there are ways to get around the quotas, he says. His latest scheme is to try to get on board a cargo ship in Constanţa that is being kitted out for refugees. An advance party has gone to Lwów to meet with a representative of the Jewish Underground from the Land. Hugo uses words that Lonia doesn't understand: *yishuv, ma'apilim, aliyah bet.*

She has been studying the map. From the coast of Romania, the ship would have to make it past the Turkish guards at the Straight of Bosphorus, across the rough Aegean and the eastern Mediterranean, then past the British blockade to the port of Haifa or the beach at Tel Aviv.

Isaac says the British will throw them into prison if they don't first sink or run aground. Lonia has never been on a ship before. She doesn't even know how to swim.

"Papa won't approve," she says to Hugo, even though she knows this is the least persuasive of all the arguments she could make.

Hugo just glares at her. "You do what you want, Lonia," he says finally. "I don't care."

Lonia turns away. *Families should stick together*, the Hanoar girl said.

There was one moment, she remembers, after they'd emerged from the mine, when through the silence of the colliery there came the sudden sound of voices and a dog's sharp bark. She saw panic flash in Hugo's eyes. They had been betrayed.

The older of the red-haired brothers scrambled to his feet. A blade flashed in his hand.

"Hold still," the guide hissed between his teeth.

Lonia held still. The dog barked again. Hunched beside her, Hugo grabbed her arm. His fingernails dug into her skin. He was as powerless and as afraid as she was, she realized then.

The guide had the hungry look of a wolf, an anti-Semite's eyes. They all knew what would happen now. The border guards would arrest them or just shoot them on the spot. The guide would top off the sum they'd already paid him with a fat reward. Probably that had been his plan all along.

But it was not the border guards. It was just an old couple in oily hiking boots and woolen caps, out for a Sunday walk in the forest, a spaniel trotting before them on its lead, barking at squirrels, wagging its tail. The couple didn't even look their way.

The red-haired brother folded his knife and put it back in his pocket. Hugo let go her arm and grinned, stupid with relief.

Now Hugo is leaning on the windowsill with his back to her, his shirt stretched across his bony shoulders, the sleeves rolled up. When they were little, he used to pretend sometimes that he was a knight and she his vassal and make her swear an oath of loyalty. She had to kneel before him and bow her head. *I promise never to betray thee*, she pledged.

But now she's tired of following him around, tired of doing what he says. She'll be eighteen in a couple of weeks. She has her own life to live.

Today the breeze along the river smells of river weeds and grass, a summer smell, the smell of the lazy walks they used to take with their grandparents along the Opava towpath, scavenging for wild strawberries and lady's slippers beneath the brambles and dead leaves. The sun is hot. The sky is clear. Isaac is leaning back on his elbows, his ankles crossed. Then he turns toward her, reaching into his jacket pocket with one hand.

"Lonia—"

For a second, she thinks he is going to propose. Maybe he has not sold her mother's ring? But what he gives her is not a ring but a small blue booklet. It is a passport. She flips it open. It is a passport. There is her photograph in black and white. There, in purple ink, sealed with official-looking stamps, is a visa for the United Kingdom. And there, tucked into the pages of the booklet, is a pink slip of paper, a ticket for a ship. The date stamped on the ticket is three days away.

"How on earth——? Is it real?"

He ignores her. "What do you say?"

Static fills her head. England was an island where it rained. The British had stiff upper lips and wore pith helmets and tweeds. They ate mutton and porridge, drank milky tea. Of the English language, she can remember only useless phrases from the primer: *I am sure to leave to-morrow. He is likely to arrive by the evening train.*

Isaac is watching her closely. "Will you come with me?"

"And Hugo?"

He shakes his head. "I'm sorry."

She runs her finger along the cloth cover of the passport, over the gold-stamped words and seal. She cannot speak. She just nods, *Okay.*

All this time, she has not known how to choose, when in fact there was no choice at all.

The refugee hall is nearly empty now. The three of them sit at the end of a table near the back, awkwardly sipping glasses of tea.

Isaac's tone is formal, his manner stiff. "I would ask your father's permission," he says, "but I ask you now instead. I promise you I will take good care of her."

Lonia feels like a piece of livestock being bartered for a prize. "It's *my* decision," she says, but no one is listening.

"I should hope so," Hugo says.

"If you can wait another week or two," Isaac is saying to Hugo, "it's possible something will come through for you as well. If Hitler doesn't attack before then."

Hugo pulls himself up straighter. "Don't go to any trouble for

me—I don't need your help. I wouldn't go to England anyway.
I've told you that."

Lonia feels as if her heart has swollen and grown as porous as
a sponge. She knows her brother's stubbornness and pride. He'll
never admit to being afraid.

Isaac pushes back his chair and extends his hand. "I wish you
luck," he says.

She wants to say she's sorry, but Hugo's jaw is set. He will not
meet her eyes.

Later, she washes and folds her sheets and towel and the clothes
borrowed from the old cousins' grownup daughter and sets a
note atop the stack. She writes a letter to her father as well. *Do
not worry, Papa*, she writes, her pen scratching at the onionskin
page. *It is for the best*, she writes, then adds, *and only for a couple
of months at most, I'm sure*. She taps the rounded end of her Pe-
likan pen against her teeth. She is finding it difficult to breathe,
as if a band around her chest has been cinched tight. She flips the
words around in her head, unable to decide what to write. *Hugo
has refused to come along with us*. No. *Hugo has booked passage on a
special ship to Palestine*. No. She tries to inhale, but her lungs have
turned to lead. *Hugo wants me to go with him but I cannot*. No. She
sets her pen down and covers her face with her hands and weeps.

The ship belches smoke from one tall smokestack and the docks of
Gdynia fall away. She stands by Isaac at the rail and breathes the
briny, coal-smoke air. Far below, the water churns into a widening wake. The coast fades to a thin gray line.

The ship's third-class cabins are tiny slots, six narrow bunks
in each, bolted to the wall. Isaac sleeps below her, a Dutch phy-
sician overhead, three snoring merchants on the other side. She

spends the rest of the time on deck, wrapped in Isaac's coat, the sleeves dwarfing her hands. They chug past Swedish freighters, Danish fishing skiffs, German warships flying huge red swastika-emblazoned flags. The flat green fields of Schleswig-Holstein stretch into the distance beyond the Kiel Canal. The crossing of the North Sea is rough. She vomits in the latrine.

At Tilbury, she wobbles weak-kneed down the gangplank to a shed where a dough-faced British officer stamps her passport, making her an official refugee. Then they board an autobus to London where an immigrant reception center has been arranged inside a primary school, the narrow beds crammed into class-rooms lined with dusty chalkboard walls. She drinks endless cups of milky tea. She memorizes the phrase: *I am sorry, but I do not understand.*

In the washed-out light of England, Isaac's hat and coat look shabby, his face pale and strained. Although he is fluent in five languages, his English is inadequate, his accent guttural and hard for the Brits to understand. How will they find work, a place to live? She twists her phony wedding band around her finger. In the refugee center, alone in the cold toilet that reeks of piss, she weeps.

Less than three weeks later, the Germans invade Poland and two days after that the British and the French attack. *WAR*, the newspaper headlines scream. *Lucky, lucky,* everybody says. They are lucky they got out. But lucky is not what Lonia feels. She is marooned now on this dismal island, cut off, the borders closed. No telegrams will reach behind enemy lines. No telephone calls. No post. She writes letter after letter that she cannot send.

At the newsstand on Bayswater Road, she peers at the grainy black-and-white photographs on the front pages of the English papers: Hitler and Chamberlain, goose-stepping Nazi soldiers, bombed-out buildings and rubble-covered streets. She can make out only that new word—*blitzkrieg*—and a smattering of familiar names: *Danzig, Warsaw,* Łódź. Poland is surrounded by German tanks, Isaac says, the cities pulverized by bombs.

Here in London, there are fears of air raids too. Children are being evacuated to the countryside. Gas masks are being prepared. People are queuing up outside the shops for blackout curtains and petrol, blue low-light bulbs, sugar, lard.

Isaac finds a place as a school cleaner in Taunton, and a family in Wolverhampton that needs a nanny takes Lonia in. Lonia and Isaac see each other once a month on weekends when he comes up on the train. She shares a bed with the five-year-old who teaches her words in English and kicks violently in his sleep. As her English improves, she tells him bedtime stories, the fairy tales her father once told her, about the twelve princesses and the underground cavern with the gold and silver trees.

"At the beginning of a story, you must say, 'once upon a time,'" the boy solemnly instructs her. "And at the end, you must say, 'happily ever after.' That's the way it is with stories," he says.

Lonia pushes down the hollow feeling in her chest. *Happily ever after*, she thinks. She prays that her father has enough to eat, that Hugo has reached Palestine aboard his clandestine ship. She pictures him leaning on the rail, looking out toward the distant coast of Romania or Turkey, passing rocky Aegean islands or the green flank of Cyprus, squinting in the sun reflecting off the waves. She pictures him in Palestine, picking oranges at dawn, his chest tanned and bare. He is now a pioneer. He has changed his name to Ziv.

In German, at the end of a story, one said: *Und wenn sie nicht gestorben sind, dann leben sie noch heute,* which meant, *If they haven't died, then they're still alive today.* Lonia crosses her fingers and holds her thumbs and tells herself that everything will be okay.

There are many stories, Lonia comes to understand much later, that have no endings. For years, long after the war has ended, she hopes and waits. Letters are returned unread. Inquiries to the Red Cross turn up documents revealing that her father was transported to Nisko nad Lanem in October 1939, sent back to Ostrava in March 1940 after the dissolution of the labor camp, and deported to Terezin two years after that. Of the 3,567 Jews deported from Ostrava during the war, she eventually learns, only 253 survived. Of Hugo, there is no trace. He is unaccounted for, uncounted, lost. Did he perish trying to reach Palestine? Or might he have traveled east instead and somehow, somewhere, survived?

How could you lose a person? Lonia wants to know what happened. She wants a body, a record; she wants to leave a pebble on a grave. Isaac tries to work his contacts in Israel and behind the Iron Curtain but turns up nothing. In place of knowing, Lonia has only the inexorable arithmetic of time. On the day her father would have turned one hundred, she lights a Yahrzeit candle and fills in a Page of Testimony for the Hall of Names at Yad Vashem. The row on the Testimony form marked "Circumstances of Death" lists a grim litany of possibilities: *prison/ deportation/ghetto/camp/death march/hiding/escape/resistance/ combat/unknown*. She leaves it blank.

She does not light a candle for Hugo. She does not fill in a form. Maybe, maybe, maybe, she thinks. Maybe he was alive and living in Vladivostok, Sverdlovsk, Magadan. Maybe he was driving a tractor in the wheat fields of the Kazakh oblast, or hidden in a remote valley in the Siberian taiga, living off the land. Maybe he didn't want to be found. She realizes that by now he would have aged, his skin gone slack, his hair turned white, like hers. But she cannot picture him as anything but young.

In Lonia's morphine dreams, she is underground. She is drifting through a glittering stalagmite-studded cavern. She is crawling through the blackness of the Tešin mine. She is huddled on a platform in the Underground, sirens wailing, Stukas roaring, bombs thudding overhead. She is streaming through the darkness of a tunnel toward a glimmering white light. Everything is shattered, everything is smashed to bits.

Somewhere, far away, music is playing. The melody splits into fractals, circles, repeats. The great gears turn. Voices rise and fall, spinning beyond the reach of time. *Kyrie, Gloria, Sanctus*, the voices sing.

There is a hand. She reaches out to grasp it, squinting in the light.

"Tell him—"

Her fingers are slipping.

"Tell—"

SIX

JAVAD

He swings his briefcase as he makes his way along the quiet residential streets toward the Tube. It is a damp, gray Thursday morning. There is a feeling of expansiveness, a ringing in the air. The harmonies resonate around him: that mossy wall, that white-blossomed bush, the dappled play of shade and light. He has felt this way since his night with Esther. The memory comes to him in gentle waves, catching him by surprise: the softness of her body, the sweetness of her lips. This is happiness, he thinks.

At Finchley Road, Javad waits at the pelican crossing for the light. Four lanes of traffic sweep away the peaceful curving streets, the equilibrium of the morning, in a blur of exhaust fumes wafting up off the concrete. He checks his watch. He's due at a committee meeting at 9:00. He's running late.

He'd stayed up too late the night before watching the news—good news for once—of London's successful Olympic bid. Smug Lord Coe and grinning Beckham, Tony Blair dancing his little victory jig. The 2012 summer games, here in London. God only knows how they'd manage the security for an event like that. *2012* still sounds like science fiction. Maybe the world would be a better place by then. One could hope, at least.

The light turns green. The signal bleeps. He crosses, makes

his way around the plastic tubs of flowers, the crates of fruit, the crowds of commuters elbowing their way into the Tube.

On Platform 4, the electronic departure board reads ALDGATE 2 MINS. It's 8:38 a.m. Six station stops to King's Cross, then a change for Russell Square. He sighs. He'll almost certainly be late.

With a rhythmic clatter, the train pulls up and squeals to a stop. The doors hiss open. The carriages are packed. He squeezes his way in and grabs a pole, setting his briefcase between his feet. It is hot and claustrophobic. Why is it so crowded? The closing bell beeps.

At Baker Street, he grasps the pole as a mass of passengers pushes out around him and a fresh mass surges in. Again the doors hiss shut and the train jolts forward. He shoves his hand into his pocket and flips his phone open, shut. He wonders, for a fleeting moment, whether he should try calling Amir again or just leave him be. *No news is good news*, people always said. He has not heard from him now for going on two weeks.

They are just a minute or two out from Great Portland Street Station, deep inside the tunnel, when the train lurches abruptly to a stop. He staggers against the passengers standing by him around the pole. The engine moans and then the lights blink out and everything is dark.

The darkness is dense and absolute, as if he's underwater, or in a mine. He expects that the engine will rev back up and the lights will switch back on after a few moments, but nothing happens. He pulls out his mobile and flips it open, squinting at the blue square of the screen. 8:52 a.m. Now he'll certainly be late. No signal bars, of course.

The mass of bodies pulses around him in the darkness. He dislikes enclosed spaces. He is not fond of crowded cinemas, narrow corridors, small planes, lifts. He tugs at his tie. The woman seated in front of him starts to fan herself with a magazine. People shift in their seats. There are too many bodies, too little air, too many people crammed into this metal cylinder stopped inside this tunnel, two hundred meters underground. Panic begins to squeeze him in its python grip.

Just breathe, he tells himself. Slowly in and out. Out and in.

It is nearly fifteen minutes before a voice comes over the tannoy, a garbled South Asian drone. Through the static Javad thinks he makes out the words *power surge . . . electrical fault.*

A ripple of grumbling passes through the carriage. "It's absolutely shambolic!" a man's voice says. "How the hell are they going to manage the Olympics if they can't even run the bloody trains?"

Javad wipes his forehead on his sleeve. His lower back is beginning to ache. Surely an electrical fault was something they could fix? Surely they were working on it already. How long would it take? He checks the time again. He feels as if he's been down here, trapped, forever, but it's only 9:08 a.m.

Panic squeezes his throat. This is the way people feel in the MRI tube. Some hyperventilate, shake, scream. Most clinics pipe music into the tube to help relieve the anxiety. Others give patients mirrored glasses that create an optical illusion of greater space. He tries closing his eyes, wishing there were soothing music, and tries to breathe.

After an interminable wait—he feels as if he has been standing here for days—a torch flashes in the tunnel outside the train. The driver's voice comes on again. They are to be evacuated. "Hallelujah," someone calls out.

Slowly, they move forward through the train. He shuffles to the far end of the carriage, then the next. It is quiet, close, and hot. At the very front of the train, a door has been opened. He climbs down a short ladder and steps onto the tracks.

The tunnel is dark and dank. It smells of burnt brake shoes, mold, and piss. People are holding up their mobiles as makeshift torches, blue-lit squares like miner's lights. Javad takes his phone out and holds it up as well, although it is of little help. No one speaks. He picks his way into the darkness along the tracks. At least there's no live rail. There is a faint scrabbling noise of mice. How horrid it must have been down here during the Blitz.

Finally, they emerge into the dim space of a station. Emergency lights give off a weak glow. The younger and more impatient passengers are heaving themselves up onto the platform, which rises at chest height from where they stand down on the rails. Now another ladder is being propped against the platform's edge. The driver, a turbaned Sikh, positions himself at the base, begins helping people up. His long beard is twisted into a thick strap beneath his chin. Gibberish squawks from the two-way radio strapped to his chest. "Mind your step," he mumbles. "Mind your step."

"What in hell is going on?" demands the man in front of Javad, but the driver only shrugs.

Javad climbs the ladder, stumbles up the stilled escalator steps and out of the station. And then he is on the street.

Daylight stabs his eyes. The Euston Road is a gridlocked mass of cars and taxis and vans and double-decker busses lined up as far as he can see, a few intrepid motorbikers and cyclists weaving along the edge. Two pumper trucks are idling outside the Tube station, lights flashing. But he smells no smoke, sees no sign of an emergency. Thank god, he's out.

It is 9:46 a.m. His committee meeting will be nearly over—there's no point hurrying now. Never mind. It's a short walk from here, ten minutes at most. There is the reassurance of the air and trees and the concrete of the pavement firm beneath his feet. The tinted façade of the Wellcome Trust building reflects the fluttering leaves, the scudding clouds, the summer sky.

———

He walks east along the Euston Road, the crowd of stranded commuters deepening as he goes. Men and women are waving frantically at occupied taxis, shouting into their mobile phones. It is madness. An entire city is late for work.

He has not gone far when a man in a filthy, rumpled suit staggers into him, hard, bumping shoulders on his way past. Piss drunk, Javad thinks—how pathetic, so early in the day, and on a day like this. But there is something strange. It takes a moment before it comes to him that the far side of the man's face and suit were black with soot. Javad wheels around, but the man has disappeared.

His breath catches in his chest. What has happened? Not just a power surge, he thinks. Ahead a phalanx of police have blocked off the entire Euston Road and are diverting traffic and pedestrians south toward Tavistock Square. Red and yellow emergency lights flash. He follows the throngs funneling into Upper Woburn Place. The banners hanging above the tall red doors of the St. Pancras parish church flutter in the morning breeze. They seem to belong to a different dimension of time and space.

He has just passed the entrance to the Hilton when it happens. The sound comes first: a massive crunching thud, like cars colliding, only louder—a great whooshing pop. It is followed by a strange, slow, silent puff of movement: a cloud of debris and shattered glass spraying into the air, a plume of white smoke rising up. A cordite smell. Amid it all, a metallic ribbon floats, twisting and flashing almost lazily, in the summer light.

All around him, everything is frozen on a blast wave of shock. Cars and vans are stopped. The people standing along the pavement are stopped. Just ahead, at the northwest corner of Tavistock Square, a red bus is stopped. It's one of those sightseeing busses with an open-air upper deck. It's strange, Javad thinks—one didn't ordinarily see tourist busses like that here. But then the image shifts and he realizes that it is not a tourist bus but a regular red double-decker bus, blown to bits.

The roof of the bus is peeled back like the lid of a sardine tin, the upper deck exposed. People are hanging over the shattered sides, slumped forward in the seats. Bile rises in his throat.

Somewhere, through the frozen stasis, comes the sound of pigeons cooing in the park. Very far away, a siren wails.

Javad does not move. The air smells of melted plastic, acrid smoke, burnt flesh.

And then a black Ford Focus is screeching up onto the pavement right in front of where he's standing and four policemen are leaping out and running toward the bus. One policeman's helmet falls off as he runs. It drops to the pavement, bounces twice, rolls to a stop amid the twisted shards of metal, bits of paper, blue shreds of blown-up seats. The policeman does not turn back.

Suddenly everyone is running. People are stampeding down the street, streaming out of the British Medical Association building, hands pressed to their lips. The stone facade is splattered red with blood. A man with a TV camera on his shoulder is slowly turning in a circle, filming blind. Someone is shouting for people to move into the courtyard before more bombs go off.

Javad becomes dimly aware that his mobile is vibrating in his pocket. He pulls it out and tries to hear above the clamor, digging a finger into his other ear.

"Oh, thank god," Caroline says.

But she's not calling to check up on him. It's Amir she's trying to reach.

"How should I know?" he says. "I haven't seen him in the past two weeks."

"What are you talking about? I thought he was with you."

"I thought he was with *you*." A clanging fills his ears.

"Jesus fucking Christ."

The line cuts out. He tries to ring her back, but he can't get a signal now.

Two men struggle past, carrying a café table repurposed as a stretcher, a man in a gray business suit lying limp across the top. The man looks unscathed, and Javad wonders if he's suffered a blow to the head. But then he sees that both his legs have been blown off beneath the knees.

He tries texting Caroline, his fingers trembling, clumsy on the keys, but the message will not go through. The circuits must be jammed.

Somewhere nearby, a siren whoops.

A woman with a soot-black and bloodied face stumbles toward him. A man runs up and drapes a cloth over her shoulders. She is trembling, in shock. Javad crosses the street.

A woman comes out of the BMA house archway, her arms full of water bottles.

"I'm a doctor," he says. "How can I help?"

"Over there," the woman says, gesturing with her chin. There are bodies lying in the street. The police are cordoning off the square with yellow tape, pushing people back.

Where in god's name was Amir?

It is past noon by the time he finally makes it over to the Institute. Everyone is in the staff lounge, gathered around the TV. On the screen is the blown-up double-decker bus, empty now, looking like a broken toy. A banner scrolling across the bottom reads *Remain where you are. Do not travel.*

Li is hunched over his laptop at the table. "Now police say seven bombs," he reports. "Edgware Road. King's Cross. Liverpool Street. Russell Square. Aldgate East. Moorgate. Tavistock Square."

Seven bombs.

Evelyn, the secretary, hands him a cup of tea. "We were all so worried you were on the Tube," she says.

"I was," he says. "Fortunately, I was running late."

Somehow everyone in his lab has been accounted for. Everyone
is safe. Thank god. His hands tremble as he takes the tea. His hands.
He sets the cup down and goes over to the sink and washes them,
scrubbing at his nails. The water is hot. He lets it burn. He feels de-
tached from his body, light-headed with panic. Where was Amir?

On TV, the camera cuts to the G8 Summit up in Scotland, Tony
Blair on a podium, flanked by George Bush and Jacques Chirac.
Blair's mouth is moving. The closed captions read *It is reasonably
clear that there has been a series of terrorist attacks in London* . . . *All
leaders share our complete resolution to defeat terrorism* . . .

Lalitha is sniffling into Wolff-Dieter's broad Teutonic shoulder. Black rivulets of mascara smear her cheeks. "Who would do
such a thing?" she says.

Xiang Li glances up. "No one claims responsibility yet."

"Bastards," Wolff-Dieter says.

He turns back to the TV. The Metropolitan Police Commissioner, Sir Ian Blair, looks beleaguered. *We are working to return
order to the situation. The entire Underground and bus and train networks have been suspended. Millions of commuters are stranded in
Central London. The mobile phone network is overwhelmed.*

Javad stuffs his hand in his pocket, flips his mobile open and
shut. A helicopter is throbbing dully overhead. Out the window,
the view is the same as always: the chimneys and brick roof peaks
of the hospital, the green treetops of Queen Square.

There was no reason to think Amir would have been on the
Tube so early on a Thursday morning, Javad tells himself. There
was no reason for him to be in Bloomsbury over the summer
break, or for that matter anywhere near Edgware Road or Liverpool Street or King's Cross or Russell Square. The circuits were
just jammed. He was probably perfectly okay.

Behind him, voices rise and fall.

"Is your phone working yet?"

"Do you think it's Al Qaeda? Maybe it's a response to the
Olympic bid."

"Only four bombs, they're saying now. But there could be more to come."

Amir had said he was going to Caroline's. Surely he'd said that. Hadn't he?

Again Javad hears the front door slam. Again the floorboards shake.

Right, whatever, I won't be around.

They've been instructed to stay in place until the situation is secure. Javad goes into his office and shuts the door. He tries Amir's mobile again, but the call will not connect. He tries Caroline on her landline, but she does not pick up. He jiggles the mouse on his computer. The little rainbow wheel spins and spins. The BBC website will not refresh.

His desk is covered in piles of papers, printouts, scans. On top is a series of fMRI images of prefrontal cortices—Li's first few volunteers. He absently picks up the sheet. Reduced prefrontal cortex mass was linked to violent behavior, he thinks. What sort of person sets off bombs on public transport? Who would do such a horrific thing?

He has little faith that the police will identify the bombers any time soon. Three months on and they still hadn't worked out the identity of that poor bloke, the Piano Man. Of course, all sorts of people had thought they recognized him. People rang in claiming he was their next-door neighbor, their long-lost friend. A Danish woman even said on television that she thought he was her Algerian-born husband. Facial recognition was a complex process, involving visual perception, pattern recognition, expert discrimination, and long-term memory. It was prone to error. People were constantly seeing patterns in random data, or perceiving faces in random objects, like clouds or trees.

On top of the filing cabinet stands an old framed photograph of Amir at nine or ten in football kit—a fancy Barcelona jersey and silver Nike boots. Javad remembers him begging for those boots. Pricey buggers, they were, too, that he outgrew within the year. In the photograph, Amir's face is round and sweet. He hardly recognizes his features now.

Javad puts his head down on the desk. But the moment he shuts his eyes he is down again in that dark, hot, claustrophobic tunnel, picking his way along the tracks. Again there is that strange loud, whooshing pop, debris spraying through the air. Again, people are running, a helmet is dropping, a steel ribbon is twisting in the light. A man's legs have been sheared off below the knees. A woman with a bloodied face is shaking. Again he is tying tourniquets with tablecloths, splinting shattered limbs with two-by-fours and duct tape. Sirens screaming in the background. Alarm bells clanging in his brain.

He lifts his head and covers his face with his hands.

His son, his son.

Four bombs, one bus, three trains. His boy.

ESTHER

Until the phone rings in the early afternoon, she has no idea.

It's the Marie Curie nurse, Jane. She just woke up and saw it on TV. Hasn't Esther heard? Bombs in the Underground. Bombs on busses. Bombs on trains.

"Oh my god," Esther says.

"There's more than thirty dead, apparently, and hundreds, possibly even thousands, wounded! The city is completely shut down. It's absolutely horrific. An utter catastrophe."

"Oh my god. I had no idea."

"Nothing's running, and the public are being strongly advised to stay clear of Central London. So I'm stuck out in Bromley for the time being, I'm afraid. I'm terribly sorry. I'll be there tomorrow, if I can."

"Who did it? Al Qaeda?"

"They didn't say."

Esther pulls the phone over to the window. The street is quiet. Parked cars, a little drizzle. The sky is gray. Through the phone she can hear the faint sound of sirens on Jane's TV, as if the police cars and the fire trucks and ambulances were out in Kent instead of less than two miles from here.

"Right during rush hour, it was, too," Jane says. "Timed to cause maximum harm."

This was the world in which they now lived. Everything had changed.

Already she is counting, accounting, just like on that other day four years ago, the names clicking through her head: Zofia, Myrna, Vivian, Ruth, Phil, Javad, Amir. Her throat constricts.

"I'm sorry to leave you on your own tonight," Jane says. "I'll ring back if there's any change."

"Don't worry about us," Esther says. "Stay safe."

Upstairs in her mother's room, she turns on the TV, puts the sound on mute. It's the same on every channel, block letters on red banners across the bottom of the screen: *LIVE BREAKING NEWS, LONDON BLASTS*. Over and over, the images repeat. Flashing ambulances and fire trucks, streets cordoned off with barricades and caution tape, rescue workers in bulky trousers and yellow vests. Dazed survivors, their faces bloodied or black with soot. People being carried off on stretchers. Mangled subway cars. The exploded bus, its side panels bent back like wings.

Beyond it all, the towers burned. Smoke churned into the perfect blue.

Nothing will ever be the same.

That other day, they'd waited out in front of Noah's school in a crush of parents frantic on their cell phones, teachers waving clipboards, kids crowding onto the sidewalk, hugging and crying and holding hands. At last Noah had emerged at his usual slow, ambling pace, his hair combed across his forehead, his backpack on his shoulders, his clarinet case and lunchbox in his hands. He was in ninth grade. He'd just turned fourteen. He was old enough to understand but not yet old enough to imagine that a thing like this could actually touch him.

Aldgate, Liverpool Street, Edgware Road, King's Cross, Russell Square.

Russell Square. That was right where Javad worked.

She tries ringing his mobile, but the call will not connect. She tries again but gets nothing but a busy tone. Finally, she dashes outside and runs across and rings his bell. She presses her face against the glass. The interior is dark.

Just the other night, she lay there in the dark, her limbs entwined with his. His breath was soft in sleep, his face unguarded as a child's. She slipped out of bed and dressed. The cat brushed against her ankles and leapt up onto the bed. It curled up in the warm, wet spot she left behind.

There were eight million people in this city, she tells herself now. Only thirty-something dead. The odds were good. More than good. She tries to breathe.

All day long, her mother drifts in and out of sleep, oblivious to the disaster playing out on the city's streets. The end, the nurses say, is very near. Her mother's face is gaunt, the whites of her eyes stained yellow, her breathing erratic, strained. But still the blood flows through her veins, still her heart taps out its beat. Every time she opens her eyes, she gives Esther a startled look, as if she's surprised to find that she's still there.

Esther turns her mother from one side onto the other, changes the bed pad, sponges her off and checks for pressure sores, applies glycerin to her lips, administers her meds. The bedside table is piled with pill packets, boxes of latex gloves, tissues, wet wipes, syringes, tubes of cream. She wouldn't have thought she could manage this, just a few weeks back. But none of it bothers her now.

From time to time, the telephone rings, and Esther's heart flips. But it's just Ruth, then Myrna, making sure that she's all right. Of course she's all right, she says. She hasn't even left the house. She never goes anywhere, anyway.

That other day, there had been a stream of calls and emails as well, many from people she hadn't heard from in years, wanting to make sure they were safe. It was kind of them to call, but she wanted to tell them that she was much more likely to die of cancer or get run over by a bus than to have been in the World Trade Center that day. She lived and worked uptown; she hadn't been south of Canal Street in ages, maybe years. Still, they were close. They could hear the sirens. They could smell the burning in the air.

Everybody had their near-miss story. Gil's younger brother, who had an office in the South Tower, had flown out the day before for a conference in L.A. Esther's college roommate had just stepped off the PATH. The cousin of one of the doormen in her building, a security guard, had called in sick that day. Of course, some were not so lucky. The father of one of Noah's classmates had gone to work as usual and was at his desk on the 102nd floor of One World Trade when the first plane hit. The odds were always in your favor until they weren't. Some people called it luck. Some called it fate.

She keeps the radio on all day in the kitchen, the TV on upstairs. Grave reporters and officials offer the same formulaic sound bites again and again. Already the attacks have their own logo, their own theme song and sound effects. By late afternoon, four attacks have been confirmed: one on a Metropolitan line train at Aldgate, one on a Circle line train between Paddington and Edgware Road, one on a Piccadilly line train between King's Cross and Russell Square, and one on a Number 30 bus at Tavistock Square. By early evening, the BBC is reporting thirty-seven verified fatalities, more than three hundred injured and hospitalized, hundreds more "walking wounded" wandering the streets. It is apparent that it was a coordinated terrorist attack. A group affiliated with Al Qaeda may have claimed responsibility. CCTV footage is being studied by the police.

Esther leans back and shuts her eyes. Her temples throb. She would like to beam herself somewhere the hatred could not reach. But it was everywhere, bubbling like magma beneath the earth's mantle, pressure building at the seams. There were those who said America had had it coming, that bullies had to pay the price. This

was payback for Kandahar and Tora Bora, Fallujah and Najaf,
Guantanamo and Abu Ghraib. Retribution for the materialism,
the hedonism, the blithe cultural imperialism, the arrogance of
the West. And hadn't she too been caught up with the rest of them
in that end-of-century surge of hedge fund wealth and dotcom
speculation, that blinkered optimistic swell? It had felt like prog-
ress, then. The rich cigar-and-martini bankers growing richer,
the great slick cities getting slicker, the Dow soaring, mortgage
rates falling, the old communist empires collapsing, peace breaking out in places like Belfast and the West Bank. Swords were
being beaten into ploughshares! They thought they'd left their
parents' bloody century far behind.

But it was still there, all along, just beneath the surface—the
seismic fault of hate.

When she hears from Javad at last, it's late. He has had to walk all
the way home from Bloomsbury. She is so relieved that she can
hardly speak.

He tells her about the Tube, the bus. About Amir.

His voice is flat. "I don't know where he could be."

There's a buzzing in her ears, a swarm of fear. "Come over,"
she says.

"I'm absolutely knackered."

"You shouldn't be alone. Not now. Come on, I'll make you
something to eat."

It is more than an hour before he shows up. He has taken a
shower, changed into jeans. His hair is wet. He has been trying
to ring through to the emergency helpline, he says. He follows
her into the kitchen. She sweeps the newspapers to the side of the
table and gestures to a seat.

"What can I get you?"

"Maybe just a cup of tea. I haven't got much of an appetite,
I'm afraid." He takes his phone out of his pocket and sets it before

him on the table. He rests his forehead on his hands. "I just can't imagine where he could be."

"He's probably just stranded somewhere, like everybody else," she says.

"He could still ring."

"Maybe his battery is dead."

He pushes up his glasses and rubs the bridge of his nose. "We had our little tiff and he stomped off and I thought, right, that's it then, he's gone back to his mum's. And here I was, feeling guilty that he was nursing her and her broken ankle instead of being off on holiday with me. And it turns out he only stayed a couple days and then took off! It's been well over a week, and no one has a clue as to where he could be. And now, nothing, not a peep. You'd think, at a time like this, he'd ring, just to say that he's all right. Unless—"

"Javad, don't."

The electric kettle puffs out steam. She pours the tea and comes to sit.

"It's not like him," he says. "He's never done anything like this. He's not that sort of kid." He takes a breath, looks down at the silent phone, the untouched cup of tea. "I went into his room the other day," he says. "I'm ashamed to say it—I had a bit of a snoop. There were all these weird photographs on his laptop . . . dilapidated buildings, tunnels, what seemed to be building sites . . . some of the images looked like the Underground, others seemed to have been taken from a great height. And then on his desk, he's got all these books on Islam, Arabic grammars, flyers for political protest marches. The Qur'an. I don't know what to make of it." His eyes are clouded with pain. "The truth is I don't know him. I don't know what he gets up to, who he hangs around with. I don't know anything at all."

She crosses her arms and presses them into her stomach. "What does his mother think?"

His jaw tightens. "Who knows? Half the time she's drunk."

"I'm sorry. I didn't know."

He picks up the teacup, then sets it down again without drinking. "You know, when he was small, he used to beg me to let him come and live with me. I had him only every other weekend. I could have taken her to court, tried to overturn the custody decree. He begged me. But I was selfish. I didn't know how I'd manage with a child all on my own. I worried about my career. And she was desperate, absolutely desperate, to keep him. He seemed to cope all right. He *has* coped all right. Or so I thought." He exhales a shuddering breath. "I should have fought harder for him. It was a mistake."

"It's not your fault."

"I don't know." He picks up the phone and flips it open and shut, as if willing it to ring.

"You can't blame yourself. Trust me, I know."

His face constricts. "I'm sorry. I didn't——"

She pushes her chair back. "Please let me get you something to eat. You must be starving."

"No, really, I can't."

"Are you sure? Have you eaten anything today? I've got cheese, grapes, coffee cake, eggs, soup . . ."

"I'd better be getting back," he says, standing. "Just in case."

She stands as well. "I wish I could come with you."

"I know you can't. I understand."

She wraps her arms around him and presses her face into his chest and breathes in his shirt's starchy, laundered smell. She can feel his heart pulsing behind his ribs. Was it really just the other night that they'd had sex? Things were only just beginning—and now this. She clings to him even as she feels his grip release. She wishes there were something she could do. But she can only cross her fingers, hold her thumbs, pray to a god she does not believe exists.

"Let me know if you hear anything," she says into his shoulder. "Please."

"Okay."

"No matter how late it is." She steps back and looks at him. "You won't wake me up. Since Jane's not here, I'm sure I won't sleep at all tonight."

He nods.

"Promise?"

He tries to smile. "Yes."

She sits beside her mother's bed, the TV on, the volume low. Her mother's chest is pumping like a bellows. In and out, in and out. It is hard labor, dying. Just like birth. Abruptly, all movement stops. Esther waits. Nothing. Every time this happens, she panics and thinks, *this is it*. But then her mother gasps and shudders and the shallow, raspy breaths start up again. Her ribcage rises and falls, her mouth agape. Cheyne-Stokes breathing, it is called, the nurses said. It is quite common at the end. Yet another normal, abnormal thing.

"She's a stubborn one," Jane said. "She must be waiting for something."

"The other day I could have sworn she kept saying 'I'm sorry.' I don't know who she imagined she was talking to."

"Sometimes they do that," Jane said. "They're waiting to set the past in order so they can move on."

Esther just prays it's not tonight.

The *News at Ten* is given over exclusively to the bombings. There are more eyewitness reports from shell-shocked survivors with blackened clothes and bloody, lacerated skin. More images of the blown-up bus cordoned off with caution tape. Blurry cell phone photographs of the mangled, smoke-filled trains. Hundreds of people still missing. Rescue efforts are being hampered by the toxic dust and heat. Clearing the deep Underground tunnels of all the bodies could take days.

Please don't let Amir be lost down in that hell, she prays. Please, please, please.

She remembers little now of those awful hours of limbo between the sergeant's phone call and the confirmation, squawking over the squad car radio from the search crews down the river, that her son was dead. She'd stood there at the pullout. Down the gorge the green-flecked water spilled. Her teeth chattered and her knees shook. Possibilities swung back and forth, like saloon doors. Nothing had happened. The worst had happened. Her son was fine. Her son was dead. Marcie Ellis, her voice high and false with guilty relief that her sons were not the ones gone missing, had said, "I'm sure everything will be okay." It was a lie. Everything had already, irrevocably, changed.

She looks over now at her mother's purple eyelids, her cracked, pale lips, the loose cords of mottled yellow skin. It was just a body like all those other bodies. Skin and bone and blood and piss and shit. The body, her mother had once told her long ago when she was little, was like a suit of clothes. Eventually, after many years, you got tired of it and didn't want it any more. After that she'd imagined old people unzipping their wrinkled skins and casting them aside like the blown cocoons she'd sometimes find in spring, stuck to the underside of a broad leaf. This body was not her mother. Her mother was already gone.

On TV, Ken Livingstone is at the mic. *We will not be afraid, intimidated, or cowed by this cowardly act of terrorism.* Citizens are being urged to be vigilant. Muslims are being advised for the time being to stay off the streets.

Emergency telephone numbers scroll across the bottom of the screen. One 0800 number is the Missing Persons Helpline. Another 0800 number is the Anti-Terrorist Hotline. *Anyone*

*with any information whatsoever in connection to the bombings
should call the intelligence investigation line immediately.*

Now, amid the worry, sounds a higher, sharper drone of fear.
Javad's words from earlier ricochet inside her head. What did any
of it mean? Those photographs on the computer, the Tube, that
first late night, the Qur'an, the mosque. Pattern or coincidence?
How could you tell?

You couldn't know anybody, really.

She should know that by now.

The TV flickers in the darkness. The 0800 numbers scroll
across the bottom of the screen. Her cell phone lies beside her on
the bedside table. She wishes Javad would call. If only he would
say, *He's back, he's safe, everything's all right.* But a sinkhole has
opened up inside her and hope has fallen in.

On TV, the police commissioner is speaking. *The most important thing is we need the community's help. They always come up
trumps giving us information.*

What had happened to Amir?

Beside her, her mother continues to breathe erratically. A gasp.
A long pause. Another breath.

The buzzing swarm inside her head is growing louder. Again
she is following Amir down the steep, rumbling escalators at
Warren Street onto the Tube. Again she is standing outside the
Finsbury Park Tube station, scanning the empty street. Again she
sees those mud-caked boots, that cap pulled low, those eyes.

The look he gave her now feels like a warning: *Don't you dare
say a word.*

What does she know?

She is afraid of what will happen if she speaks. She is afraid of
what will happen if she does not. The details flap and swirl like
swifts.

She reaches over for her phone and taps in the number of the
Anti-Terrorist Hotline. The screen glows bright blue in the dark.

She takes a breath and presses *Talk.*

JAVAD

He spends the night in front of the computer, clicking between the news and message boards and back to email again. He checks his mobile. He paces. He passes the closed door to his son's room, does not go in. He takes off his clothes and lies down on the bed, but his perseverating mind just races, chasing away sleep, running over and over the things he knows, or thought he did: that his son hardly ever got up that early in the morning, that he had no reason to be anywhere near Central London now that term was out, that he was a sensible, good kid. But above it all, the questions keep circling like buzzards. Where is he? Why doesn't he call? Where has he been?

Near dawn, unable to stand it any longer, he throws on his clothes and leaves the house. The early morning air is cool, the streets quiet, as if nothing has happened. A frayed moon hangs low over the London rooftops. Delivery vans are unloading. A street sweeper chugs past. How could the daily business of the world be going on at a time like this? Overhead, a plane blinks along the flight path to Heathrow.

He walks fast, aimlessly, in a white fog of fear. The words *missing* beat inside his head. Hands in his pockets, he flips his silent phone open and shut. The streets seem strange, as if all the familiar landmarks have been erased. He registers only disconnected elements: brick, glass, stone, concrete. A lamppost, a phone box, a plane tree, a shop window, a sign marked with letters he cannot understand.

A fortnight ago, they'd quarreled. Over what? Over money. Over nothing. Over a stupid comment—a joke. He would take his words back in an instant if he could.

He looks up at the empty sky. He will be more generous in the future, he vows. He will be more patient, more understanding, less caught up in his work. He will do anything it takes.

The boy had stomped upstairs; the door had slammed. He'd gone off to his mother's, Javad assumed. It was a reasonable assumption. She was laid up with a broken ankle. She needed him there—she'd practically begged. But when Niels returned at the weekend, Amir had taken off. Where had he gone? Back home, Caroline had assumed. It was a reasonable assumption too. Why would she have thought to check?

Neither of them had a bloody clue.

He thinks of the little boy in the photograph in Caroline's collage, running away along the white-foam line left by the waves along the Margate sand. If he looked closely, in the far corner of the image he could see faint traces of what must have been his own footprints in the sand. So long ago. If only he could take that moment back.

In the photograph he'd seen on Esther's mother's chest of drawers, her son had the open, guileless, faintly freckled face of a boy who hadn't hit his growth spurt yet. He looked like her, especially about the eyes. A terrible thing, he'd thought then, looking at the photograph, the missing pieces of her story clicking into place. The worst. He couldn't fathom how one went on after such a loss, how one could bear that kind of grief.

It had bothered him, at first, that she hadn't told him, although he understood. It threw everything he'd thought he knew about her in a different light. But mostly, it was tenderness that he felt.

He had wanted to make it better, to hold her and tell her everything would be all right.

It was a bad omen, he thinks now, then feels ashamed. He is as bad as his old superstitious grandmother, dangling blue amulets and burning *esfand* to ward off the evil eye. It wasn't as if bad luck were a communicable disease. But right now the thought is more than he can stand.

You can't blame yourself, she'd said. But of course he did. If only they'd gone on holiday, as he'd originally planned, they'd be together right this moment, gazing out at the blue Aegean from some idyllic isle. But he hadn't done it. He'd chosen to be with Esther instead. He was a fool.

Caroline glares at him from across her kitchen table, her broken foot in its pink cast propped on a chair. Her short blond hair is disheveled, and she is still in her dressing gown even though it's nearly night. He has gone over there in hopes that she might be able to provide the names or phone numbers of Amir's friends—some kind of clue—but he should have known better. She's no use. All they can do is sit and wait. Their phones lie inert between them on the table. No calls, no texts.

Sky News is playing on a little flat-screen TV suspended above the sleek quartz countertop. Niels leans back in his chair, watching the TV. His longish hair is combed back from a high forehead, and he is wearing an expensive gray linen shirt and black, expensive jeans. Dutch, not Swedish, Javad reminds himself.

There is no new news. They have heard it all already many times, and yet they cannot turn away. Most overground trains and bus services are back up and running, but there will be no Underground service on the Circle line or the Hammersmith and City lines for several days at least. King's Cross Station will remain closed indefinitely too. The camera zooms in on the pop-up shrines that have appeared at the sites of all the bombings: bouquets of wilted flowers, candles, stuffed animals, hand-lettered notes and signs. Pictures of the missing. The numbers have gone up again. More than seven hundred injured. More than fifty dead.

Niels turns to him. "Where were you yesterday? Did you get caught in all the mess?"

In all his worry about Amir, Javad has hardly thought of his own near miss. It seems irrelevant, even self-indulgent, to speak about it now. Besides, he doesn't want to think about those claustrophobic minutes down in the tunnel, stopped dead in darkness—the crackling announcements, the dark trek out along the tracks, the throngs at Euston Square. He doesn't want to think about the exploded bus, the black and bloodied faces, the blown-off limbs. He wonders if those images will ever leave him. Trauma, he is well aware, like history, repeats.

"I was on the Tube, actually, when it happened," he says. "We got held up just out of Great Portland Street. They evacuated us through the tunnel to Euston Square."

"You didn't tell me that," Caroline says.

He looks away. "You didn't ask."

"You're a lucky man," Niels says.

Caroline's mobile phone lights up, vibrating as it bleeps. Across the table, their eyes meet and freeze. For a long moment, neither of them moves. Then she reaches forward and picks it up.

Alarm sirens are shrieking. He can't breathe.

"Hallo?" she says.

He waits, straightjacketed in fear.

Her eyes grow wide. "Oh my god, Amir!"

For a moment, he is afraid he hasn't heard her right. Then she says the name again and relief floods in. Thank god. Not dead. It's him.

And then he and Niels are on their feet and shouting questions, but Caroline just keeps saying "oh my god" and waving them away with her free hand. Finally, she sets down the phone. Her eyes are red and wet.

"What happened? Where is he? Is he all right?"

She nods, then shakes her head. "He's been arrested," she says.

Javad spends the rest of the night and all the next morning placing fruitless calls. His solicitor, Charles, still has not responded. The bugger was probably off playing golf. Javad leaves yet another message and hangs up. Nothing ever gets done at the weekend. He sits at the computer, trying different combinations of search terms: *arrested, custody, rights*.

His efforts are interrupted by a rapping at his door. A loud, sharp *rat-a-tat*. He has a bad feeling even before he opens it and sees the two police officers in their black uniforms and white shirts and peaked caps. A police car is double parked in front of the house, bright blue lights flashing, blocking half the street. His first irrational thought is that Amir is dead. His second thought is that he too is under arrest. His heart knocks against his ribs.

"Mr. Javad Asghari?" the taller of the two constable says, looking down at his clipboard. He pronounces the words slowly, flattening the vowels with the confused distaste reserved for a foreign name.

"Yes. It's Dr., actually."

"Right. We need to have a word."

Javad steps aside and lets them in. The constables' expressions are flat and grim. It's clear from the start that this it is not a polite inquiry but an inquisition. The taller officer does most of the talking. He has thin lips, a beefy face. The shorter cop looks on, pen poised. From time to time, his walkie-talkie squawks like a parrot on his chest. When exactly was Javad last in contact with his son? What was his son studying, what were his politics, what

were his beliefs? Had he traveled recently to the Middle East? Did
he still have relatives in Iran? Was he in contact with them? What
did Javad know about his son's activities at the Finsbury Park
mosque? What was his relationship with the youth groups there?
What was he doing in King's Cross Station early in the morning
of July the second?

Javad tries to hold his voice steady. "Why have you arrested
my son?"

"Please answer the question, Mr. Asghari."

"Look, I don't know what you're playing at, but this is all a big
mistake."

The policemen shake their heads. There was no mistake. They
had it on closed-circuit TV.

He stands by, helpless, as they rifle through the contents of
Amir's drawers, turn over every object on his desk. They confis-
cate a flash drive, a stack of notebooks, a map of London, the leaf-
let for the protest march, a broken radio scanner, the paperback
Qur'an. They seize Javad's computer from his office and a jug
of hydrogen peroxide from the cupboard beneath the bathroom
sink. They pull the SIM card out of his mobile phone. They shove
the lot into plastic bags and haul them out to the police car.

The street is quiet, watching. His neighbors are probably wondering what terrible thing he has done. Opposite, someone has set
out planters of geraniums on a second-story balcony, a flare of
red. The blue strobe lights of the squad car flash. The officers get
in and slam the doors and drive away.

Back inside, Javad pours himself a glass of Scotch even though
it's not yet noon. His hands are shaking. Jesus. He feels filthy,
flayed. He reaches into his pocket for his phone, then remembers
that it's dead.

His head is filled with static, like a TV station gone off air.
They said they'd identified Amir on CCTV, at the Finsbury

Park mosque, at King's Cross. What the hell was he doing there?

It was all a misunderstanding. A terrible mistake. It had to be.

The relief he'd felt after Amir's phone call the day before has crystallized into an icy rime of fear. They must think Amir had played some role in the bombings. Under the Terrorism Act, suspects could be held in custody without charge for up to fourteen days. The bags of evidence they'd just seized would be used to build their case.

Good god. It couldn't be.

But the brain, as he knows well, was hardwired for prejudice and suspicion. Human beings were predisposed to perceiving meaning in coincidence, to seeing outsiders as threats. And he was an outsider. A foreigner with a hard-to-pronounce name—worse, a Muslim from the Middle East. The fact that his son was born in London of an English mother didn't matter. People looked at blokes like them and they saw what they expected to see.

He knocks back the Scotch and lies down on the sofa. Anger swirls inside him, hot and red. This was London, not Tehran, he tells himself. This was a democracy, governed by the rule of law.

But who was to say such things couldn't happen here? Human beings were human beings. Bad things could happen anywhere.

He was already in England when they came to arrest his father in Tehran. Javad had spoken to him on the telephone the previous week. The line was poor. His father's voice was hoarse and flat. The Shah was dead. The universities had been shut down. The war against Saddam Hussein would never end. "I didn't think that it would come to this," his father said.

That was the last time he heard his father's voice. Security agents came to the door the following Tuesday at 5:00 a.m. They blindfolded his father and pushed him into an unmarked car and drove away. His precise and gentle father, the engineer. There were no charges, no trial. He just disappeared. Everybody knew what that meant. Everybody knew the grim hulk of the Evin

Prison, had seen the rows of bodies hanging from makeshift gallows rigged from mobile cranes.

The sound of hammering jolts him awake. He moves too fast, without thinking, jerking forward, and his lumbar seizes with a searing wrench of pain.

Shit. His goddamn back.

The hammering stops, then starts up again. Not hammering, knocking. Someone is at the door. What now? Anger flares above the pain.

He staggers up and hobbles to the door. Clenching pain radiates along his spine, through his pelvis, down his leg. A muscle spasm pressing on a nerve. This wasn't good.

It's Esther. Her hair is loose around her face, tired circles beneath her eyes.

"Please," he says, "come in."

"I can only stay for a moment," she says. "I saw the police and— I wanted to see if—" She frowns. "Are you okay?

He grimaces. "I've just thrown out my back, I'm afraid."

"I've been calling and calling, but you didn't pick up."

"I know. I'm sorry. They took away my SIM card."

"Who? What?"

"The police. They searched the house. Amir has been arrested, it seems."

She presses her hands to her mouth, her eyes growing wide. "Oh! I was so worried! I thought—when you didn't call—"

"I know. We finally heard from him last night. I'm sorry—I should have rung to tell you—"

"What happened?"

"I don't know." He digs his hands into his back. "They said just now that they had footage of him on CCTV at Finsbury Park and King's Cross. I don't know what that's about. I don't know what's going on." The pain is searing, deep. He needs to lie down.

He needs to get hold of his bloody solicitor, get his son released.

"I'm so sorry," she says. She has an odd expression on her face—one he can't quite read.

He feigns a shrug. "We'll sort things out."

She is backing up. "I'm so sorry—" Still that odd look. "I have to get back—my mother—"

"I understand."

Her eyes are shining as she turns away.

SEVEN

ESTHER

Her mother dies on Sunday. It is three days after the bombings, July the tenth, three years to the day since Noah's death. A black day. Jane says her mother's soul must be meeting up with Noah's up in heaven, but Esther has no faith. At least this time she is prepared. She has been holding vigil since the night before when Jane came in and touched her shoulder and said, "It's time." Out the window, there was just the grayest veil of light.

She sat with Jane beside her mother's bed and waited. She held her mother's hand. It was cold and mottled purple blue. Her face was a yellow, wrinkled, shrunken mask. Her lips were bluish gray. She was breathing in the shallow and erratic pattern of the dying, as she had been for the last several days. At last she exhaled a long and jagged breath and seemed to hold it, and they waited, holding their breaths too, and then Jane took her mother's wrist between her fingers and counted, and then she said that she was gone.

Gone, through that porous membrane. Out of time.

Downstairs, now, Zofia is talking on the phone in her lilting Polish voice. She is taking care of the death certificate and registration. She is ringing the Burial Office at the synagogue. Arrangements are being made.

Jane has covered the body with a sheet. It must not be left alone, according to Jewish law. Esther stands at the bedroom window.

The sound of hammering reverberates across the street. Work continued. Life went on. The sunlight brightens, then dims. It is chilly, or maybe it is only her fatigue. The stilled fan sits on the chair, a copy of last Friday's *Evening Standard* tucked behind its rusty cage. Jane must have left it there. *Terror Attacks: Pictures of the Missing*, the headline reads. Even now, three days later, bodies were still being pulled from the wreckage of the exploded trains.

Thank god Amir was not among them. But what had he done? He must have done something—he was in jail. What had *she* done? What would happen to him now? Her stomach twists beneath an acid wash of guilt and shame.

She had followed him that day to Finsbury Park the way you followed someone in a dream: semiconscious, blind. She'd followed him as if he could lead her into that other underworld where the lost and missing dwelt.

As if he could lead her to her son.

Jane enters the bedroom and sets down a tray with a rack of toast and a pot of tea. "Here you are, then," she says. "You must eat."

"I'll try," Esther says.

"Are you all right?"

"It hasn't really sunk in yet."

"It takes time," Jane says.

"Oh, I know. Believe me."

Jane smiles gently. "She's in a better place."

"You think?"

"I do, yes."

"I wish I did."

Jane folds her into a hug. She feels soft and smells of lavender and bleach. Esther doesn't want her to leave.

A weight of exhaustion drops over her. Her skull feels welded tight. The interment has been scheduled for tomorrow. A funeral home van is on the way. She'll need to notify Myrna,

Vivian, Ruth. She should call Gil, too. She wonders if he'll go out today to visit Noah's grave in Queens. These past two years, she hadn't gone with him. Wherever Noah was, she felt, it wasn't there.

She turns back to the window. The Byzantines found comfort, she supposes, in their golden angels with their placid, somber faces, their golden-haloed heads. The Hasidim imagined side-curled rabbis dancing in Messianic ecstasy with the risen dead. Muslims dreamed of shahids languishing in Paradise, sloe-eyed houris feeding them pomegranates and grapes. It was the same old story, whichever version you believed. But she believes in nothing. You just stop being—that is it.

Her mother's body is a rigid hump beneath the sheet. What is a body? Just minerals and water, atoms of carbon, oxygen, hydrogen, nitrogen. Traces of copper, cobalt, iron, zinc. It is the stuff that everything in the universe is made of, indistinguishable from the stars, the earth.

In the cemetery at Willesden, she stands by as the casket is lowered into the open grave. They are a small group, just her mother's few remaining friends. They bend and toss handfuls of dirt into the grave as the rabbi chants the Kaddish. The dirt is damp and black. She wipes her hand off on her skirt. The sun is hot. Sweat beads across Ruth's husband Gerry's bald head. Myrna fans herself with her hat. Sunlight reflects off the polished headstones. Esther fingers the strand of pearls around her neck. Her mother's pearls. Esther will wear them now to keep them alive and lustrous against her skin.

"Good thing the plot isn't over in West Ham," Gerry huffs as they file back to the car park. "Eighty-seven graves were desecrated there the other day. The thugs pushed over and broke the headstones. They even tried to kick in the door to the Rothschild mausoleum. Spray-painted a swastika on the side."

"Despicable," mutters Vivian's husband Joseph, a gray-bearded gnome of a man.

"Gerry, not now," says Ruth.

Gerry ignores her. "Do you know how many anti-Semitic incidents there have been here in England so far this year?"

"Spare us, Gerry, please," Ruth says.

Gerry ignores her. "Five hundred and thirty-two. Can you believe it?"

Joseph pushes out his lower lip. "Despicable," he repeats.

"That's nearly two hate crimes per day," says Gerry. "But you wouldn't know it from reading the papers, would you?"

Their shoes crunch along the gravel path. Rows of headstones stretch to either side. She squints at the familiar Jewish names: *Meyer, Marcus, Levy, Adler, Woolf.* Were things really as bad as these old men feared?

She thinks of her clever, crooked father, always trying to finagle things the way he'd done during the war. When people looked at him, what did they see? Did they see Shylock, Barabbas, another Fagin? Did they see the hook-nosed, crafty-eyed Eternal Jew?

Ruth is at her elbow, Myrna on the other side. They are going on about bringing over food and keeping her company during the coming week.

"I'm not sitting shiva," Esther says.

"How long will you be staying on in London?" Myrna asks.

"Myrna, really," Ruth says. "It's much too soon for her to know, I'm sure."

"I should have thought she'd want to get away as soon as possible, after the events of this past week," Myrna says.

They talk about as if she isn't there, as if she has already gone.

What should she do? Was it really just last week that she'd told Javad she might stay? Oh, Javad, she thinks. How could she ever face him now?

That night, she had lain there in Javad's bed for a long time, watching him sleep. Her head rested on his shoulder, their legs entwined. His breath was soft and shallow. His lashes curled against his cheeks. She ran her fingertip along his stubbled jaw, along the crease that framed the tragus of his ear, his tender lower lip. He was beautiful. He was a stranger. She shifted her legs out from between his. He stirred and turned, his eyes still closed, and kissed her. "Don't go," he whispered. "Don't ever leave."

For one brief moment, it had all seemed possible. The three of them, a family.

Now everything was ruined. Everything was blown to bits.

After the funeral, alone in the house for the first time in nearly fourteen weeks, she pulls back the curtains and throws open the windows, lets out the smells of medicine and death. In the grip of a surge of energy born of exhaustion, she clears away the dirty dishes and bottles and packets of pills, the oxygen tank and cannula and plastic mask, the used-up morphine syringes, the tubes of ointment and cream. Bach is playing on Radio 3. A fugue. She turns the volume up. The music swirls and swells. The voices intertwine, repeat.

She strips the bed, bundles up the sheets, and stuffs them outside in the rubbish bin. She sits down on the top step, shakes out a cigarette, and puts it to her lips, but does not light it. She will quit now, she thinks.

It has clouded in. The sky is a field of rippled gray. The air smells faintly of the sea. A memory rises to the surface, a memory from the time before America, before her father's death, when it was still the three of them, a family. They were driving down to the seaside from the city, her father at the wheel, the smoke of his Rothmans mingling with the smells of motorway exhaust and the musky rapeseed fields. She bounced on the back seat, excited, counting number plates. She must have been seven or eight. In front of her, her mother reached across the seat and rubbed the back of her father's neck, tracing the protrusions of his vertebrae, the follicles and moles. A private smile turned up the corners of her lips. Her father kept his gaze fixed on the road, his cigarette tipped out the open window, his other hand loose atop the wheel.

She remembers kicking off her shoes and running to touch the water. Where were they? Somewhere like Margate or Weymouth or Poole. The tide was out. The sand was smooth and flat, marked with the faint claw prints of crabs and birds, the sky the palest watercolor wash of blue. Gulls were reeling overhead. She had not understood until that moment that England really was an island, surrounded by the sea. Of course, it was only the English Channel; the coast of France was not even fifty miles away. But she didn't know that then.

How many had fled, like her parents, to the shores of this green isle? She pictures them approaching—Romans, Angles, Saxons, Normans, South Asians, Eastern Europeans, Muslims, Jews. A line of black dots slowly growing larger: a flotilla of invaders, opportunists, asylum seekers, refugees. The headlands rise out of the mist. Did they find what they were searching for? They should have listened to the ancient Greeks, who understood the beguilement of islands, the fickleness of the sea.

The next thing she knew, her father had grabbed her mother by the wrist and was pulling her toward the water's edge. Come on, Lonia! he was shouting. You can't come to the seaside and not even get your feet wet! Her mother was squealing and pulling back, trying to wedge her heels into the sand, crying, Stop it, Isaac, I mean it, stop! You know that I can't swim! They wrestled and splashed through the shallow water, her mother's rolled-up trousers turning dark and wet as she pulled free and lunged away, her father kicking water at her in great shining sheets, until he stumbled and lost his balance and went down into the little waves, and then she was laughing or crying and running back and he was yelling *Scheiße*! trying to stand, droplets of water flying from his hair.

She remembers standing there, rooted in a kind of fascinated fear, until she worked out that they were not struggling any longer but embracing, her father pinioning her mother's arms behind her back with one hand, the other hand behind her neck, pulling her lips to his, and they were kissing, up to their knees in sea-water, dripping wet in all their clothes, twined like the caduceus's twin snakes, the familiar turned dangerous and strange.

He saved my life, her mother always said.

She misses them. She misses the child she used to be.

Something rubs against her ankles. It's Javad's gray cat. She crouches down and rubs her fingers along the silky fur between its ears. It purrs and doesn't run away.

The story breaks the following day. In her mother's bedroom, Esther clicks on the TV. The identities of four suicide bombers have been confirmed. Raids in West Yorkshire have been carried out by the police. Blurry CCTV images show four figures entering the Luton train station, heading toward the platform for the Thameslink train that would take them to King's Cross. Four boys with dark hair, black T-shirts, backpacks, jeans. British boys. *Homegrown radicals.* The oldest was thirty, the youngest was nineteen. Shehzad Tanweer, Mohammad Sidique Khan, Germaine Lindsay, Hasib Hussain.

The driver's license mug shot of Hussain, the youngest bomber, shows a dogged, loyal face with small black eyes, a broad nose, an adolescent scruff of beard. His license was recovered from the wreckage of the Number 30 bus at Tavistock Square. When Hussain's mother rang the helpline to report him missing, the identification was made.

Esther takes a step backward and sits down on the edge of the bare mattress. She can scarcely breathe. How was it possible for an ID card to survive a blast like that intact when so many were dead? The absurdity of the detail jangles like an out of tune note.

She puts her hands over her face and starts to weep. Four boys from West Yorkshire had blown themselves up. Four boys were dead. They had done this. Not Amir.

It is the first time she has cried since her mother's death, the first time she has cried in all these weeks. Great waves roil up from deep inside her, raw and wracked. She sobs so hard her chest aches. She could not have said why she is crying, but she cannot stop. She is crying for Amir, locked away in jail. It was her fault, her terrible mistake. She is crying for those four boys and for her boy and for all the lost boys, everywhere and in all time, for the dead boys and for their mothers and fathers who would miss them forever, despite everything they did, for the yearning that will never cease. She is crying for herself. She sobs and sobs. She pulls her knees into her chest and rolls over on the mattress and cries until she is empty, turned inside out, a hollow gourd, her eyes burning and swollen, her throat raw, until she falls asleep.

AMIR

The walls of the cell are stained brown as nicotine, the floor a vinyl slab. A bare bulb hanging from the high concrete ceiling casts a sallow glare. The low shelf bunk is covered with a thin plastic pad. Pipes hiss beneath the bunk, too hot to touch even in the July heat. The open toilet reeks. The only window is a tiny Plexiglas peephole in the door. The door is two inches thick. They've confiscated his rucksack, his iPod, his wallet, his belt, his shoes, his phone.

The lights never go out. There is no way to tell if it is day or night. The silence swells. He wedges the bog roll beneath his head for a pillow, but still he cannot sleep. He counts the filthy tiles that line the walls, gets nearly to one hundred, loses track, starts again. He stands up and paces out the area of the cell. Barely twelve-foot square.

There's nothing to do, not even a magazine to read. Time has stopped. He tries to remember stuff he memorized in school: capital cities of Europe, Latin conjugations, the genealogies of the kings of England (he still gets all the Henrys and the Edwards bolloxed up). He tried to recite his favorite football team rosters, the playlists on his iPod. Panic sirens inside his head. In places like this, he knows, people go mad.

In his memory, he revisits the places they've explored: sewers and the drains, an abandoned asylum out in Surrey, the Pimlico steam tunnel, the disused platform at King's Cross. How easily they'd trespassed. How easily they'd crossed the line. Now he's crossed the other way. His grandfather died in prison in Tehran. The fact of it had been nothing but an abstract concept until now.

They arrested him when he got back to London. It was the day after the attacks. The whole transport system was still in chaos, security on high alert. The cops surrounded him as he stepped off the train onto the platform. They cuffed his hands with tight plastic ties behind his back. They emptied the contents of his pockets into their helmets and patted him down, loosening his belt. One of the policemen took his rucksack and disappeared.

"We're doing this for your own safety," a cop with a South London accent said.

There was nothing but dirty clothes and climbing gear inside that rucksack. "I didn't do anything!" he said.

Then they took him by the elbows and marched him out of the station and into a police van and dumped him out at Paddington Green.

In the custody suite, he filled in forms. Polaroids were taken; his right hand was washed and his fingertips dipped in grease and pressed onto a glass-topped scanner. His heart clenched like a fist. He had a right to a solicitor, didn't he? A right to make a phone call to let someone know that he was here? The custody sergeant laughed. "Open up, mate," he said, swabbing DNA from the inside of his cheeks.

He'd gone up north to Yorkshire with Bigsby—a spur-of-the-moment trip. He was still pissed off at his parents, tired of sleeping on grotty couches, ready for a change of pace. Miranda was busy at work; Mole had gone off to explore the Paris sewers with some froggy friends. So when Bigsby proposed a laddered-up one-hundred-footer at the top of Farsley, he agreed. They hopped on a train to Leeds.

The countryside blurred past the rain-smeared windows of the carriage. The drab backs of buildings gave way to wooded stretches interspersed by rolling fields studded with golden wheels of hay. Bigsby pulled out a paperback Baudrillard and read. Amir put his feet up on the facing seat and let the rocking of the train lull him to sleep.

Bigsby came from a long line of colliers and keelmen who worked the drift mines and bell pits and piloted barges along the Aire, big ruddy men with lantern jaws like his. He was the youngest of five siblings, the only one to go to university. His family treated him with the bemusement accorded an eccentric, and paid little heed to where they went or what they did. They stayed out late, cycling back half-drunk along the towpath, and then slept in until noon. They stuffed themselves with the massive amounts of meat and veg his mum served up for tea. Amir had expected the usual questions—where are you from, what's with the funny name—but no one said a thing.

The mill Bigsby had his eye on was an old Victorian hulk with broken windows and decrepit brickwork in a dingy little town halfway between Bradford and Leeds. The chimney was to be torn down, the building converted into a housing estate. They tramped around the property. The mill had once made woolen cloth for army uniforms, Bigsby said. When the chimney was first built, they'd hoisted the townspeople to the top in a barrel run up the inside of the stack. The local band played polkas at the base. Afterward, a few of the band members went up with their instruments and played from the open chimney top.

An old wooden ladder was bolted to the chimney's crumbling exterior brick. Bigsby led off, running a fixed line up the ladder's edge. From the top, he flashed his torch and waved. Amir double-checked his carabiner, tugged on the figure eight. It was a soggy night and the splintered rungs were slick. A few were broken, others missing. From above, Bigsby pulled the rope tight, yanking at the harness around his waist. Halfway up, Amir paused to catch his breath and his knees began to shake. His neck and fingers ached. Far below stretched a web of sodium vapor lights. He told himself to focus on the ring of light his headlamp cast against the brick. He trusted Bigsby, but he didn't want to think about what would happen if he fell.

But oh! That dizzy twinge that sparked along his coccyx as he reached the chimney top, a hundred and thirty feet up in the air. If he'd had a trumpet, he would have played a fanfare like a member of that Farsley band from long ago, sending triumphal notes of victory out across the wet West Yorkshire night. Oh, the height, the view, the free-drop thrill! And even better was the feeling when his feet touched back on solid ground.

"To new heights," he and Bigsby toasted the next day at the pub. They drew up a new list on a bar coaster: bridges, rooftops, towers, tower cranes. The vertical city. The freedom of the night.

But here he is now, stuck underground in the bowels of the Paddington Green nick. Other than the duty officer who brings him watery coffee and ham sandwiches on limp wheat bread, he has not seen or spoken to a single person since they locked him up.

Panic refluxes in his chest. The cell walls contract. The hot pipes hiss like snakes. His shirt is damp with sweat. He shuts his eyes and the light bulb glows on in afterimage, the filament a crimson streak. He understands now, for the first time, what power meant. He'd lived within its great machinery his entire life without even knowing it was there. He listened to the news and read the history books, he used the words—*order, governance, surveillance, law enforcement, state*—like everybody did, without understanding. Power: from the Latin *posse*, root of *possible* and *possess*. He got Bigsby's theories now. Even paranoid Tawfiq was right.

He swings his legs over the edge of the bunk and leans forward, head in hands. The air is stale. The toilet stinks. He wants to go home. He wants his father. He wants his mother. He was screwed. He'd never get out of here. He'd never see any of them again.

He stands up and kicks the door, sending a shock of pain through his sock-covered toes and up his leg. For a second, the peephole darkens and an eye appears. Then the sound of footsteps, fading away.

The cell door swings open and the officer says, "Get up and come with me."

Amir sits up and runs his fingers through his hair. Had he fallen asleep? He's had the same clothes on since the day he was picked up. He probably stinks.

They step out of the lift and he blinks in the unaccustomed daylight. What day was it?

"Tuesday, July the twelfth," the officer says. "Your lucky day, if you're released."

He is led into an interrogation room. A plainclothes CID officer, dressed in jeans and a blue polo shirt, is sitting at a table. A tape recorder has been placed between them. A rectangular, archaic thing. The officer pops in a tape.

"Do you know why you've been arrested?" the officer says.

Amir shakes his head.

The officer sets two large plastic evidence bags on the table. Amir recognizes his own belongings: notebooks, a paperback, the broken radio scanner he'd dismantled when he was twelve or thirteen. How did they get his things out of his room at home? In a smaller bag were items from his rucksack: his phone, wallet, iPod, keys.

"This is what we have determined," the officer says. He counts off the items on his fingers as he speaks.

One, left thumb up. He was in possession of suspicious documents—ambiguous drawings in his notebooks, an Islamic protest march pamphlet, the copy of the Qur'an, various incriminating maps.

Two, first finger. He associated with a radical Islamic group at SOAS.

Three. He had close personal connections to Iran.

Four. He'd made visits to the North London mosque on three occasions between 21 May and 30 June, all documented on CCTV. All three visits were at times when the youth group, long suspected of radical activity, met.

Five. He was spotted on CCTV in King's Cross Station at 2:45 a.m. on July the second along with two other young men. Photographs on the camera found in his rucksack confirmed that they'd been inside a restricted area to which they must have broken in.

Six. Right thumb up. Two hands now. He had visited Leeds, possibly in connection with a known terrorist cell.

Seven. When they picked him up in London, he had on a hoodie that was too warm for the season and was carrying a bulky rucksack.

Eight. Wires were observed to be protruding from a pocket in the rucksack.

Nine. He was fiddling in a suspicious way with his mobile phone.

Ten. There is no ten. The officer lowers his hands. "Is there anything you want to say?" His narrative has the quality of a dream. Everything is wrong and yet everything still fits.

"We had a poke around King's Cross, that's the truth," Amir says. "We're into exploring, my mates and me—abandoned buildings, restricted places, stuff like that. But that's it. That's all we were doing there, I swear."

The officer takes out a pile of photographs, glossy black and whites. "Do you know any of these men?"

Amir shakes his head. He has never seen them before in his life.

"Do you recognize these names? Germaine Lindsay? Hasib Hussain? Shehzad Tanweer? Mohammad Sidique Kahn?"

Again, he shakes his head.

"You did not make contact with them in Leeds?"

He was with his mate, John Biggs, he tells the detective. You could ask him or his parents. On July seventh, he was in Leeds with them.

"You're a lucky bugger," the officer says, sweeping the photographs away. "These bastards blew themselves up last week. We know what they did and how they did it."

It was a series of coincidences, circumstantial evidence. They were looking for a fifth bomber, but they had no proof that it was Amir.

"You'll likely be charged with trespassing and possibly burglary in connection with the King's Cross incident," the detective says. "In the meantime, it's your lucky day. You're being released on bail."

He slides a typed form and a pen across the table. Amir signs his name.

"The conditions of police bail stipulate that you may not leave the country," the officer recites. "You must remain in residence at your permanent address. You must adhere to a nighttime curfew between 7:00 p.m. and 7:00 a.m. You must refrain from contacting or associating with Mr. Martin Conway and Mr. John Biggs. You must sign on at a police station once a week until your magistrate's court hearing date. Failure to comply with these conditions is a criminal offense. Do you understand?"

"Yes, sir," Amir says.

"Get the hell out of here, then," he says.

JAVAD

He is lying flat on his back, in corpse pose, zoned out on muscle relaxants, thinking about the amygdala: the two almond-shaped nuclei lodged deep in the temporal lobes of the brain. The anxiety response is triggered here—a chemical reaction that travels out along the ventral amygdalofugal pathway, governing one's conditioned fear of dangers, real or perceived—loud noises, for instance, or certain facial features, or the color of a person's skin. When activated, it shows up as a little red and yellow blob on the gray fMRI scan. An isolated thunderstorm, a little fugue of fear.

The landline rings. He rolls over and fumbles for the telephone. The amygdala signals the hypothalamus. Cortisol, norepinephrine, vasopressin flood in.

"Baba. It's me."

He's been released.

By the time Javad arrives at Paddington, twenty minutes later, numbness has overtaken the first shock of relief. There he is, his son, standing across the concrete plaza on the steps in front of the police station. His son's hair is dirty, his cheeks scruffy with a four-day growth of beard. A rucksack is propped between his feet. Javad tells the taxi driver to wait. He gets out and waves and Amir breaks into a run. He takes his son in his arms and grasps him tight.

This. This child he has made. This musky smell. This heft. This is the infant he held in the palm of one hand, naked and new, blinking in the light. This the skinny boy he chased, the boy he tried to teach and care for, now become a man. He has failed. He presses his face into his hair and shoulder, breathes in, holds him tight.

He wants to say, How could you do this to me? Anger licks his heart. His heart so swollen he can scarcely breathe.

"Camden," Javad tells the taxi driver as they climb in. The boy insists on stopping at Caroline's place first.

Around the corner, the Edgware Road Station is still cordoned off, the pavement still heaped with cellophane-wrapped bouquets.

Along the way, his son tells him the story. The urban exploration, the unfortunate coincidences, the mistakes.

"We weren't doing anything wrong, honestly, Baba," he says. "There's loads of people out there doing it. Biggs is writing his anthropology thesis on it. We're very careful. We're not destructive. It's really very safe."

Javad braces himself with the strap, each jounce of the taxi sending a stab of pain through his pelvis and down his legs. "So the only charge is trespassing?"

"Probably. I think that's what he said."

"I'll ring Charles first thing."

The taxi crawls along the Marylebone Road through the rush-hour traffic. Just ahead Euston Road, King's Cross. He hasn't been back to work since the bombings. The taxi turns north along the edge of Regent's Park.

The boy talks too fast, animated with exhaustion and relief. He has no idea. Javad looks out the taxi window at the green blur of the park. Had he, too, been this oblivious to his parents' pain?

Caroline can't stop weeping. Tears streaming down her cheeks, she is piling food onto the counter: containers of hummus and tzatziki, pots of yoghurt, packets of cold cuts, wedges of cheese, a bowl of cherries, another bowl of grapes. Niels has his phone pressed to his ear, trying to get through to some connection at Grey's Inn. Amir sits on a barstool on the other side of the counter, digging in.

Javad has the disconnected feeling that he's high above them, looking down onto Niels's kitchen with its quartz counters and expensive stainless steel appliances and barstools with leather seats. His son. The mother of his son. It seems as if months, not days, have passed since he was last here in this kitchen.

"I can't believe it," Caroline is saying to Amir, dabbing at her eyes with a tissue. "I can't believe you're here. I can't believe you truly are all right."

Amir makes a face. Caroline looks so small next to Amir. Without heels—she's got a trainer on one foot and the cast on the other—she has to stand on tiptoe to kiss his cheek. From a certain angle, they look so much alike. It's the smile, Javad thinks.

His back is killing him. He pulls the blister packet of pills out of his pocket, pops one out, and swallows it with a handful of water from the sink. He straightens, digging his fists into his spine.

"His secretary says he'll ring when he gets out of court," says Niels, setting down the phone. "Are you okay?"

"Threw out my wonky back."

"Ach, that's the worst."

Amir has taken out his camera. Caroline hobbles around to look. "These are the ones from Farsley," Amir says, holding it up so she can see the screen.

"It's magistrate's court, you know," Javad tells Niels. "A solicitor is all we'll need."

"It's not only the charges that you have to worry about," Niels says, "but the data—the fingerprints, the interviewing tapes, the phone records, the DNA. It's a privacy matter. You cannot trust the police."

"I still haven't gotten my own things back. The stuff they took when they searched my place."

"That's exactly what I mean."

Caroline and Amir are hunched over the camera, his dark head beside her blond. "That one's Pimlico," Amir says. "And that's Cane Hill."

"These are gorgeous, my god," Caroline says. "Beautiful dereliction!"

Was it? Javad wonders. Was that the lure of squalor and blight? It was dangerous to romanticize destruction, he thinks. It wasn't beauty. It wasn't art.

"These shots are phenomenal," Caroline calls over. "You two, come have a look."

He walks around and wedges himself in beside his son. Caroline is resting her head against Amir's other shoulder, her eyes shiny. She loves him, Javad thinks. How long had it been since they had been together, the three of them, like this? He thinks of Margate. The summer sky, the foamy wave line at his feet, Amir running along the beach, his scapulae like a fledgling's wings. That might have been the last time they did anything together as a family. He feels a wash of sadness. But here they are. Here and now—that was the important thing. The three of them, bound together, as they would always be.

It is getting late. Better not to violate the curfew on his first night out. They were all exhausted. They'd best be getting back.

"Already?" says Caroline. "Oh no, not yet."

Niels puts his arm around her shoulder. Niels is the first of Caroline's long line of boyfriends that he actually might not dislike, Javad thinks. A bit stiff, they were, the Dutch, but Niels seemed all right.

Would he ever find someone? He hasn't spoken to Esther since Saturday afternoon. He knows her mother has passed away; he saw the funeral director's van. He left a message on her mobile, but she hasn't rung him back. He has been caught up in his troubles too. Was she angry? He feels bad. How difficult it was to know another person. He shouldn't have allowed himself to imagine it, these past few weeks. How quickly hope unfurled! Better to have kept it locked away like those old, abandoned places in Amir's photographs. Derelict, his heart.

"I'll see you soon, Mum," Amir says, bending to kiss her on the cheek.

Niels says, "I should think we'll all sleep well tonight."

It is late on Wednesday afternoon before Javad finally goes next door and rings the bell. He's been wrapped up all day in phone calls with the solicitor. There will be hearings, filings, meetings, motions—all the endless details of a legal mess.

Esther comes to the door. She is wearing a summer shift and sandals, her hair pulled back. "Oh!" she says.

He hands her the bouquet of lilies he has brought, feeling awkward. He is not sure of the Jewish custom. *White for funerals*, the girl at the flower stand had said.

"Thank you," she says. "You didn't need to do that. Come in."

He follows her into the sitting room. She gestures for him to sit down on the sofa. There is a green-tiled gas fire, just like his. There is the piano. It has been a long time, he realizes, since he has heard her play. A clock rests on the mantel above the fireplace. Through the glass case, he can see the golden clockwork moving—the tiny gears, the beating pendulum, the spinning heart.

"I'm so sorry for your loss," he says. He feels a coolness radiating from her that he's not sure how to place.

She perches on the arm of an upholstered chair. "It was a long time coming."

"I feel really terrible. I would have liked to pay my respects."

"It's fine. You had a lot going on. It was just me and a few of her old friends, anyway. She didn't want any kind of to-do. Nothing religious, no ceremony."

"I know, but—I'm sorry."

The patio doors are open onto the garden, the afternoon sun

illuminating the angles of her pale face with its gentle glow. She is so beautiful, he thinks, with a feeling almost like surprise.

"So Amir is home again?" she says. "I was so worried. I'm so relieved."

"Yes—they released him yesterday."

"And he's okay?"

"He's fine, thank God. He spent a couple of nights in a nasty holding cell at Paddington Green, but he's none the worse for wear, I shouldn't think."

He outlines for her the events as he now knows them: The urban exploration, Finsbury Park, King's Cross, the trip to Yorkshire, the arrest, the release. The unfortunate coincidences, the horrible timing. But the police sorted it out. He was impressed, actually, that they got it right. They'd brought a minor charge of trespassing; there would be a fine. The lad had learned his lesson, or so one hoped. End of story. And that's all it is now, he thinks—a story. Once upon a time, and then, and then, happily ever after, the end.

Her expression is pained. She crosses her arms around her waist. "I'm really sorry," she says.

"There's no need to apologize."

She shakes her head. A hard, swift shake. "Yes, there is."

"Whatever for? It's not your fault."

She looks away. "You don't know. You have no idea. I was suspicious—I misunderstood. I mean, if I hadn't—"

He waits, but she doesn't complete the sentence. She looks so miserable. What is she talking about? He has a sinking feeling. She is right there and yet he cannot reach her.

"We were all very frightened," he says and pauses. "It's been a rough time for both of us, hasn't it? But it's over now, at least."

"Is it?"

She stands up and walks over to the patio doors, turning her back to him. Beyond her, in the garden, the weeping mulberry's long branches are trembling in the wind. He'd like to go to her, to touch and hold her, but somehow, he understands that he cannot. They have fallen out of orbit, spun apart.

When she turns back, her eyes are wet. "I'm putting the house on the market, Javad. I can't stay. I'm sorry."

He thinks of the first time he saw her, that April afternoon, out on the front steps. She took his breath away. It was a cliché, he knows, but there is no other way he can think of to describe it—the compression in his lungs, the breath stifled in his chest. The quick, hopeful, ridiculous thought had crossed his mind then that maybe she was Persian, too. That heart-shaped face, that corona of dark hair.

"What's the hurry?" he says. His heart is knotted tight. "Why don't you give it some time?" *Give us some time* is what he means. *You can't keep running away forever* is what he wants to say.

She shakes her head. "I don't know." She sweeps her arm across the room. "All this—it's just too much. I can't."

"You've been through a lot," he says carefully. "But I think you should give it a chance."

Her eyes are dark and flat. "I really like you, Javad," she says at last. "I really, truly do. But—I don't know. Maybe it's just bad timing. Or maybe we're just too different. I'd like to think that wasn't true, but I'm afraid it is."

On the mantel, the gold clock sounds the hour—five tinkling chimes. They have missed their moment. The words they should have said, all the things they should have done, have slipped away. He stands and says, "I'm sorry, Esther, I really am."

She says, "I'm sorry too."

At the door, she stops and turns to him. "I'm just curious. What was Amir doing in Finsbury Park, anyway?"

"It seems he's got a girl."

"A girl!" Her eyebrows rise. "And you were so sure he didn't!"

He almost smiles. "I was, it's true."

She opens the door for him. "I'm just really glad that he's all right."

The wind is pushing gray-white thunderheads across the sky. Leaves are fluttering on the trees. The light shifts and dims. He steps closer and pulls her to him and kisses her softly on the lips. "I'll be here, Esther," he says. "If you change your mind. Just know that I'll be here."

ESTHER

The movers have come and gone. A crew of stocky Romanians with the barrel chests and massive shoulders of Olympic weight lifters arrived and swathed the furniture in quilted padding and hauled it all away: the sofa, the walnut bedroom set, the dining table, the glass-fronted vitrine, assorted chairs. It will all be sold, auctioned off to antiques dealers and other collectors of such things. She likes the idea of her mother's belongings taking on new lives in other peoples' homes. All that remains now is the piano, which she will store. The specialist movers will be coming for it soon.

Her suitcases are packed and waiting. The keys are in the lockbox for the estate agent. In a little while, she'll take a taxi to St. Pancras and then the Eurostar to Paris and from there the TGV to southern France. She has never taken the train beneath the Channel before. It is strange to think that Paris is the same distance from London as Buffalo is from New York City. In just a couple of hours, she'll be eating dinner in a French café.

It is the end of August. She is going to stay with old friends who have a country house near Nîmes. She imagines long walks along quiet streets lined with shuttered houses, hillside vineyards, ancient ruins, open-air *marchés*. Her host and her husband have no children. They'll eat dinner outside on the flagstone terrace.

They'll keep her glass filled with the local wine. She will fly back to New York from there. She doesn't want to think about what will happen after that.

Stripped of objects, the house seems larger, dingier, strange. *The Last Resort.* Soon it would belong to someone else. Already she feels ectoplasmic, as if she already is already a ghost. The FOR SALE sign has been posted out in front. Once this house is gone, there will be nothing left.

She moves from room to room, checking the empty cupboards, running her fingers along shelves, peeking behind doors. Way at the back of a kitchen cabinet, she finds a dusty platter with a chipped rim. In the sitting room, she retrieves a few abandoned paperbacks that have slipped behind a shelf. The cleaners can throw them out.

She thinks of Javad and Amir, just there, a few yards away on the other side of their shared wall. She thinks of the boy's dark eyes, the slight gap between his teeth. She thinks of Javad's body, vulnerable in sleep, his sweet and tender kiss. They had their moment, she thinks. They had that, at least.

Through the windows, bare of curtains, the light shifts. It is just a place. Four walls, a roof, a space.

Downstairs in the sitting room, she wanders over to the piano and runs her fingertips along the keys. She hasn't played in weeks. She is thinking of that Beethoven sonata, *Les Adieux.* She must have the sheet music here somewhere.

She lifts the lid to the piano bench and rummages through the music books. They smell of mildew and must. Bits of yellowed paper and glue crumble off the spines. She pulls out the thick blue Henle Verlag volume of Beethoven sonatas. She flips through it, clean pages of notation alternating with the scribbled pages of the pieces she once played. A piece of folded paper slips out, a child's drawing. Her lungs squeeze tight.

It is a picture of a jet plane, the red and blue waves of the British Airways logo traced across the tail, engines shaded in pencil beneath the wings. The landing gear has been retracted; the plane's in flight. In the middle of the row of oval windows are three tiny smiling faces. Arrows point to names, written in block letters at the top of the page. *Mommy. Daddy. Noah.* The one in the middle with the mess of black scribbled hair must be her. To the side, in smaller, careful letters, he has written *I love you* inside a crayoned heart.

Oh, Noah, she thinks.

She touches the paper to her lips. Her hands are trembling. She can see him at seven or eight, his dark head down on one arm stretched out across the kitchen table, a pencil gripped in his little hand. She thinks of his room, back in New York, dim and dusty now, the model fighter jets and bombers grounded, the glow-in-the-dark stars dimmed.

Fly away, the drawing says. Let go.

There is a knock at the door. She tucks the picture back into the book and puts it in the bench and goes to let the piano movers in.

There are three of them, armed with ramps and trolleys and padded cloths and heavy-duty ratchet straps.

"Moving back to the States, then, eh?" the foreman says.

"Maybe."

"Nice instruments, the Blüthners," he says. "Don't see too many of them these days."

"It was my mother's," she says, and stands back and lets them work.

One man removes the music stand as the other crawls underneath the keyboard to unscrew the pedals. They wrap padded cloths around the lid and case. Then they wheel a trolley underneath the center of the piano, unscrew the front left leg, then tilt the piano over onto the trolley so that it is resting on its side. Thick straps are looped on and tightened. The piano weighs close to one thousand pounds. Strapped and swaddled, it is the size of a small car or giant coffin.

The men lay rubber mats over the thresholds and set a wooden ramp over the front steps. Two men position themselves on the down-ramp end of the piano; the foreman takes the top. They grunt and strain as they ease the trolley down the ramp. Esther stands in the doorway and holds her breath. She cannot watch. As they hit the bottom, she hears a sound, the reverberation of the sounding board, a low, deep, groaning *bong*. And then the piano is safely on the pavement, and they are pushing it up the van, securing it inside. The other men hand up the swaddled bench and legs. The job is done.

"Yikes," she says, coming down the steps.

"Oh, that was nothing. You should see the ones where we have to use a crane," the foreman says.

She signs the paperwork, and they climb into the van and pull away.

She stands out on the pavement, watching them go. She turns back and looks up at the twin blue doors, the twin front steps, the matching windows, the shared line of the roof. All the windows are mirror dark—Javad's, her own.

The summer air is still. Sounds of the city drift upward: a barking dog, the rev of a shifting engine, the brake-squeal of a bus, a helicopter's growling hum. In the sky, the crisscrossed contrails of a vanished plane are dissipating, two tight lines at one end, spreading into cirrus at the other, milky brushstrokes against the blue.

AMIR

His father is in the kitchen, elbow deep, as usual, in work. Piles of scans and printouts are spread out across the table, along with a mug half-full of coffee, long since gone cold, a half-eaten piece of toast. Miranda pads in behind him. She is barefoot, her painted toenails red against the white tiled floor. She's wearing one of his old black T-shirts that drapes below the hemline of her shorts so that it looks as if she isn't wearing anything under it at all. He is happy she is here, officially his girlfriend now. Her presence shifts the balance between him and his father. A counterweight. His father likes her, he can tell. His father is glad to have her here, at least, if that means that he'll stay home. She calls him "Dr. Asghari" even though he tells her not to. She smiles at him with her kohl-rimmed eyes.

His father shakes out *The Guardian* and folds it back. "Bloody hell!" he says. "He speaks!"

Amir opens the refrigerator and squints into the cold, bright light. "Who speaks?"

"The Piano Man. Looks like all has been revealed! Amir, don't let all the cold air out of the fridge."

What is he looking for? Orange juice, right. He takes out the carton and drinks from it, then extends it to Miranda, who shakes her head. "You're disgusting," she says.

He shakes the carton to demonstrate. "It's nearly empty."

"You finish it, then."

His father is still looking at the paper, shaking his head. "Apparently, a nurse went into the fellow's room yesterday morning and said, 'So are you going to speak to us today?' And he simply replied 'Yes!'"

"That's a bit embarrassing, isn't it," Miranda says. "After all that fuss."

"He's from Germany, it seems," his father continues. "Grew up in the Bavarian countryside, near the Czech border. His father owns a dairy farm. He came over to England on the Eurostar from France. He says that he is gay, that he was trying to commit suicide the night they picked him up. Claims he remembers little of what happened after that."

Miranda twists her lips. "Is he a hoaxer, then?"

His father shrugs. "Not necessarily. It's more complicated than one might think." He pushes up his glasses and rubs the bridge of his nose. "The brain sometimes shuts down and erases things, rather like a computer hard drive crash. Abnormal memory functioning can result from psychological trauma or severe stress."

"I feel sorry for him," Miranda says. "You have to be quite desperate to pull a stunt like that."

"Hoaxer or not, he's a nutter either way," says Amir. But he can understand it. He can understand the desire to flee, to start afresh, to be washed clean.

They take their coffee and head out back into the garden. The earth is cool beneath his bare feet. Miranda follows, the cat rubbing against her heels. It's the end of August. The sky is full of low-slung clouds with dark gray underbellies. The air is cool and smells of rain. He sits down on the ground and plucks at the weeds.

Miranda pulls the cat onto her lap and nuzzles it between the ears. "So all that buildup, and it turns out he's just an ordinary bloke."

Everybody wants a story with a happy ending, Amir thinks. Man lost, man found. Mystery solved.

"I'm not too surprised, really," he says. "The whole prodigy thing always seemed pretty farfetched."

"I should think his parents are chuffed to have him back, in any case."

"Yeah. He's probably back home already, milking the cows."

"Poor sod!"

His parents are glad to have *him* back, that much is sure. After the July bombings and the police murder of Jean Charles de Menezes down in the Tube, his father had actually looked scared. Watching the news on TV, it hardly seemed as if it could be real: the man's dark jacket, his brown Brazilian skin, the seven police bullets fired at close range, the photograph of Menezes's ordinary legs, in cheap blue jeans and white socks and trainers, sprawled dead across the aisle of the train. "That could have been you," his father said.

But it wasn't Amir. He was right here, safe.

Miranda lies back on the grass, her knees bent, arms stretched out, looking up at the sky. She looks like a child in his too-big T-shirt, her hair fanned out on the grass around her head. The shirt says *UK Decay*—a relic from his post-punk/goth phase at school. He doesn't much care for their music anymore, but he still likes the name.

"Have a look at the sky," Miranda says. "Look how fast the earth is spinning!"

"It's just the wind."

"I know. But we are spinning. And at a rate of a thousand miles per hour, they say."

He reaches out and takes her hand. For days after his release, he had faint brown marks along his wrists where the handcuffs had chafed. The ground beneath him is damp. It smells of mud and earthworms, decaying plants and weeds. Her body is close beside him, expanding and contracting with her breath. Its warmth radiates toward him. He can feel her blood faintly pulsing beneath the fine bones of her wrist. Her beating heart, alive beneath her skin.

They are high above the city, surrounded by points of light. The lights stretch out in all directions, yellow and white and here and there a dot of red, glimmering like stars. Iconic London. St. Paul's, the Gherkin, Big Ben, the London Eye. The river is a blue-black ribbon, laced with silver and gold. Above them, the four great smokestacks rise. The ziggurat of the power station laid out underneath. Battersea, at last.

It's their coming-out party. The curfew has been lifted, the fines paid, the charges cleared. "Time to get back on the fucking horse," Mole said.

Bigsby is unfurling rope, singing Pink Floyd under his breath. *Ha ha, charade you are.*

Since the arrest, since the horrible days in the holding cell, since the questioning and the release, he feels as if he has returned from a long and arduous journey. Now it's all a blur. Time has bent. Where has he been?

"Do you remember—?"

Mole and Bigsby laugh. Bloody wanker.

At the base of the nearest smokestack, Mole is double-checking the buckles on his harness. Mole's the third to climb; Bigsby's on belay. Iron bolts stretch like eyelets up the chimney, the static line that Bigsby set earlier that night threaded through them to the top.

Mole clips in. He breathes out once, hard. He's not too fond of heights.

"Climbing," he says.

Bigsby says, "Climb on."

Amir is sitting on the flat roof, Miranda beside him, leaning against him. His limbs are slack with fatigue and relief. He wraps his arm around her and pulls her close. It's her first time on an expedition. He is glad she's here.

It is the end of summer. Already the wind smells different. Already it is edged with the chill of autumn, that undertone of regret. He'll be glad to put this summer far behind him. Up here, though, for the moment, he is free.

Ha ha, charade you are.

At the base of the chimney, Mole leans back into the harness and places his boots against the side of the smokestack. He steps up, shifts the ascender, steps and shifts, working his way like a giant inchworm up the stack. He moves tentatively at first, then starts to find a rhythm. Bigsby leans back against the rope, craning his neck, watching. He shifts his hands along the rope as Mole moves up and pulls it tight.

Even here, below the four great smokestacks, on this vast, flat slate playing field of roof, they're at least a hundred meters up. Getting this far up was easy. Over the wall they went and up the scaffolding that conveniently stretched like a climbing frame all the way up the A-side building's flank. Mole and Bigsby led. Miranda clambered after them. Amir took up the rear.

Halfway up she turned and looked at him, her black cap pulled low over her eyebrows, like a spy's. "It feels like flying!" she said, making a sweeping motion with her arm. "I can't believe we're doing this!"

"Yeah. Be careful. Hang on tight."

The sky seemed to grow larger as they climbed, expanding like a dome. The ground was a winking circuit board of lights. The scaffolding's steel bars were cold beneath his hands. His heart raced. Gear clipped to his harness clanked around his thighs. As they rose, pigeons roused and flapped into the night.

Bigsby slides his hands along the rope, still humming.

Ha ha, charade you are.

The hulk of the power plant lies beneath them like a sleeping beast, a great stilled wreck. Here, there are no illusions, no pretense. This is as close as you could get to reality, hard and clear as ice. Here time caught fast and stopped. You came and witnessed. You touched but left no trace.

There is a faint drumbeat, growing louder. The thrum of rotors. Amir squints. It's a helicopter, flying low along the Thames at Chelsea Reach. He says, "shit."

Miranda stiffens. "Do you think they've spotted us?"

"Better not have done."

Amir looks up. Mole is just a small black speck against the smokestack. Could he be seen? The helicopter blinks slowly across the skyline. Then it veers north and turns away. Amir lets out his breath.

"I get it now," Miranda says.

"Get what?"

"Why you lot do this."

"Yeah?"

"I couldn't work it out, before. I thought it was just another thrill-seeker's sport. The sort of thing adrenaline junkies get off on. When you showed me the photos of those grotty tunnels, those disgusting sewer pipes, I thought you were cracked. But this," she says, gesturing. "It's so beautiful. Like, *spiritual*. No cathedral even comes close. Know what I mean?"

"Yeah."

"I want to go everywhere now."

He draws his legs up and wraps his arms around his knees. The sky is slowly deepening to violet. The earth is turning. In an hour, it will be dawn. Mole has nearly reached the top rim of the smokestack, tiny as an ant. An hour ago, he had been that ant.

"This might be it for me," he says. He hasn't meant to say this, but as he speaks the words aloud, they sound sure and true. "I think I'm done. Hanging up my hat, so to speak, now that I've been here."

"What? Really? Why?"

"I've done what I needed to do, I guess." He shrugs. "Time to quit."

"That's not fair!" For once, she isn't smiling. He understands her disappointment. He has let her in on this great secret, hidden world, and just like that, he's slammed the door. But it's not about her, or them.

His father was waiting for him when he came out of the police station after his release. It felt strange to be outdoors, to have shoes back on his feet. His father stood beside the idling taxi. The skin on his face was gray and slack, his shoulders bent. He looked diminished, as if it had been years, not just a fortnight, since he'd seen him last. He ran to him and they embraced. His father grasped him tight. He thought he felt him shake. His father was the one in need of consolation, he understood then.

He could no longer remember why they'd fought, why he'd been so angry, why he'd run away. He'd always taken his parents' love for granted, chafed against it, pushed against its bounds. But it was fragile, he saw in that moment—an egg in the palm of his hand. His father had pulled back, pushed up his glasses, and swiped his fingers across his eyes. Nothing needed to be said. But that love, he understood now, would keep him tethered to the ground.

A whoop erupts. Mole's down. He's high-fiving Bigsby, giddy with relief.

"A good night's work," Mole says.

"Aye," Bigsby says.

"Good thing we got to do it before it's gone."

It is strange, the way you always remember the outset of a journey, but never the trip back. The anticipation is what remains—the anxiety of preparation, the serrated edge of fear, the gut-dropping liftoff. The return is just a blur.

Soon they'd be climbing down the scaffolding. Soon the world would shrink back into scale. Soon they'd be home, easing open the front door, sneaking in. The street would be dark and quiet. The house next door had been put up for sale. The old woman who lived there had passed away, and the American had gone back to the States.

It is the end of summer, the end of his exploring, but it doesn't feel like the end. Maybe there is no such thing as resolution. Maybe time is just a series of endless variations, spiraling outward, expanding into space. He was home again and yet it wouldn't ever be the same. His sleep remained uneasy, turbulent with dreams. Water dripped inside the walls. A ghostly hand disturbed the curtains. Lying in bed in the dark, awake, he looked over at his mum's collage, at the scratched picture of himself when he was little, chasing birds along the beach. "You were a wild one at that age," his father said. His mother said, "Rubbish, you were just a normal kid." He remembered the picture, not the actual moment, but to him they felt the same, the emotion and the image, the feeling of running, free as music, down the wave-smoothed sand.

Now, at the top of Battersea, Miranda rests her head against his shoulder. Mole and Bigsby stand to either side. They stand like ancient conquerors on a hilltop surveying captured ground. Far below and all around them, London glitters like a geode in the gray light of dawn. Even the wind smells prehistoric, of stone and dust and ice.

They coil their ropes and hoist their packs and drop over the side of the roof and onto the scaffolding. The rusty rungs are cold. Below, the dogs awaken and begin to bark. They are on their way.

ACKNOWLEDGMENTS

This book began with an NPR piece on the "Piano Man" that I found myself listening to, sitting in my parked car in my driveway, one afternoon in May 2005. It has taken me many drafts and many years to find the story sparked by the image of that lost, mute man, and to all those who have helped me along the way, I am more grateful than I can say.

Thanks first of all to the James Jones First Novel Fellowship—and to Kaylie Jones, Bonnie Culver, Laurie Loewenstein, Taylor Polites, and the members of the James Jones Literary Society—for giving me the boost I needed at a crucial time. I am also thankful to the Ucross Foundation for granting me a two-week residency in the fall of 2011; I wrote the first thirty pages looking out onto the Bighorn Mountains from my lovely studio on the Ucross ranch. I am also indebted to the National Endowment for the Arts Literature Fellowship, which gave me a semester off, during which I wrote (and discarded) this project's earliest draft. I am most grateful for the generous flexibility I have found at Denison University over the past twelve years, and for the R. C. Good fellowship, which gave me much-needed time to write.

I would not have completed this project without the encouragement and support of my wonderful friends and colleagues, especially Peter Grandbois, whose smart, generous feedback and friendship helped me more than I can say. I am indebted to Nicole Walker, Holly Goddard Jones, and Rae Meadows for their helpful readings of early drafts, and to Susan Kanter for meeting me at the coffee shop and encouraging me to write when I was at my lowest point. Heartfelt thanks go out as well to Mike Croley and David Baker for taking the time to read and talk and offer sage advice. Much gratitude is also due to Ann Townsend, Linda Krumholz, Jack Shuler, Joan Krone, Cookie Sunkle, Peter Slevin, David McGlynn, Sue Davis, Jessica Rettig, Andrea Ziegert and to all my wonderful running friends for their conversation, encouragement, and moral support. Maxine Hong Kingston led a one-week workshop at Denison in 2007, in which I created a collage that has guided me in this project for many years. Finally, a very special thank-you to Rosamund Bartlett, who invited me into her lovely Oxford home for a desperately needed two-week writing "retreat."

I am deeply grateful to Irene Skolnick (I owe you lunch!) for believing in this book. And to Dennis Johnson, Taylor Sperry, Kait Howard, Nikki Griffiths, and all the rest of the talented team at Melville House, thank you for all the amazing work you do.

And finally, to my family—my parents, Dan and Barbara Singer; my children, Micaela and Rafi DeGenero; and above all to my husband, Tim—my love goes beyond words.

1.   Why does Lonia find the resolution of "The Twelve Princesses" fairy tale so unsatisfying? What does this say about her as a character, given what we know as readers?

2.   Does *Underground Fugue*'s shifting point of view affect how we interact with the characters and their relationships? If so, how?

3.   Parents figure largely in *Underground Fugue*. What point do you think the author is making by linking the stories of three seemingly estranged parent figures: Javad, Esther, and Lonia?

4.   How is the relationship between Amir and Javad similar to the relationship between Esther and Lonia? How is it different?

5.   Discuss the scene in which Esther mistakes Amir for a burglar. Is it racially coded? Does it change your perception of Esther's relationship with Javad? Does it change your perception of the moments when Esther criticizes Lonia for calling their neighbors "Arabs" and Lonia's friends for spouting anti-Muslim rhetoric?

6.   How do the differences in passive and active prejudice play out in this novel? Is one more dangerous than the other?

7. Amir reminds Esther of her son, Noah. How might this imagined resemblance influence Esther's actions?

8. How are Esther's and Javad's definitions of the word "fugue" similar? How are they different?

9. At one point, Javad thinks about his patient (a "fuguer") as someone who's trying to "run away from something," perhaps "some kind of trauma." In what ways is Javad himself running away from something? Are any other characters running away from trauma? Consider minor characters as well as the novel's protagonists.

10. What does "fugue state" mean to you? Would you consider either Esther or Javad themselves to be in a kind of "fugue state?" What about people in your own life?

11. In what ways are diaspora and emigration key themes in this novel? Is Esther more an emigrant, or, using her own term, an exile? What about Javad? Lonia? Amir?

12. How do Esther's deep-seated, unrevealed prejudices affect her relationship with Javad, with whom she obviously feels an unspoken kinship?

13. The ethnic violence of Lonia's past is a constant presence in this novel. Is there anything ironic about how Lonia (and her friends) recycle prejudicial/anti-Muslim rhetoric? How might we draw connections between that past, and the current-day events in *Underground Fugue*?

ABOUT THE AUTHOR

MARGOT SINGER won the Flannery O'Connor Award for Short Fiction, the Reform Judaism Prize for Jewish Fiction, the Glasgow Prize for Emerging Writers, and an Honorable Mention for the PEN/Hemingway Award for her story collection, *The Pale Settlement*. Her work has been featured on NPR and in *The Kenyon Review*, *The Gettysburg Review*, *Agni*, and *Conjunctions*, among other publications. She teaches English at Denison University in Granville, Ohio. *Underground Fugue* is her first novel.